NORTH STAR RISING

The Lindisfarne Series
Book Five

BY THE SAME AUTHOR

THE LINDISFARNE SERIES
In Darkened Corners (A Lindisfarne Series short story)
Firelight Rising (Book 1)
Moonlight Rising (Book 2)
Midnight Rising (Book 3)
The Rising Tide (Book 4-Prequel)

THE WEST COUNTRY TRILOGY
Moonshine (Prequel)
Bridles Lane (Book 1)
Hills of Silver (Book 2)
Wild Light (Book 3)

FAR FROM MY NATIVE SHORE: A COLLECTION OF AUSTRALIAN HISTORICAL NOVELS
One of Us Buried
Forgotten Places
Playing the Ghost

STANDALONE TITLES
The Devil and the Deep Blue Sea

NORTH STAR RISING

THE LINDISFARNE SERIES
BOOK FIVE

JOHANNA CRAVEN

NORTHUMBERLAND, ENGLAND

NOVEMBER
1725

CHAPTER ONE

His earliest memory is this: salted windows and firelight, sea at all the edges. A father who had made this rock his world. Surrendered his own freedom to save the lives of strangers. Back then, Finn had not understood. Had run instead; sought adventure, danger, a broader life of cannon fire and privateers. Almost lost that life on far too many occasions.

But this wind-crashed island has always been here waiting for him. This place of unlikely shelter, where tides rise to his doorstep and cloud sweeps stone. Shelter, once, for his mother, his father, his short-lived childhood. And now, for the last decade, his own unlikely, growing family. They have weathered Longstone through Jacobite plots and failed Risings, births and deaths; lives saved, lost and reunited. His wife, sons, tottering daughter—some days they all still feel impossible. Even now, after all this time, Finn is still waiting for them to be a moonshine dream.

He turns up the collar of his coat and marches down the stairs at the front of the cottage to refill the firebasket. The night is deep and silver-black, a cold late-autumn wind whipping across the sea. In the brassy glow of the flames, he can see the ocean pushing up against the edges of the island. The tide is rising, drawing pieces of the Farnes below the surface.

The sound comes to him like a memory; distant, haunting. A ship's bell, tolling across the water. Finn secures the chain of the firebasket to the hook. Turns in the vague direction of the sound. Again, it comes. A metallic, musical echo.

It's rolling in from the south, out behind the cottage, where nothing but the Crumstone islet interrupts sheets of dark sea. A light there too, he realises; disappearing, reappearing, dancing back and forth behind unseen castles of rock. And suddenly, vividly, a gunpowder roar. A streak of fire brightening the sky.

Finn runs inside, taking the stairs two at a time. Snatches the spying glass from the mantel.

Eva wakes at his urgency. Slides out of bed. "What is it? What do you see?"

"Flares," he says. "Out near the Crumstone."

Eva pulls her shoes on over bare feet and grabs her cloak from the hook beside the door. Takes the lamp from the mantel as she passes. Finn hurries down the steps of the cottage and lifts the spying glass. These early-morning hours, the sea, the cloud—it changes things, makes the world hazy. Makes you see things that aren't there.

It's not the first time he has imagined a ship foundering.

There have been incidents before, of course. Near misses of herring boats. Passenger ships venturing a little too close to the reef on rainy, lightless nights. The battered dinghy that had tossed his future wife onto Longstone in the wake of

Donald Macauley's death.

This feels like more than a near miss.

The ship's bell clatters through the darkness again. A scream drifts across the water. Tells him this is not the night, or the sea, or the cloud playing tricks. Tells him the ship has struck the reef, and he needs to act.

He hands Eva the spying glass. Panic in her eyes, but she does not attempt to stop him as he hurries to the jetty and unwinds the mooring ropes of the skiff. She just wraps her hand around his wrist and pulls him close for the briefest of moments. "Be safe," she says. "Come back to us."

He squeezes her fingers, thin and cold in his gloved hand. "Of course."

Finn leaps into the boat as Eva hooks the lamp to the bow. He guides the skiff carefully away from Longstone towards the light rising and plunging on the Crumstone. A second roar of gunpowder is followed by another flare, illuminating, for seconds, the peaks and troughs of the sea. It's a treacherous patch of ocean, yes, rippled with currents and hatched with reefs. But visibility is fair tonight and the sea is often far harsher than this. The fog far thicker. There are days when attempting this trip out to the Crumstone would end in certain disaster. Why a wreck tonight? A navigational error, he guesses. A compass variation. A quadrant wavering in the hand of a sailor tossed by the sea. A misreading of the stars. Perhaps they had not seen the beacon in time to correct their course.

Finn looks over his shoulder as he approaches the scarps of the Crumstone. He can see the ship now, run aground on the reef, the bulk of it emerging from the darkness. Two masts at a violent tilt, her portside languishing below the waterline. It's a packet boat, he guesses, trapped sails thudding and straining. He can tell the reef has torn one side of the ship open. He hears the screams and cries of the passengers, hears the sea thunder as it roars into cabins and crevices, the animal groan of the ship writhing against rock.

Bodies struggle over the sloping deck, straining towards the cold solidity of the Crumstone. It's a nugget of rock far smaller than Longstone. Will disappear almost entirely beneath the sea once the tide is at its highest. Finn eases his boat past the flailing hulk of the ship.

He hears shouting from the water. Looks down to see three figures thrashing towards him.

Finn reaches over the gunwale. Hauls out three young men in sailors' slops. The skiff rocks violently as they tumble inside.

"How many aboard?" Finn asks.

The responses are tangled, but he makes them out: eight passengers. Five members of crew. Passenger ship: London to Edinburgh.

"Take the lamp," he tells one of the men. "Guide my way."

Getting closer to the Crumstone is risky. He knows he is right above shards of rock that could slice the hull of the skiff from below. Men and women are scrambling up over the jagged island, trying to outrun the swell of the rising tide. A child wails in its mother's arms. Finn sees torn skin, bloodied faces, horrified eyes. Two figures—a man and a woman—lie motionless on the rock. The ship groans loudly, pummelled by the swell. It lurches, rolls, another inch of its gunwale disappearing beneath the surface.

A pull on one oar, the other, careful, muscles straining,

and the skiff is close enough. Finn steadies the boat against the white water glowing at the base of the islet. The crewmen help the passengers climb aboard.

He looks down at the two motionless figures. The man, older, with a thready grey beard, has a deep gash on his head, his face awash with crimson. The woman is wearing only a thin white nightshift and dark cloak, long pale hair clinging to her face and neck. No sign of an injury—Finn guesses she has succumbed to the cold. He knows from experience how quickly the chill of the water can steal your senses. But the woman's chest is moving with slow, shallow breath. A survivor, if he gets her back to the cottage quickly enough.

A man with a thick black beard is hovering by her side. "Make room for her in the boat," he barks, stumbling back to let the sailors lift the woman into the skiff.

"She your wife?" Finn asks him as he clambers over the gunwale after her.

"No. Just someone I met on the voyage. I think she was travelling alone."

Finn takes off his greatcoat and lays it over the woman's body.

"Don't freeze to death on her account," one of the crewmen tells him bitterly. "She tried to jump from the ship before we even ran aground. Caused quite the commotion. Think she'd prefer for us to leave her out here."

Finn eyes him warily. Feels a pull of unease as he glances back at the woman. "I'll take her with us if it's all the same to you."

Too many people for the tiny skiff. He feels it sitting low in the water. One of the sailors takes an oar and together, they shove the boat away from the Crumstone. Finn looks over his shoulder. Pulls towards the light blazing on the edge of his island.

———————⸭◈⸭———————

Fire, thinks Eva. Blankets. Tea and broth and warming pans. She restokes and fills, and gathers bowls and cups and spoons and cloths, mind fixed on nothing but the task at hand.

And so this is how it is: this desperate need to act, without thought of what might lie ahead. Eva has wondered. Ten years she has spent out here in the glow of the Longstone light, and at the edges, there has always been this uncertainty. This unsureness of how she would react if faced with a situation like this, with a ship foundering on their doorstep and screams echoing across the water. There has always been a fear that she might close down. Freeze up. Fail to be of use. In the past, her panic has not served her well.

But somehow, it feels as though she has always been waiting for this. Standing in the firelight and watching the sea for this moment of disaster.

She has banked up the fire and filled the kettle and pot from the rainwater barrel behind the cottage. Hung both over the flames to heat. Has gathered the blankets from her and Finn's bed, collected the covers kicked to the bottom of the boys' mattress, plucked the old shawl from the corner of Maggie's cradle. The warming pan waits beside the hearth, ready to be filled with embers and slid between the sheets of the bed.

Act, and it will stop her from thinking. From fearing.

She laces her quilted skirts and bodice on over her nightshift. Knocks the tin cups from the table in the panic she is trying not to give life to. The clatter brings Noah out of the children's bedroom, dark hair tangled on his shoulders, brown eyes hazy with sleep. He looks around the living area at the piles of blankets, the simmering pot, his mother crouched beside the table with her arms full of fallen cups.

"What's happening?" he asks, rubbing an eye with his palm.

Little point trying to shield him. Out here, they are too exposed to be shielded. Besides, he's nine now, her eldest child. Too old to believe untruths told to protect him.

"A wreck," Eva says, splattering the cups on the table. "On the Crumstone. Da has gone out to help them."

Noah's eyes widen slightly. He hurries to the window. "What kind of wreck?"

"I don't know." Eva can't tell if it's excitement or fear in his voice. A little of both, perhaps.

Noah's cousin Tom slips out of the bedroom. "A wreck?" he echoes.

Noah throws open the door, letting a blast of cold air inside. The fire dances, throwing wild shadows across the walls as the boys fly down the stairs at the front of the cottage. Somewhere distant, Eva thinks *coat, hat, shoes, gloves*; but then her son says:

"The boat, Mama. I see Da's boat."

At once it's chaos, the cottage overflowing with tearful passengers and blood-streaked crewmen, and trails of water streaking the floorboards silver. Eva helps men from sodden greatcoats, wrestles women from drenched and weighted bodices. She pours tea and serves steaming broth. Wraps shivering bodies in blankets and sponges blood from cheeks and foreheads, straps the swollen arm of a woman who holds a thrashing child upon her hip. She ushers people towards the fireplace, cramming them in between the table and chairs and fireguard hung with drying clothes. There's sobbing and murmuring, and stunned, colourless faces.

Finn carries a woman into the house; lays her on their bed in the corner of the room. Eva looks over. A motionless figure, sprawled beneath Finn's greatcoat. "Is she alive?"

"Aye. Just. We need to get her warm."

Eva hangs the kettle back on the hook and hurries towards the bed. She freezes suddenly, shock striking her beneath the ribs.

The room is shadowed. Firelit. And it's been ten years since they've stood face to face. But Eva knows without a doubt that the woman lying on the bed is her sister.

CHAPTER TWO

Eva slides the wet cloak from Harriet's shoulders, and it falls to the floor with a metallic thud. A coin pouch in the pocket, she supposes. She kicks it beneath the bed, away from prying eyes. She tugs the sodden nightdress from Harriet's body and wrangles her into one of her own dry shifts. Pulls the blankets up over her sister and shoves the warming pan into the bed.

"Some tea," Eva says loudly, panicked, not entirely sure who she is speaking to. "Bring me some tea." Her heart is hammering, her thoughts colliding. Distantly, she thinks, *there are not enough cups.* Not enough cups, not enough blankets. Not enough, not enough, not enough. The baby on the woman's lap shrieks.

On the edge of her vision, Eva sees Noah take a cup from a man by the fire. He fills it from the teapot on the table. Uses two hands to carry it over to her.

Eva slides a hand beneath her sister's head. Drizzles a little of the warm liquid down her throat. Harriet's eyelids flutter faintly. A swell of relief.

Finn had not recognised Harriet when he had brought her into the cottage, Eva is sure of it. And why would he? She and Finn had only been married weeks when Harriet had disappeared without a word ten years ago. The two of them had barely known each other.

"I'll go for help at first light," Eva hears Finn say. "I don't know if anyone on the mainland will have seen the flares." When she doesn't speak, he squeezes her shoulder. "Evie. Did you hear me?"

"It's Harriet," she says. "It's my sister."

Finn comes to stand close beside her at the bed. He is dressed in a knitted shirt and woollen cap, droplets of water shining in his beard. Eva can feel the cold radiating from him. He looks down at Harriet, and is silent for a long moment. "Did you know she was coming here?" he asks finally.

Eva shakes her head. "I've not heard a word from her since she ran away. I never imagined I'd hear from her again." Why her sister has come back is something she cannot even begin to consider right now. It's far too complicated a prospect.

She glances through the window to the dark reams of sea beyond the firebasket. "Were there any that didn't survive?"

"Aye. Several were lost on the ship, including the captain. One man passed while I was bringing them back. Bled out from a gash to the head."

Eva's stomach rolls. "Is he in the skiff?"

Finn nods. Glances over his shoulder at Noah and Tom. "It'll do him no good to be brought inside."

Eva reaches for his hand and squeezes, needing the steadying feel of him.

"They're saying…" Finn begins, then changes his mind.

"They're saying what?"

He hesitates. "One of the crewmen told me there was an incident. Involving Harriet."

Eva frowns. "What kind of incident?"

"I can't be certain. But he seemed to suggest she was trying to make her way off the ship before they were wrecked."

"Make her way off the ship?" Eva repeats. "You mean, she tried to jump into the sea?" She feels a hot pull of dread. "Do you think she was trying to… end things?"

"Try not to jump to conclusions. These people have been through a hell of an ordeal. They're likely confused about what they saw."

Eva feels eyes on her. One of the men at the hearth stumbles to his feet and makes his way towards the bed. He's tall and dark-haired, with a thick black beard and close-set grey eyes. A blanket is pulled around his shoulders and she sees the little finger on his left hand is missing at the knuckle—an old injury. He tries to peer past Eva to Harriet. "Is she alive?"

"Yes." Eva says no more. Cannot bring herself to consider why he is asking, who this man might be to her sister. She glances around the living area at the passengers and crew piled into her tiny cottage, huddled close to the fire. Noah and Tom are moving between them, refilling teacups and bowls of broth, throwing extra logs on the fire. On some sudden instinct, Eva finds herself shifting to block Tom's view of Harriet.

Finn takes the bearded man's elbow, guiding him away from the bed. "Sit," he says. "Rest. My wife will take care of her."

Eva touches her fingers to her sister's wrist, relieved to find a steady pulse. As she sits on the bed, making the mattress shift, Harriet opens her eyes. Takes Eva in. There's a look of distant bewilderment on her face, as though she is unable to determine if she is alive or dead. Or how she has ended up here.

Eva cannot make sense of it either. Was Harriet on her way to Lindisfarne? To see her family? Her son?

The son who is running around their living quarters with his cousin, completely unaware of his estranged mother's presence?

Eva fights the urge to pull Harriet into her arms. To ask questions. Demand answers. She has no thought of how any of it would be received. Has ten years washed away the bitterness that had existed between them the last time they had spoken? Eva has no idea. No idea of her own thoughts on the matter. And no idea who her sister is these days. If she is honest with herself, Harriet has always been a stranger.

But she is here, she is safe, she is alive. And right now, that is all Eva can find room for.

Harriet closes her eyes again, as though unable to even begin comprehending. Finally, eyes still closed, she says, "So, I'm alive then?"

Eva smiles faintly. "Yes, Harriet," she says. "You are."

And from the long, wavering breath that Harriet lets out, Eva cannot help but wonder if she might have been hoping for the alternative.

CHAPTER THREE

Nathan stands outside the house, squinting up at the loose boards dangling from the window casing. The oriel frame is a convoluted mess of Tudor woodwork that has spent the last century and a half rotting away in cold sea-salted air.

"See," Theodora says from beside him. "I told you it was in a state."

"Mm." She's right. The window needs fixing—but so does the back step and the rotten floorboard in the front guest room, and the loose hinge on the door of Mrs Brodie's quarters. And then there's that half-rebuilt fireplace in his mother's old dressing room he has never bothered to finish. Really, it's a rare day that there's not something wrong with this house.

Nathan has done little to the place in terms of upkeep—at least not since he'd been horsing about with his sham restoration on a search for Henry Ward's Jacobite letter. A part of him is holding his breath waiting for the house to collapse around him. And after years of to-ing and fro-ing and simultaneously loving and hating the place, he has come to the conclusion that this is not the outcome he wants. Unbidden, Highfield House has worked its way under his skin. The same way, Nathan thinks distantly, that he feels about Holy Island as a whole. Somehow, this place of stone and sea and pink-grey light has begun to feel like home. Or rather, he is reminded that it always has been this.

He shivers as wind blusters off the water, carrying the scent of drying kelp. The broken window casing shudders violently. "I'm sure there's someone in the village who can fix the thing."

Theodora leaps in with a touch too much enthusiasm. "I know someone who can help. I met a lad last week who's just arrived on the island. He's been doing odd jobs around the place for some extra coin. He fixed Mrs Emmett's roof a few days ago."

Nathan eyes her. "And how exactly did you meet this lad?"

His daughter shrugs with a nonchalance he feels certain is cultivated to annoy him. "I was just out walking. Happened to cross paths with him."

He gives her a withering look. "As a fine storyteller, you might come up with something a little more convincing."

Theodora smiles. Says nothing.

"I don't know, Thea," says Nathan. "This lad could be anyone." The thought of his pretty seventeen-year-old daughter flitting about the island with some itinerant roof-man is not sitting particularly well.

"Don't be silly. He's not *anyone*." She nods towards the window. "Besides, that thing could have someone's head off. We need to fix it."

Nathan is pleased to see their stable hand trudging over

14

the dunes towards the house.

"You know anything about carpentry, Lewis?" Nathan calls to him, gesturing up to the window.

Lewis chuckles. "You want me to fix that? Not a chance, sir. I'm the last fellow you want with a hammer in his hand." He digs his hands into the pockets of his coat, a seriousness falling over his eyes. "You been into town this morning, Mr Blake?"

"No. Why?"

"A passenger ship was wrecked out near Longstone last night. Survivors are with your sister and her husband."

"What?" Nathan's attention is drawn away from the window. "Was anyone hurt?"

"Don't know much more than that, I'm afraid," says Lewis. "But a few of the fishermen are heading out there once the tide lifts to help take the passengers to the mainland. I'm sure one of them will take a message over to the island for you."

"Write the message, Papa," Theodora says with a shine in her eyes. "I'll take it down to the anchorage. And I'll ask this fellow about fixing the window while I'm there."

And for far from the first time in his daughter's life, Nathan knows there's little point in protesting.

Boats come. Jostling and creaking against the Longstone jetty to ferry the survivors to the mainland. The morning is bright now, with fierce shards of sunlight straining into the cottage through the gaps in the shutters. Light falls on the aftermath of the night: on bloodied cloths and scattered cups, on bruised and sleepless faces. The sailors of the rescue boats—Trinity House seamen and a horde of local fishermen—pour into the crowded living space, helping survivors to their feet, shepherding them out of the cottage.

Eva steers the people past the bedroom door, hoping they won't wake the children. She would like, when her sons and daughter next open their eyes, for the worst of this to be over. Through the window, she can see the man in the skiff being wrapped in hessian. She watches the lifeless weight of him being passed over the gunwale into one of the rescue boats. She wraps her arms around herself, suddenly cold.

"A note from your brother, Mrs Murray." She turns at the sound of a fisherman's voice. He holds a folded page out to her. "Your niece gave it to me this morning after they heard about the wreck."

Eva takes the note, nodding her thanks. Unfolds the page and skims over it.

Finn catches her eye. "All right?"

She nods. "Just asking after us." She glances over at Harriet in the bed in the corner of the room. "I think I've a little too much to tell Nathan in writing," she says, voice low. "I'll call on him when I can."

The officer has pencil and notebook in hand now, a hundred questions on his lips. Questions for Finn, for the lost ship's crewmen, for the passengers. Time of impact? How many souls lost? Your captain among them? Cause of the wreck?

He scrawls down answers. Promises an investigation.

Eva glances at her sister. Her eyes are closed, but her breathing is shallow, eyelids fluttering. Eva can tell she is awake.

One of the fishermen steps up to the bed, nodding towards Harriet's still form. "She's the last one?"

Eva steps in front of him, blocking his way. "Yes. But she'll stay here." She cannot let her go. Not now that she has just found her again. She waits for a protest from Harriet, but it doesn't come.

Finn guides the last of the men out of the house and closes the door behind them. Shouted instructions carry in from outside, then a thick stillness falls over the cottage. The sound of voices is replaced by sea against the jetty; the rattle of the firebasket's chain. A chaotic choir of birdsong.

Eva moves around the cottage, throwing blood-splattered cloths into the washbin, collecting empty soup bowls from beside the hearth, folding blankets over the backs of chairs.

Finn reaches for her. Pulls her into him. "There's no need to do all this now."

A wave of exhaustion breaks over her and for long moments, she stands with her head pressed to his chest, inhaling the scent of sea, feeling the coarse wool of his shirt against her cheek. She had not allowed herself to consider the danger he had been in out on the Crumstone, but now the relief at his safety threatens to break over her. She tightens her arms around him, craving his nearness.

Finally, she steps away. Opens the bedroom door a crack and peeks in at the children. After being up and down throughout the night, all four are now sleeping heavily; Noah, Tom, and Archie sprawled out across the bed in a tangle of legs and blankets, Maggie on her back in one corner of her crib.

Eva pulls the door closed and looks down at Harriet. Her body is limp and weighted, and Eva guesses that this time, her sleep is genuine. Her chest is rising and falling steadily, a little of the colour returned to her cheeks.

"She seems better," says Finn.

Eva nods. "Perhaps we could take her to the bedroom? Make up a bed for the children out here by the fire? At least there she can have a little privacy."

"Aye. Of course."

When the boys are curled up in blankets by the simmering hearth, and Maggie's crib brought out to stand beside the fire, Finn scoops Harriet into his arms and carries her into the children's room. Eva watches from the doorway as he settles her onto the bed. Pulls the blankets up to her chin. Harriet stirs in her sleep but doesn't wake.

Finn steps out of the bedroom, closing the door behind him. His eyes drift to Tom. "Have you told her?"

"Not yet." Eva sinks wearily onto her bed. Her sister's wet hair has left dampness on the sheets, but it doesn't stop fatigue from tugging her down. She hopes the children are as exhausted as she is. Hopes they will sleep for a little longer yet.

Finn pulls off his boots and climbs onto the bed beside her. He wraps an arm around her, lies with his forehead pressed to hers. "All right?"

Eva meets his gaze. She sees the gold flecks in his brown eyes, threads of silver in the crags of his beard. "I ought to be asking you that. After all you did tonight."

"Aye, but are you all right with your sister being here?"

Eva cannot deny it: she feels on edge at Harriet's nearness. She is infinitely grateful that her sister is alive. But there's an old unease there; a discomfort she has not felt for years. It's just nerves, she tells herself. Nerves that come from not having seen her for so long.

But she knows there's more to it than that. A fear of what pieces of the past her sister might see fit to dredge up when she next opens her eyes. The last time Eva had seen her, Harriet had been wild with anger at her for keeping the truth of Oliver's death a secret. For marrying the man who had killed their brother. It is something they have never really discussed. A truth Eva has tucked away, buried deep. One she would be happy never to go near again. Certainly, she and Finn never speak of it; their children do not know—will never know, if Eva has her way. But with Harriet sleeping beneath her roof, the peace they have spent the last ten years cultivating suddenly feels far too precarious.

CHAPTER FOUR

When she opens her eyes, it takes Harriet a long time to remember where she is. Pale light is struggling through curtained windows, the sea hissing constant and unseen. The sound makes her feel painfully enclosed. She had hated being on the ocean, unable to escape the confines of the ship.

An easy target.

Trapped at first—and then the sea was everywhere; cold and dark and flooding into places it was never meant to be. Last night is made up of fragmented memories—the roar of the ship against rock, the shouts of the crew, the pitching of the deck, water sweeping her off her feet and stealing her breath. When she tries to grasp hold of it all, the only clear notion she comes away with is fear, and a cold so fiercely all-consuming she had ceased to be aware of it.

She is not on the ship now. Her addled brain grasps this, yes. Because that ship had succumbed to the ocean, straddled and splintered upon the reef.

Eva's cottage.

In the pale afternoon light, Harriet sees pieces of the life her sister has built: children's breeches tossed on the back of the chair in the corner, nine-pins tipped over beside the bed, a rag doll lying face down on the dresser. She hears muffled voices on the other side of the door. How many voices? Eva and Finn. Three children? Four? How do they all fit in this crumb of a cottage? How many small bodies squeeze into this bed each night? Harriet feels faint regret at taking up so much space.

The muffled voices grow steadily louder, then are hushed by their mother.

Tom, she hears. *Would you like some more bread, Tom?* The name nudges at her; an ache. She does her best to push it away. Push all of this away.

The last of her sleep is sloughed off her when Eva shoulders open the door, a wooden bowl in one hand and a water jug in the other. She gives Harriet a tentative smile. Sets the bowl on the side table and empties the jug into the washbin in the corner of the room.

Harriet takes her sister in in the daylight. Eva seems to have grown into her life here, eyes clear and blue against her tanned skin, a dark knot of hair piled messily on top of her head. She looks less coltish and willowy than last time Harriet had seen her, her body made curved and muscular by motherhood and firelight. There's a rugged strength to her that seems completely at odds with her London self—Harriet realises her sister has become an islander. Perhaps she has always been one.

"How are you feeling?" Eva asks.

"A little better." She feels cold again now she is sitting up with her arms out of the blankets; supposes it's a good thing

21

that she's able to recognise the sensation again. She still feels drained to the core. And more than a little surprised she is still alive. Her mind goes to dark water and shouting crewmen. Arms grabbing a hold of her, tugging her back from the railings. The ship groaning, splintering.

She sits up suddenly. "My cloak. Where is it?"

"Out in the living area, drying by the fire," says Eva. "I put your coin pouch in the sideboard to keep it safe."

Harriet lets out her breath in relief. After all this, at least she will not be reduced to a penniless charity case. "Were my travel documents in there too?"

"I don't know. I'll fetch it for you."

Eva disappears for a moment and returns with the pouch in her hand. She passes it to Harriet, who opens it carefully. Her folded papers are at the top of the pouch, sodden but intact. The sight of them goes some small way to steadying her.

"There's a lot of money in there," Eva says.

Harriet eyes her. Sets the pouch on the side table. "The other survivors were all brought here?"

"Yes. No one from the mainland came until morning."

Harriet's heart quickens. "Was a man with a missing finger among them? A dark beard? Is he here?"

"He was taken to Berwick with the others," says Eva. "He was asking after you. Is he… a friend?"

Harriet looks away. "He's no one. Just an acquaintance."

"He and the other survivors will go on to Edinburgh by coach," Eva tells her. "It's where the ship was headed, was it not?"

Harriet nods. They had been due to reach Edinburgh this morning. Not that she herself was ever destined to make it to

Scotland. She is fairly certain the man with the beard will not go to Edinburgh either. Likely, he will bide his time here in Northumberland until he finds her again.

Eva reaches for the door, then seems to change her mind. She turns back slowly, hesitantly. "Did something happen to you aboard the ship?" she asks carefully. "Before it foundered, I mean. The other passengers said there was a commotion."

Harriet tries to laugh away the question. "A commotion? Of course there was a commotion. The ship was sinking."

Her sister presses her lips together—an attempt, Harriet can tell, not to rise to her sharp response. Eva may have become an islander, but she has always been easy to read. "One of the crewmen says he saw..." She knots her hands together. "He thought he saw you try to throw yourself off the ship."

Harriet gives another short laugh; too forced and brassy. "Why on earth would I do that?"

Eva chews her lip. "You weren't trying to..."

"Kill myself?" Harriet finishes. "Good God, Eva, of course not. The crewman was obviously confused about what he saw in all that chaos."

Eva studies her, as though trying to find the truth behind her eyes. Finally, she says, "I'm very glad to hear that. Very glad you're safe." She hovers beside the bed, clearly waiting for more. A piece of information about what her long-lost sister was doing aboard that ship. Why she has come up here, to this part of the country she had once been so desperate to escape.

When Harriet doesn't speak, Eva takes the bowl from the side table and holds it out towards her. It's filled with a thin, watery soup, unappetising chunks of vegetables floating on the surface. "You ought to eat something," she says. "It will help you regain your strength." A clatter, then a boyish giggle from the other side of the door. Eva glances towards the sound. "You're welcome, of course, to join us outside if you wish." The offer sounds tentative, uncertain.

Harriet shakes her head. The thought of stepping out there, into all that life, feels far too overwhelming. Being face to face with her sister is hard enough. "I'd prefer to stay in here for now." She takes the bowl. Forces down a mouthful, surprised to find the soup almost edible.

Eva drags the rickety wooden chair over from the corner of the room and perches on the edge.

"You did not have to keep me here," Harriet says, cutting off her sister's questions before she can ask them. "I could have gone to Berwick with the others." She is infinitely glad, of course, not to be in the company of the man with the missing finger—although she is not entirely certain that being marooned here on Eva's island is any better. There are far too many unresolved poisons hanging in the air between them. "I'm sure it's enough of a squeeze here without a house guest."

Eva smiles slightly. "We shall manage."

Harriet swallows down another mouthful of soup. Her gaze drifts towards the door, towards the voices. *Would you like some more bread, Tom?* She swallows heavily. Feels that ache again. And she has to ask. "Your son's name is Tom?"

Eva tilts her head, taking her in. Doesn't speak for a moment. Then: "He's your son, Harriet."

Harriet closes her eyes. The answer is not a surprise, despite the sudden thumping in her chest the confirmation brings. She sets the bowl back on the side table, her stomach suddenly weighted and tight. "Why is he here?" she dares to ask. "Why is he not with his father? Is Edwin... Is he dead?" The waver in her voice surprises her.

"No," says Eva, and it brings Harriet a swell of relief. Thomas has gone ten years without his mother. She does not want him to be without his father too. "Edwin is away in Bath," Eva tells her. "He's had a string of pains and illnesses since he suffered the bullet wound during the fight with Ward's men. He brought Tom up to stay with Nathan and Thea at the house while he convalesces." She smiles slightly. "I think the adventure of staying out here held more appeal. He and Noah are the best of friends."

For a long time, Harriet doesn't speak. A thousand questions war inside her head. Questions she knows she has no right to ask. Finally, she manages, "Does he know anything about me?"

There's a brief moment of silence before Eva says, "Edwin told him you had passed. He asked that Nathan and I not speak of you to Thomas." Her voice is soft, and faintly guilty.

Harriet lets Eva's words fall into the silence. She feels the ache of them, though she knows she can expect little else. Of course Edwin had told their son she was dead. What was the alternative? To let him know his mother had seen fit to abandon him?

What was it she had told herself when she had left Thomas that night, a decade ago? That he was better off without her? That is far truer now than it ever was back then.

It feels impossibly fateful that she has ended up here, stranded on this rock with her estranged sister and son. But really, what coincidence is it? She had come to Northumberland because her family is here. As for the wreck, well, she had been anticipating disaster from the moment they had slipped out of the mouth of the Thames.

And Thomas being here? Unexpected, yes. But perhaps fate knows well she deserves this kind of punishment.

"Good," she says finally. "Then you must do as Edwin asked. It's for the best."

Eva says nothing. She takes the breeches from the back of the chair and folds them pointlessly in her lap.

"Miss Haywood," Harriet says suddenly. "That's who I am now. Miss Haywood." Their mother's unmarried name. The name she has chosen to hide behind.

Eva hesitates for a moment, uncertain. But then she nods; seems to catch the thread. Beneath this roof, Harriet is not an aunt, nor a sister. Not a mother. She is just Miss Haywood, wrecked upon the reef.

Eva swallows heavily, toying with the hem of the breeches. "Were you on your way to Lindisfarne? To see us?"

"Yes." It's not a lie. Not a lie at all. And right now, Harriet cannot find the will to give anything other than the simplest answer.

CHAPTER FIVE

Finn sits at the table in a pool of lamplight, turning through the pages of the logbook. His pencil scratches across the page.

November 8: Passenger vessel wrecked on Crumstone.
At least four lives lost on packet boat Cygnus. *Survivors taken to mainland. Trinity House investigation to follow.*

The abrupt phrases feel cold, hollow. Dehumanised pieces of the story. And so he adds: *Survivors spent the night on Longstone.* No mention of Harriet. He has no idea what the outcome of that debacle will be.

Well. He suspects. But he is willing to give Harriet the benefit of the doubt. As long as Eva comes out of this unscathed.

He leans back in his chair, looking out the window at the firebasket glowing against the darkness. The first hint of dawn is pushing at the bottom of the sky. Around him, the cottage is still and quiet; Eva and the boys all piled into the bed, Maggie snuffling softly in the crib beside the fire.

He's glad his wife and children are sleeping. All too often, their nights are broken and firelit, as he and Eva manage a juggle of lightkeeping and childrearing, and stolen, silent moments. Precious hours curled up in bed together as the beacon burns out with the dawn. Last night has broken the chaotic rhythm of their lives.

Finn stretches his arms up over his head, the muscles in his back and shoulders tired and aching. He's exhausted after last night too, and still a little on edge. Something of a wonder, he supposes, that it had taken fifteen years of him keeping the Longstone light to have had a ship founder on his doorstep. After all, it was the death of Finn's two uncles in a wreck on the Knavestone that had caused his father to build the cottage and beacon out here in the first place. To the log, he adds: *Grateful to be of use.*

Over the years, the logbooks have become far more than just a record of the weather and tides. There are entries written in Eva's neat hand; their sons' broad tangles: *Lots of seals in the water today.* Precious records: Noah's arrival; Archie's, Maggie's—born, like their mother, in the rigid safety of Highfield House. The scrawled grief of their Longstone-born daughter, arrived months too early and lost before the dawn.

Finn looks up at the soft creak of the bed. Noah's footsteps sigh over the floorboards.

"The lady in our room," he says. "Who is she?"

"Just someone your mama knows." It seems like the simplest response.

Noah slides onto the chair opposite Finn at the table; tugs the logbook towards him. "'Passenger vessel...'" He frowns in thought, a furrow appearing on the bridge of his nose.

"What's that word?"

"'Wrecked.'"

"'Wrecked on Crumstone.'" Noah glances up at his father with a weighted look in his eyes. A new seriousness that makes him look like more than a child. It catches Finn by surprise.

"All right?" he asks.

Noah nods. "I'm glad all those people are gone."

"So am I."

"There was so many of them."

"Aye. Too many for this place. But they were lucky we were here."

Noah nods again slowly, still frowning over the page.

Tom rolls over in the bed, murmuring in his sleep. "Get dressed," Finn tells his son, closing the logbook. "Let's go outside. Let everyone sleep."

Noah rifles through the pile of clothes at the bottom of the bed and steps into his breeches. Finds his coat and woollen cap hung on the hook beside the door. He pulls them on, following Finn out of the cottage.

A pale grey light is settling over the archipelago, absorbing the line of smoke coiling upwards from the firebasket. Finn walks the island slowly, carefully, peering into rockpools and crevices. There will be pieces of the wreck in these waters now. Pieces of lost lives.

"What are we doing?" Noah asks.

"Just seeing what we can see."

"Pieces of the wreck?"

"Aye." Archie will be out here exploring the pools soon, like he does at every low tide. Pulling flotsam from the water, to clutter up the mantel. Finn does not want him finding anything untoward. He'd prefer for Noah not to see anything either. But then again, he'd seen plenty worse when he was his son's age.

Finn is all too aware that Noah, at nine years old, is the very same age he was when he had fled Longstone on Henry Ward's ship. When he had decided life on this island was not enough for him. He has found himself watching his son more closely these past months, trying to catch any hint of unhappiness, of discontent.

Finn reminds himself that Noah has a far different life to what he had had: he has his mother, his siblings. And, Finn hopes, better relations with his father.

None of that knowledge stops him from wondering, from worrying. It's a concern he has never shared with Eva—can't quite tell if it's because he knows how foolish and unfounded his fear is, or because it's a concern he does not want to pass on to her. A concern, he knows, that's rooted in his own regret at the way he had left Longstone without a word to his father. Left him to fret and fear, and eventually to die alone on this island. Fearing that his own son might do the same feels like the penance he has to pay.

Out on the Crumstone, the masts of the foundered ship are silhouettes against the dawn, torn sails caught by the breeze.

"It's still there," says Noah.

Finn nods. "Trinity House'll be out here soon. Examining the wreck for their investigation. Salvaging what they can."

"An investigation? To find out why it got wrecked?"

"Aye."

Noah squints. "Why *did* it get wrecked?"

"I don't know," Finn admits. *A commotion*, he thinks. But

even if the crew were right about what Harriet was trying to do, that would not have caused the ship to founder. "A navigation error, I imagine."

"Maybe they got blown off course."

"Aye, maybe."

The sun has fully risen by the time they finish their circuit of the island, having found nothing more than a few stray pieces of driftwood. Finn hears voices floating out from the cottage. Fishing boats are dotting the water now. One, he realises, is drawing close to the island.

He goes out to the jetty, Noah trailing. Watches the cutter approach. He recognises the mainsail—misshapen, torn, and badly stitched. Knows the boat belongs to Martin Macauley.

It's Macauley at the tiller, two other Lindisfarne fishermen with him. The sight of them makes Finn uneasy. Macauley has been here in the past, stealing back the coal Finn had stolen from him—and then some. But that was all many years ago; these days, Finn has been doing his best to let his family's long-standing feud with the Macauleys fade.

The boat shudders as it knocks against the jetty. Finn is faintly surprised the thing is seaworthy. It feels like only a matter of time before he's pulling Martin Macauley off the Crumstone.

Macauley climbs out, leaving one of the other fishermen to secure the cutter to the moorings.

"Can I help you?" Finn asks guardedly. He slides a protective hand over Noah's shoulder.

Macauley reaches into the boat and produces a small hessian sack. "A gift from the villagers," he says stiffly.

Finn raises his eyebrows. "What?"

"For your efforts the other night."

Hesitant, Finn takes the bag with a faint nod of thanks. It's heavier than he expected—he feels the solid shape of a bottle inside. Smells a metallic trace of raw meat.

Noah wriggles a hand into the bag. "Look, Da. Apples." He holds one up with a flourish.

Finn turns to see Eva making her way down the cottage stairs, Maggie on her hip. It's the sight of Martin Macauley that has brought her out, he knows. Always, Martin Macauley is able to bring this look of unease to Eva's eyes.

Ten years ago, Martin's father had taken Eva out to sea and tried to kill her, on the belief she was spying for the government against the Jacobites. And Finn knows Eva has never forgiven herself for Donald Macauley's resulting death. Knows there has always been a part of her that fears Martin finding out the truth.

"Is there trouble?" she asks, eyes darting between the men.

"No trouble, Mrs Murray. We're just bringing over a gift from the villagers."

"A gift?" Eva asks doubtfully. "For us?"

"Aye. Father Morgan thought to put around the village for a collection as a show of thanks. Asked us to bring it over on our way out here."

"There's apples, Mama. Look." Noah waves it under Eva's nose, then holds it out for his sister to prod.

Finn wishes he didn't feel so suspicious. But trust between himself and the villagers has always felt like a fragile thing. He knows he's largely to blame—in the days before Eva, he'd stolen coal and peat from the villagers' sheds on more than one occasion. But this visit seems to suggest the villagers might willing to put the past behind them. Why is he finding it so hard to do the same? Is it because of the knowledge he carries of what truly happened to Martin's father?

"Thank you," he says finally. "That's very generous of you all. Please give everyone our thanks."

Macauley nods. He hesitates a moment, and Finn wonders if he is expecting to be invited inside. Finally, he turns to the other two men, gesturing back to the boat. "We'll leave you be then," he says gruffly.

Finn nods. Eva takes a step towards him and pulls Noah in close. Watches as the cutter slides away from the island.

Finn allows himself a faint smile. "I'm surprised he didn't choke himself trying to get those words out his mouth."

———— ⬥ ————

Harriet pulls the curtains back a crack. Watches through the window of the children's bedroom as the boat disappears back towards Lindisfarne. She recognises the men inside, although two have little more than a faint familiarity. Martin Macauley, though, she remembers him well. The son of the man Eva had sent to his death. He's worn and grey from his cap to his boots, hunched and rounded at the shoulders. He seems to have aged much more than a decade. So does his boat.

Through the window, Harriet sees Finn and Eva standing close to one another on the jetty. Watches them speak, eye to eye, his fingers grazing her elbow. A bonneted, pink-cheeked child is pressed between them, nightshift bunched, little stockinged legs hooked around Eva's waist. Their son is crouched at the end of the jetty, rifling through a hessian bag and exhibiting carrots like he's never seen anything so exciting. The sight of all that togetherness manages to dredge up an old jealousy Harriet had long forgotten.

Ten years ago, in a fit of rage, she had sent the authorities after the pirate ship of her father, Henry Ward, not knowing Eva's husband was aboard. Thanks to her, forty men had been sent to their deaths. Thanks to her father, Finn Murray had not been among them.

She'd followed the executions with a bleak obsession. Had felt no small amount of relief when her sister's husband had not faced the hangman. Finn's survival had felt like a reprieve from her guilt, however small. As many as forty women widowed. But her sister was not one of them.

A reprieve from her guilt, yes, but not her anger. Because Eva had knowingly married the man who had killed their brother.

But right now, Harriet is too exhausted to give any energy to that anger. Finn Murray may have taken Oliver's life. But he had saved hers.

How long this amnesty towards Finn will last, she has no idea.

Harriet can tell, by the haunted look on Eva's face as she watches the boat disappear, that there has been no resolution between her and Martin Macauley. Can tell she is still carrying the secret of how Martin's father died.

Two more boys burst from the cottage and Harriet whirls away before she catches more than a glimpse of her son. That faint, fleeting glance is enough to strike her breathless, and she stands for long moments with her back pressed to the wall, hidden from the window, trying to steady herself.

She knows she cannot stay in this room forever. This tiny island, this tiny cottage, feels stifling—far more so with Thomas here. And there is nowhere to run if the man with the missing finger shows himself. Harriet knows she needs to leave as soon as possible.

Eva has left clothes for her on the end of the bed: stays and plain linen petticoats, woollen skirts and a shortjacket the colour of rain-washed slate. Harriet goes to the washbin. Her skin is still sticky with salt, and despite the chill of the water, she scrubs until her body feels raw. She laces the bodice slowly, still heavy with fatigue, though her heart is thumping in the aftermath of Thomas. Eva's jump stays, lined only with cord, feel soft and pliable compared to the whale-boned corset Harriet is used to wearing; the storm-cloud skirts impossibly dour. She longs for her sack gowns and ribboned trims, for stomachers splashed in colour. Those purples and crimsons and fine trails of embroidery are all at the bottom of the German Ocean now. Harriet is just thankful she had her coin pouch in her cloak—with her travel documents inside—when the ship had disappeared beneath her.

She searches the dresser in the corner of the room for anything to make herself more presentable. No hairbrush, but a small wooden comb, which she runs through her tangled curls, wincing as the teeth catch on the salt-hardened snarls of her hair. She peers into the hand-mirror she finds next to the comb. Lowers it quickly. She is too pale, too weary, too colourless. Looks as though she has narrowly survived a shipwreck.

She sets the mirror back on the dresser and tugs at the shortjacket to straighten it. Then she draws in her courage and unclicks the latch of the bedroom door.

Finn and Eva are herding the children back inside as she steps out into the living area. Being in the same room as her son is an almost physical blow, and Harriet finds herself stepping backwards with the force of it.

"Oh," says Eva, her eyes widening slightly at the sight of Harriet. "I..." She gathers herself quickly. Shifts the bonneted child—a daughter, Harriet guesses—onto her other hip. "Children, this is my..." She falters. "A friend. Miss Haywood." The name—the lie—sounds awkward on her tongue. "This is Maggie and Archie," says Eva, gesturing to her daughter and younger son—five or six, perhaps—who takes one look at Harriet and disappears behind his mother. "And Noah." Eva avoids Harriet's eyes. "And this is Tom. My nephew." Harriet hears the strain in her words, the excessive, forced lightness.

"A pleasure to meet you," Harriet manages, in a voice that does not sound like her own. She tries not to let her gaze linger on Thomas. She can see herself in him, yes. Sees herself in his straw-coloured curls and sharp blue eyes. He's golden beside Eva and Finn's dark-haired flock, his coat and breeches newer and neater than Noah and Archie's, though all three boys are similarly windblown and pink-cheeked. Thomas has just an inch or two of height on Noah, though he must be more than a year older. His face is narrow and angular, Edwin's mostly, but the resemblance to her is there. Too faint, Harriet assumes—hopes—for him to see himself. She has not forgotten that unmooring feeling of standing in front of the father she had never known, and seeing herself in him for the first time. She does not want that for her son.

"Is there anything you need?" Eva asks. "Are you warm enough? Are you hungry? Thirsty? Do you—"

"I'm fine." The words come out sharper than she intended.

Archie emerges from behind Eva to inspect the bag his

father has dumped on the table. Finn glances between Harriet and Eva, then looks down at the three boys. "Come on, lads," he says suddenly. "The basket needs emptying. Best we do it now before breakfast."

He herds them back out of the cottage. As the door closes behind them, Harriet lets out a breath she had not realised she was holding.

"Are you all right?" Eva asks.

Harriet nods. Seeing her son has left a quake inside her, but she does not want Eva to know that. Leaving Thomas had been her decision—the right decision. She does not want anyone to question that. Especially not her sister.

Maggie bleats and wriggles, and Eva sets her down on the worn rug in front of the hearth. She totters off towards the table on unsteady legs. "You look better today," Eva says to Harriet. "Are you feeling any stronger?"

"A little." Harriet sidesteps the baby and perches on a chair at the table, folding her hands in her lap. She wishes she had stayed locked away in the bedroom.

Eva peers into the bag on the table, rummaging through its contents. She lifts out a bottle of claret and a misshapen seedcake. Inspects a wrapped cloth package Harriet assumes is full of meat.

"A gift from the villagers," Eva tells her, tucking the meat back into the bag. "I'm not quite sure what to make of it. They've never seen fit to thank us before."

"Well," says Harriet, "I imagine you've never rescued shipwreck survivors before either."

"No. That's true. In any case, I'm grateful. I'll not turn down such an offer with so many mouths to feed." Harriet catches her faint wince. "I mean... Not that I mind. We're very happy to have him here. And Edwin made sure he was well taken care of." Her cheeks flush as she blunders over her words. "Financially, I mean."

Harriet looks down into her hands. She has no idea what to say. An apology? A thank you? She supposes both options would be more than appropriate. But she cannot find the will to speak.

Eva pulls a cannister from the sideboard and scoops its contents into a pot sitting on the hearth. She pours in water from the kettle and hangs it on the hook above the fire, she and Maggie jabbering back and forth to each other in a dialogue Harriet can barely make sense of. She feels like an intruder.

Eva looks over her shoulder. "Tell me about your life," she says, stirring the contents of the pot with one hand and herding her daughter away from the fireguard with the other. "Did you ever make it to France? Are your paintings hung in Parisian salons?"

She speaks with forced lightness, but Harriet hears the weight of the questions. She knows Eva is probing, prying, to see if there might be anything so terrible in her life that she might have no other choice but to fling herself from a ship in the middle of the German Ocean.

"They are," Harriet says. "Yes. I've a number of patrons in France. Several in England."

Maggie stares up at her with wide brown eyes, then makes a grab for a carrot poking out of the bag. She scurries back towards Eva.

"Really? How wonderful. Thank you, Maggie. Give that to me." Eva prises the carrot from her daughter's pudgy fingers. "Sorry," she says to Harriet. "Now she's walking she's into everything. I'm pleased for you. I know it was what you always wanted." She puts the carrot back on the table. "Tell me about your patrons. Are you able to make a living from your art?"

"Yes." And it brings her no small amount of pride. "Although my commissions are not always so thrilling. Usually a patron comes to a woman artist if they want a nice, polite painting of a vase of flowers to hang above the harpsichord."

Eva smiles. "A nice, polite painting of anything has never been quite your style."

Harriet traces a finger over a knot in the wood of the table. "I signed most of my landscapes with a man's name until very recently. One of my London patrons commissioned a series of pieces for a public display. I agreed to it on the condition I could use my own name." She smiles wryly. "It was a series of pieces inspired by these islands, of all things."

Eva raises her eyebrows. "Really?" She glances at Harriet, then corrals her daughter back towards the table. "You thought to paint the islands?"

"I know. I—"

"No sweetheart, you can't have that." A screech from the baby. "It's for another time."

"Perhaps we can speak later," Harriet says stiffly.

Eva gives her apologetic eyes. "I'm sorry," she says, stuffing the bag of food into the sideboard cupboard. "I truly do want to know. I'm just—"

"Raising three children and keeping a shipping light." Harriet glances down, hit with a pang of guilt. "Four children."

Eva doesn't respond at once. "Yes," she says finally. "I

am. We are." She pauses. "But I do wish to hear about all these things. Very much so." Meets Harriet's eyes. "Are you happy?"

It's a complicated question, and in the tentative way Eva asks it, Harriet can tell she is aware of this.

In many ways, she has been happy. Eva is right: seeing her paintings on salon walls *is* the dream she has always wanted. She is slowly, steadily making a name for herself; pushing the boundaries of what is expected of her as a female artist, and tutoring other young women to refine their skills.

Once the fear of being out in the world alone had eased, Harriet had reinvented herself in London. Had detached herself from her old life as Edwin Whitley's wife, and yes, as Thomas's mother. A risk, she knew, to be living her unconstrained life in the city she shared with her estranged husband—the chance of being recognised was always there in the background. But she knew there was little enough crossover between Edwin's circles and her own. Knew, also, that he was unlikely to come looking for her, at least as the months turned into years. With time, the fear of being drawn back into her old existence began to fade.

Life as Miss Haywood was vivid and thrilling—a life lived in bright colours on the fringe of society. Days spent hunched over paper and inkpot, writing letters of introduction, seeking new commissions, managing patrons, setting tasks for her students. Long hours at lamplit canvases, wrangling pastels for her neat, patron-approved flowerpots. Storms of oil paint for the wild skies and islands that flowed most instinctively from heart to hand to brush.

Nights spent twined with Isabelle; talking of art, not talking of art, staring out through the uncovered window in the roof of the garret at the stars that strained through London fog.

Harriet had cared deeply for Isabelle. Cared for her far more intensely than every facet of society told her she ought to. Loved her? Perhaps, but it's an uncomfortable thought, and one Harriet rarely allows herself to go near. Because she had taken what she needed from her—shelter, a listening ear, the confidence to try and make something of herself as an artist—and then stepped out into the world alone.

When it was just the two of them together, being with Isabelle had been a solid, healing thing. Had taken Harriet away from the guilt and unhappiness that had followed her for so much of her life. But the secret of what they were to each other had begun to feel like just another weight to carry. Just another piece of herself she needed to keep from prying eyes. Harriet knew how damaging it would be if anyone discovered the true nature of their relationship. She and Isabelle would both lose patrons, students, commissions. They would be shunned as sinners—never hired again. The fear of it was a weight that Harriet could not bear. And leaving those she cared about, well that was what she did best wasn't it? In so many ways, life was easier on her own.

It has been more than five years since she has spoken to Isabelle. Since she has had more than fleeting glimpses of her among crowds—whether real or imagined, Harriet is never quite certain. She tells herself it is easier this way. Believes herself sometimes. Other times is sure it's a lie.

Eva takes a pile of wooden bowls from the top of the sideboard and fills them with porridge. Gives up waiting for Harriet to answer the question. "If you wish," she says, "I can take you to the house tomorrow. I'm sure it cannot be easy being around Tom. And I'm sure Nathan will be pleased to see you."

She does not sound sure. Rightfully so, Harriet assumes. She has no thought of what kind of reception she will get from her brother. But at least the vastness of Highfield House will give her a little space to breathe.

"Yes," she says finally. "I think that would be for the best."

CHAPTER SIX

This lad that Theodora has dug up from the depths of the island is much too preoccupied for Nathan's liking. As far as he can tell, the boy has been spending far more time chattering at Thea than he has mending the broken window casing. Nathan is beginning to wish he'd attempted to fix the damn thing himself.

Naively—or too hopefully—he'd assumed this to be a simple afternoon's work. How it has extended into a two-day ordeal, he is not quite certain. At least the sound of hammering that has finally started coming from outside the house suggests some work might actually be getting done this afternoon.

Nathan is at his desk now, trying his best to focus on the inventory in front of him. It's an exotic—and expensive—list of porcelain, silk and spices, and he'd really rather not be distracted by thoughts of Thea's roof-man.

Nathan had been pleasantly surprised at how quickly he had managed to rebuild his professional life once he had made the decision to stay here in Northumberland. Had fast recognised the gap in the market—and the number of gentry from Auld Reekie to Newcastle eager to part with their money for a glimpse of the Far East. In little more than a year, he'd managed to rebuild the thriving Northumbrian merchant business his father had once had—and rebuild a little respect for his family name while he was at it. The villagers had been far more welcoming once they had realised he was not spying for the government—these days, it's easy chatter and friendly greetings he gets when he walks the streets of Lindisfarne, instead of turned backs and looks of suspicion.

Nathan loves the challenge of his work, loves the scents and colours of the goods he deals in. The regular excuse to travel to Edinburgh to meet ships and retailers, and snatch a reminder of his old, chaotic city life. Usually, he returns to Holy Island exhausted, exhilarated, and glad to be home.

He realises the hammering has stopped. He looks out the window, straining to see down the side of the house to the broken casing. Hears the dull murmur of voices. A bubble of laughter from Theodora and the boy.

There is a definite ease to their interaction. This boy is no stranger to Thea—of that Nathan is certain. He does not believe for a second that she had just crossed paths with him on her way to the village.

The realisation is uncomfortable. Headstrong and self-assured as she is, Theodora has never been one to lie to him. Challenge him, frustrate him to no end, yes. But never lie.

Why is she feeling the need to do so now?

Probably, Nathan thinks dully, because she had anticipated him acting like a possessive madman at the first hint of some young lad snaring her affection.

He shoves open the window of his study and pokes his head out into the cold air. "I thought I was paying you fix my window," he calls.

Thea and the boy whirl around, starting at the sight of him glaring down on them from above.

Theodora's cheeks blaze. "Papa," she hisses. "Don't be rude. I was just telling him there are extra tools in the cart shed if he needs them."

Nathan would like to believe that. Does not believe that.

He is not looking forward to the day when Theodora marries and leaves him to start her own life. He wants her to be happy, of course. Wants that more than anything. But he cannot bear to think how empty this house will feel then. Or how much he will miss her when she is no longer sitting across the table from him at breakfast time, chattering away about the story she had stayed up all night writing. For so many years, it has just been the two of them, tucked away in the cradle of Highfield House. What will he do when she is no longer there to call out to when the sky clears and the stars light the darkness, or he sees auroras glowing at the window?

Thea is still months from her eighteenth birthday; up until now she has shown little interest in any lad she has crossed paths with—at least to the best of his knowledge. Nathan had told himself he still had a year or two at least before she settled down with a family of her own. But given the way she is creeping around the place with this boy, he is beginning to wonder if he may have misjudged the situation.

The boy glances at the broken casing, then back up to Nathan's study window. He looks distinctly uncomfortable. "Thank you, Miss Blake," he garbles at Thea. "I'm sure I'll manage to find the tools on my own." He bobs his head at Nathan. "Window should be finished this afternoon, sir. Tomorrow morning at the latest." He hurries away, disappearing around the side of the house.

Nathan watches him vanish. When he looks back down at Theodora, her hands are planted on her hips and her flushed expression suggests she is wild with either anger or embarrassment. Probably both.

"Did you really have to do that?" she demands. "I was only telling him about the tools. Honestly."

"I think that boy's done quite enough work around here," Nathan says tautly. "It's time I sent him on his way and found someone to do the job properly."

"No!" she cries. "Papa, you can't! I swear, he did nothing wrong." She stares up at him, pinning her blue eyes to his. "Do you not trust me?"

"It's that lad I don't trust."

She doesn't look away. "That's not what I asked you."

Her brassiness makes Nathan curl his hands around the windowsill in frustration. Somehow, she always manages to back him into a corner. He'd hoped he might have learnt to deal with her better after seventeen years of being her father, but he seems to be getting worse at it. Or maybe she is getting better.

"Of course I trust you," he says.

"Good. Then you'll forget this nonsense about letting him go. The job's half-finished, after all."

"That's exactly my problem. The job's half-finished. He's a little too preoccupied for my liking."

Theodora turns, catching sight of a small single-masted boat gliding towards the embankment. "Oh thank heavens," she says dramatically, tossing her cloak for full effect, "Auntie Eva is here to talk some sense into you." She frowns. Looks up at Nathan. "Who's that with her?"

Nathan looks out to watch the boat approach, and suddenly the boy at the broken window is the furthest thing from his mind. He swallows, unsure exactly what to make of this creeping sense of unease. "That's your Aunt Harriet."

CHAPTER SEVEN

Nathan has no idea how to greet her. No idea what it is he is feeling towards her, this long-lost half-sister of his, who had disappeared from all their lives—her own son included. Anger? Relief? Gratitude at finding her alive?

He realises Theodora has disappeared inside the house. It's unlike her, Nathan thinks distantly. She is usually more than welcoming of any guests.

"Harriet," he manages, as his sisters climb the embankment towards the house. "It's good to see you." He has no idea if he's speaking the truth.

Harriet nods. There's a distant, dazed look about her. The bewilderment of being back here, perhaps? It seems like something more. Harriet has always worn an invisible weight around her, but it seems to have intensified in the time she has been away. Her blue eyes feel harder, somehow. Colder. She is wearing dark-grey skirts inches too short for her, and the ill-fitting clothes only add to the discordance of her being here.

Eva puts a hand to Harriet's shoulder. "I assume you've a bed for her here, Nathan." She gives him a look that acknowledges his questions. A look that promises to answer them.

"Of course, yes. You're always welcome here." The response comes out sounding forced. He goes back to the house, Eva and Harriet following. Rings the bell in the entrance hall for the housekeeper. When Mrs Brodie appears, he says, "Please find a room upstairs for my sister."

A faint look of surprise crosses the housekeeper's face. She must remember Harriet, surely. But she asks nothing. Just says, "Of course, sir. I've a guest room already made up." She turns to Harriet. "This way, madam."

Nathan flashes his sister a strained smile. "Make yourself comfortable upstairs, Harriet. We shall talk soon. If you wish." He watches after her and Mrs Brodie as they disappear up the staircase. Whirls around to face Eva, eyebrows raised in question.

"She was on the ship that was wrecked," she tells him, voice low. "Finn pulled her from the water half frozen to death."

Nathan lets out a breath. "Did she come looking for Tom?"

Eva shakes her head. "She had no idea he was here."

"And does she know now?" Nathan asks. "Does he?"

"Harriet knows who he is. Tom doesn't know who she is."

"You mustn't tell him," says Nathan. "Edwin—"

"I know. I'll not say a word."

"Was she coming up here to see us?" he asks finally.

"That's what she says." There's a thinness to Eva's words.

"You don't believe her?"

She doesn't answer at once. Glances up the staircase. "I want to believe it," she says. "But I can't help thinking she's hiding things from us. One of the ship's crewmen said she tried to throw herself off the ship before it struck the Crumstone. Harriet denies it, but I have no thought of whether she's telling the truth."

Harriet stands in the doorway of the room the housekeeper had led her into, letting her brother and sister's voices float up the staircase. For the love of God, do they really think she cannot hear them?

"Do you really think she would do something so dreadful?" Nathan is asking. "I hope her life isn't so terrible…"

Anger flickers inside her. Is that really what Nathan and Eva think her life has become? Do they really imagine she might have failed so spectacularly out on her own that she had no choice but to end things in the black water off Northumberland, of all cursed places?

"I don't know what to believe," Eva says again. "Honestly, I have no idea who she really is these days. I'm not sure I ever have."

"Nor I. I don't think she has ever really wanted us to know."

Harriet feels a pull of bitterness. In a way, Nathan is right. There have always been parts of her she has not wanted her siblings to see. Things that are far too dangerous to ever speak of. Her feelings for Isabelle, yes, but more than that too.

Those knots of darkness she has always felt present within her—coils of selfishness and deceit and self-loathing. Things she could barely put into words, even if she wanted to. Things she knows Nathan and Eva would never understand.

Nonetheless, a part of her wants to be open with her siblings, if for no other reason than to stop their painful dithering. She wants to tell them what happened on that ship, tell them why she is really here. Wants to tell them of the beacons of light that shine in her life, beneath those knots of dark. But right now, the weight of it all feels far too great. A physical thing that has melded with the bone-deep exhaustion the wreck has left within her. She feels like a part of herself is still trapped under the waves.

Harriet closes the bedroom door, silencing her siblings' voices. She had hoped for a little trust from Eva and Nathan. But she supposes she does not deserve it. After all, isn't it honesty that leads to trust? She's never been brilliant at honesty.

Nathan and Eva have always been close. Harriet can tell their bond has only solidified over the past decade, out here in the isolation of the islands. Has she ever been anything but the outsider?

She perches on the edge of the narrow bed. This room the housekeeper has led her to is her sister's old bedroom. Harriet is glad of it. She had feared she might be shunted into the room she had once shared with Edwin, or worse, the room that had been her son's nursery.

Eva's old bedchamber is sparsely decorated, with more empty space than anything else. An old chest of drawers takes up the corner beside the washstand; the chipped gold-rimmed mirror atop the mantel the only hint of opulence. Harriet catches the faint musty smell of time and neglect that had hung in so many of these rooms the last time she was here. She imagines Nathan has few overnight visitors. Why would anyone come out to this island by choice?

She goes to the window, drawing the curtains to block the view of the Farne Islands. She can certainly do without the sight of that damn place flooding into her dreams.

She has never felt as though she belongs here, in this house of the Blakes. She feels an intruder into someone else's story. She's wrong of course, because this house is her story: it's her meeting her real father, and abandoning her son, and watching her painted moonscapes swallowed by flames. It's her lies and her betrayal of her family and all the worst parts of herself.

Harriet hates who she is inside this house.

CHAPTER EIGHT

Theodora has not slept. She has been sitting up in bed for hours, half-formed sentences scrawled in the notebook in her lap. She still feels wide awake.

Her father says it's her choice of writing topics that cause her broken sleeps. She supposes he has a point: she has been losing herself in worlds of selkies and bogles and bluecaps for as long as she can remember.

And then there's the Lady in the Dunes. A making of Theodora's own imagination.

The Lady in the Dunes has been floating around her mind for years. A character that had emerged to her half-formed, then taken shape over time, populating several of her stories. The lost and wraithlike Lady in the Dunes—not quite alive and not quite dead. Sometimes wandering the dark island alone, looking for something unknown. Sometimes standing at the water's edge, watching for a ship, waiting to be saved.

The folk tales ingrained in this part of the country have always intrigued her. Have always given a sense of magic to the place. The Lady in the Dunes feels like Theodora's own folk tale. A story grown from her own little piece of the world—the lonely dunes surrounding this lonely house on this lonely, windblown island.

A lonely house, yes, but she has always loved it, fiercely and possessively. In all likelihood, it will be hers one day, and she cannot abide the idea of having to hand it over to a husband. She loves its cobbled-together walls of stone and brick, the ivy that tickles the salt-streaked panes, loves the way the years have worked their way into everything, like the rotting old window casing she'd sent B up here to prod around at. She loves that every time she opens a door, she finds another dark corner she does not remember exploring. She loves how full of secrets Highfield House has always felt.

When her father had invited her to choose a room to make her own, she had had no hesitations about choosing this one. This room Papa had tried to keep her out of as a child; this room with the priest hole within the wall. She knows, of course, that things have happened here in this room. Knows it from the look of hesitation on Papa's face when she had told him which room she wanted. Knows it from the priest hole, and the passage going down, down into the house, blocked up at its end now to keep intruders out. And she knows it because every part of this house has its own memories and stories, as though it has been here alone on Emmanuel Head for as long as the stars have burned.

Theodora knows there are pieces of the past she has not been told. She is all right with that. Just fills the gaps with imagination and story.

But tonight, her writing is just a distraction.

Theodora remembers her Aunt Harriet. She remembers

her well. How could she not?

She had been seven years old when she had stepped into the parlour and seen Harriet with a pillow in hand, holding it over her husband's face as he lay on the settle with a bullet wound in his side.

Even at such a young age, Theodora had recognised what Harriet had been about to do. When she was younger, she had made excuses for what she'd seen; tried to convince herself that perhaps her aunt was simply tidying the bedclothes, or picking up a pillow that had fallen. But deep inside, she has always known the truth.

When Harriet had disappeared, it had loosened a knot that had begun to form in Theodora's stomach. She is well aware that her catching her aunt in the act had likely played a part in her decision to leave. Her decision to abandon her son.

Theodora has never told anyone this. Not a single piece of it. But every time she looks at her cousin Tom, she cannot help but feel guilty. If she had not barged into the parlour unannounced, would Harriet never have left him?

Perhaps. Or perhaps she would have succeeded in smothering her husband to death.

Despite everything she had seen that day, Theodora has always been fascinated by her aunt.

She remembers asking her father questions when Harriet had first disappeared. Where she had gone. Why. When she was coming back. Even as a child, it had not taken her long to realise Papa did not have the answers.

As the years turned over, Harriet became a piece of the past they rarely discussed. After all, what was there to say? No one had any knowledge of her, nothing to add to the conversation. She had been slipped into that same dark corner of family stories as Oliver, the other whispered name.

The secrecy—or rather, the lack of knowledge—had only made Harriet come alive even more vividly in Theodora's mind. She was fascinated by these flimsy pieces of her aunt's story: an artist, a woman who had fled the life she had been handed, the pirate's daughter who had vanished without a word.

Now that Harriet is here in the house, there are so many things Theodora wants to ask her. Needs to ask her. Does not know if she will ever find the courage.

She'd had to summon a sizeable helping of bravery just to venture down to the dining room for supper tonight. Had been spared the unease by Harriet staying in her bedchamber, claiming she was too tired to eat. Theodora had been grateful for the comfortable familiarity of eating just with her father. Grateful for the chance to ask questions. Harriet had been on the Crumstone wreck, Papa had told her. But he seemed to know little of why his sister was here. Just like all those years ago, Theodora had come away from her questioning with few answers.

Now, as she sits up in bed with scrawls of disjointed writing on the page in front of her, she hears the door across the hallway creak open. Sees a globe of candlelight dance through the darkness. She hears the footsteps, somehow avoiding the squeaking floorboards like she herself never manages to do.

She slips out of bed and is through the door before she can change her mind. The light is coming from the study, and for a moment, she wonders if the footsteps might just belong to her father. No. Papa is one to go clomping down the hallway regardless of the hour; these footfalls had been too light and soundless to belong to him.

She creeps down the hallway and pushes open the study door.

At the groan of the hinges, Harriet turns, looks up from where she is rifling through the desk drawer. "Theodora," she says.

Theodora is faintly surprised Harriet has recognised her so quickly. But then she supposes, *Who else would I be?*

She holds up her candle. Even with deep shadows on her cheeks, her aunt is painfully beautiful, with coils of dark gold hair spilling over her shoulders and intense blue eyes. There's something wraithlike about her, standing here pooled in candlelight, in nothing but a nightgown and shawl. Theodora thinks, *The Lady in the Dunes.*

She wonders if some intuitive part of her had pieced together the story of the Lady in the Dunes from the fragmented, weighted memories she had of her aunt. Theodora's folk tale—her way of making sense of the world. Making sense of all that had happened during those turbulent months when her family had first returned to Holy Island. Making sense of what she'd seen when she had peeked into the parlour that day.

Her Aunt Harriet has long been a mysterious, displaced figure on the fringes of Theodora's memory. Little wonder she has worked her way into her stories.

"Are you looking for something?" Theodora asks.

Harriet looks faintly guilty. "A notebook," she says. "And a pencil. Most of my belongings were lost in the wreck."

Theodora sets down her candle and pulls open the bottom drawer, where Papa keeps his spare ledgers. She has pilfered a few of them herself over the years, when struck by inspiration. She hands an empty notebook to Harriet, along with a pencil taken from the cup on Papa's desk.

"Thank you."

Theodora nods. Hesitates. "Do you make a living from your art?" she asks curiously. "Without a husband?"

"Yes. Or at least, I did."

"Why not anymore?"

Harriet shakes her head. "I don't know when I'll be back in London. That's all."

"But you do plan on going back?"

"I hope so, yes."

Theodora can tell there is plenty her aunt is not sharing. "I want to write," she blurts. "Or rather, I do write. But I want to publish my work. I want people other than my family and friends to read it."

The small smile on Harriet's face is suddenly genuine. "I remember your writing. I'm glad you're still doing it."

"Do you paint under your own name? Or do you use a man's name?"

"Both, depending on the client."

"I want to use my own name," Theodora says. "Do you think I could?"

Harriet smiles faintly. "That depends on how wild and inappropriate your stories are."

Theodora returns her smile, feeling her cheeks colour slightly. She tugs her shawl around her shoulders, suddenly awkward. Is about to leave, when Harriet says:

"Do you write about the island?"

Theodora thinks of the Lady in the Dunes wandering through streams and rises in the vast rolling centre of Lindisfarne. Standing on the shore, waiting forever for a ship that never comes. "Of course," she says. "How could I do otherwise?"

"It's like that, isn't it. The way it works its way inside you." Harriet sounds faintly bitter, as though this is inspiration she has not sought. Memories she does not want.

Theodora feels uncertain. Like an intruder in her own house. "Is there anything else you need?" she asks stiffly.

"No. Just the notebook. Thank you."

Theodora is glad of it. Glad for the excuse to hurry back to her bedchamber, close her own notebook and keep the Lady in the Dunes at a distance tonight.

Theodora remembers; Harriet knows this without a doubt. Remembers seeing her in the parlour that day. Remembers what she had tried to do.

She listens as her niece's footsteps disappear back down the passage. Waits for silence to fall over the house again.

Harriet clutches the notebook to her chest and carries it back to the guestroom. She is exhausted, wishes she could sleep. But her thoughts are charging far too rapidly for that. Thoughts of the man with the dark beard and the little finger hacked off at the knuckle. The memory of water closing in around her. And now, the aching reminder of what she allowed Theodora to see, all those years ago.

At least now she has a pencil and paper—an outlet for the storm inside her head.

She pulls the guestroom door closed and curls back beneath the covers, opening the notebook and letting the pencil glide across the page. Above her head, the thick beams of the house moan. A log shifts and turns black in the grate.

Though the curtains are closed, Harriet finds her eyes darting constantly towards the window. The man with the missing finger prowls in her mind's eye. She has only vague ideas about who he might be, but she is certain that whatever he wants with her, it is nothing good. What if he goes back to Longstone searching for her? What if, somehow, he finds her here in Highfield House?

Things have not worked out the way she planned when she had first decided to return to Northumberland. And the last thing she wants to do is to put her family in danger.

Tonight, she has too little strength to do anything but stay here with Nathan and Theodora. But in the morning, she will go to the lodging house across the water in Beal. Put some distance between herself and her family. She knows it's risky. But far less so than staying here.

CHAPTER NINE

Nathan is not surprised that Harriet is leaving. That's what she does, isn't it? Runs and hides and leaves questions and worry in her wake? At least this time she has told them where she is going. He tries not to be offended that she is choosing to stay in the Beal lodging house rather than in the family home.

He wants to be pleased his sister is here. Wants to be pleased to see her. She has been in his thoughts so much over the past ten years. He has worried for her, missed her, agonised over his own role in her fleeing. What might he have done, have said, differently, to keep her from leaving? Would such a thing even have been possible?

But when Eva had appeared yesterday with Harriet in tow, and Nathan had looked his youngest sister in the eye, all he could think of was the way she had abandoned her child. Abandoned her husband in the midst of a long, slow recovery from a bullet wound. Left them all with so many unanswered questions, so much uncertainty. Being pleased to see her feels like something of a challenge.

His anger at Harriet is not helped by the reappearance of The Boy. Unsurprisingly, the window is still not fixed.

Nathan had known from the beginning that the boy had come here with ulterior motives. But now he's starting to doubt whether he has any carpentry skills at all. Or whether his sole ambition in life is gambolling about the place with Theodora.

Nathan is out on the doorstep with Thea, reciting obligatory pleasantries to Harriet—*are you quite sure you'll not stay?*—when the boy and his futile toolbox appear over the dunes. It's a heavy, grey day, with an icy wind spitting sand up off the embankment and doing nothing to improve Nathan's mood.

Harriet climbs into the wagon Lewis has waiting. Nathan watches as it rattles away down the coast path.

"Good morning, Mr Blake," says the boy, swiping a swathe of dark hair from his eyes. He gives Thea a rakish grin. "Miss Blake."

Theodora turns away from watching the wagon. "Good morning." Her smile doesn't quite reach her eyes. She has seemed uneasy with Harriet around. Had denied any issue when Nathan had asked her about it, but he is not convinced. He wonders if his sister had said or done something to put Theodora on edge.

In spite of his irritation at the boy, he is glad to see at least a semblance of a smile back on his daughter's face.

Theodora grabs at her shawl before the wind snatches it off her shoulders. "I've asked Mrs Brodie to make some tea," she says suddenly. "Would you like a cup before you start work this morning? It's dreadfully cold." Before Nathan can react, she has opened the front door and is ushering the boy inside.

Nathan stifles the urge to follow them. Mrs Brodie is in the house, he reminds himself. It's not as though they will be left to their own dubious devices. And yes, he wants to trust Theodora. Desperately wants to trust her. As hard as she is making it right now.

He lets himself inside and hangs his coat on the hook beside the door. Hears murmured voices coming from the downstairs hallway.

"This is a bad idea," he hears the boy say. "Your da doesn't trust me. We ought to have just told him all of it from the beginning."

Nathan abandons his plan to return to his study. Sidles across the entrance hall, trying to remain silent.

"No," Theodora hisses. "It's better this way. Trust me. Papa will come around. Just finish fixing the window." She pauses. "You do know how to, don't you?"

"Of course I do. But—"

"Good," she says. "That will put you on the right side of Papa. And then we can tell him everything."

In an instant, all the calm Nathan has been trying to cultivate is washed away. "Tell me what?" he demands, marching into the hallway.

Theodora whirls around. "Oh," she says. "Papa..."

The boy blusters towards the door. "I'm sorry," he says. "This was a mistake. I should—"

She snatches his wrist. "Please just tell him. It will be all right, I promise."

Nathan's eyes dart between the two of them. "Tell me what? What in heaven's name is going on here, Theodora?"

Thea looks pleadingly at the boy. He scrubs a hand across his face, then draws in a breath, as though trying to find his courage.

"I'm Bobby Mitchell," he says. "Back when I was a child, you and my mother, Julia, were… Well, I don't really know what you were. But I hope you've not forgotten her. Because she really needs your help."

CHAPTER TEN

Forgotten her? Nathan almost laughs. In ten years, he's not come remotely close to forgetting Julia Mitchell. Has come to the conclusion that such a thing will never be possible.

He feels suddenly unsteady. Feels as though the ground is shifting beneath him. Julia has never left his thoughts, but it has been almost a decade since he has spoken of her.

"What do you mean she needs my help? What's happened? Where is she? Why—" He presses a hand to the wall in an attempt to stop the barrage of questions falling out his mouth.

"She's in Bamburgh," says Bobby.

Nathan swallows heavily. Whenever he thinks of Julia, he always imagines her in Scotland or London—somewhere far further from here than Bamburgh, just across the water. A necessary act of self-preservation. The knowledge that she might be so close—might have always been so close?—is dizzying.

"She's got caught up with some bad people," Bobby tells

him. "Thieves."

Nathan's stomach rolls. He thinks of the way Julia had packed up her beloved curiosity shop on Church Lane and left Holy Island. Had put distance between herself and him after things had fallen apart between them. "She's been thieving to survive?"

Bobby rubs the dark stubble on his jaw. Glances at Theodora. She nods at him to continue. "It's more complicated than that," he says. "There's a thieving ring been operating out of Bamburgh for years. Part of the anti-Jacobite movement. Ma got caught up with them a couple of years ago."

A thousand thoughts rush at him. Guilt and regret, mostly, at having let Julia walk out of his life—and into this one. "Why doesn't she leave?" he asks Bobby. "Money?"

Bobby shakes his head. "Once you're involved with the ring, it's hard to step away. I suppose they're afraid of turncoats going to the authorities. I've tried to convince Ma to leave. But she says it's too dangerous. Says she has nowhere else to go." He digs his hands into his pockets, broad shoulders rounding. "I'm sorry to come to you like this, Mr Blake. I don't know what there was between you and my ma. All I remember is that she used to speak well of you. But she needs help and there's no one else I can ask. My Uncle Angus is in London and Ma's other brothers died in the Rising. I even went looking for my grandfather, hoping he might help. I couldn't find him. I suspect he's dead."

Nathan nods slowly. "How can I help her?"

"She needs somewhere safe to stay."

"For how long?"

"Honestly, I don't know," Bobby admits. "She just needs

to get out of Bamburgh. Get somewhere the thieves can't find her if they decide to punish her for leaving."

Nathan leans up against the wall. Hears Mrs Brodie clattering around with the teacups in the kitchen. "Why not tell me all this straight away?" he asks. "Why all this rubbish about fixing the window?"

"I—"

"That was my doing," Theodora cuts in. "Please don't be angry with Bobby, Papa. I overheard him in the village asking for directions to the house. He told me why he was coming here, and what he planned to ask you. I said it would be best if he warmed to you a little first. I know things ended badly between you and Bobby's mother, and—"

"How do you know that?" Theodora had been a child when Julia had last been on the island. How does she have any idea that there were *things* between the two of them to have ended badly in the first place?

Theodora waves a dismissive hand. "Auntie Eva told me all about it."

"Of course she did."

"*Anyway,*" Theodora says pointedly, "I wasn't sure how you would react to what Bobby's asking. I thought you'd be more likely to agree to it if you got to know him a little first. And if he helped you with the window." Her cheeks colour. "I didn't know you were going to accuse him of trying to court me."

Nathan rubs his eyes. He's not in the least surprised by this elaborate plot of Theodora's. She has always had a flare for the dramatic. But she is wrong about one thing: none of this was necessary. It does not matter what had passed between him and Julia. How can he do anything but help her?

"Bring her back here," he says. "She can stay as long as she needs."

A look of surprise flickers over Bobby's face. "Thank you," he gushes. "Thank you so much."

Nathan nods, steeling himself against the torrent of emotion that rises in his chest. "You have the means to get out to Bamburgh and back? Before the tide cuts off the island?"

"Aye, we'll manage."

Nathan doesn't like *we'll manage*. "Lewis will be back from Beal with the wagon shortly," he says. "Have him take you over." But no, he doesn't like that either. He had left Julia to her own devices before. Has no intention of doing that now. Getting her away from the thieving ring suddenly feels like the most pressing thing he has ever had to do. He marches back into the entrance hall and takes his coat from the hook. Looks over his shoulder at Bobby. "And I shall come with you."

The lodging house in Beal is tiny; just three or four rooms upstairs and a cramped public house on the ground floor—lopsided chairs and tables jostling one another for space, and a Hanoverian flag hanging above a fireplace in desperate need of sweeping.

Harriet chooses the dormitory on the top storey. She much prefers her own space—hates cramming into shared beds with strangers—but she figures having other people around will protect her somewhat if the bearded man somehow manages to find her.

But when she pushes open the door to the communal lodging space, she finds the room empty. Two large beds, wide enough to hold four people each, are untouched, dust speckling the surface of the water in the jug beside the washbin. Harriet is reminded of what an outpost this place is. Reminded she is not in London anymore.

She sets her miserable luggage—a cloth bag containing just a clean shift and underskirts borrowed from Eva, and the notebook and pencil Theodora had stolen on her behalf— down beside the bed and perches on the edge. Runs her fingers over her bodice, feeling the swell of the purse tucked inside her stays. She coughs loudly, just to make a little noise.

She pulls the notebook from the bag and opens to a fresh page. Sketches the outlines of the image beyond the window: shimmering mudflats tying Lindisfarne to the mainland. Once, years ago, she had almost drowned out there in that patch of empty sea. What an odd thing it is to look at it waterless; to stare at the ocean floor at the place the sea had once consumed her. After the wreck, it feels like painful symmetry.

Her pencil glides and scratches, forming pools and pebbles and gulls; the gentle slope of the island on the other side of the water. She has no desire to commit this image to memory, but the simple act of putting pencil to paper has always been able to calm her. Bring order to her most chaotic thoughts. Lindisfarne has found its way into her artwork on far more than one occasion—most recently at Lord and Lady Allbridge's public exhibition. The pieces had churned their way out of her faster than anything else she had ever painted: rising water at the Pilgrims' Way; storm-tossed dunes; a castle siege. Each drawn just as instinctively and necessarily as these mudflats. A sign, Harriet knows, of how deeply Holy Island has worked its way inside her.

Notebook still in hand, she stands, peering through the glass to take in as much of the land around the lodging house as possible. She realises it has become more than the act of an artist observing her surroundings. Has become the act of prey seeking to hide from her hunter. Perhaps that's what it has always been. She sees no one, just mudflats and green. Is not sure if that stillness, that emptiness, makes her relieved, or as unsettled as this empty room does.

How long will it be before he finds her?

She appreciates the irony. She had come up here to Northumberland in the hope of finding a safe haven. Has brought the danger with her.

Now she has nowhere to go, but at least she is out of her family's way. They are safe from her and the trouble she always manages to drag along behind her. Her sister. Her brother. Nieces, nephews.

Her son.

The bearded man may come for her, but her family will not be caught up in any of her mess. And at least, she thinks; at least that is something.

"I'm sorry for all that horsing about with the window," says Bobby. He and Nathan are sitting opposite one another in the wagon as it jolts through muddy farmland towards Bamburgh. "And I'm sorry if you thought I was being too forward with your daughter."

Nathan gives him a short smile. "I know Thea well enough

to be certain most of that was her doing." He looks out the window as they rattle past rolling farmland and overgrown grass, trees bent crooked with decades of sea-wind. Focusing on their surroundings goes some small way to settling the chaos inside him. Light rain is sheening the windows, making the images blurred and hazy.

Nathan's heart is thundering at the thought of seeing Julia again. At the thought of what he might say to her; how he is to act around her; what he will feel in her presence. The last time they had stood face to face, they had spoken in bitter half-sentences, and he had let her disappear from his life.

No. The last time they had stood face to face, they had spoken in bitter half-sentences, confessed their love for one another, and then he had let her disappear from his life.

He knows that, in the wake of all the lies and distrust he and Julia had entangled themselves in, letting her go was the only way forward. But at the thought of facing her again, all that clarity is crumbling.

"Has Julia been in Bamburgh this whole time?" he asks. "Since the two of you left Lindisfarne?"

"No." Bobby looks down. "We went up to Scotland first. Were in Edinburgh for a few years."

"Why return to England?"

He hesitates. Picks at a loose thread on the cuff on his grey coat. "Things changed."

"What things?"

Bobby shrugs, avoiding Nathan's eyes. "Work. Life. Just… things…"

Nathan feels a faint needling of suspicion. "Why have you come to me now? You said she's been caught up in the ring for the past two years."

"I've been away working in North Sunderland," Bobby says. "Ma wanted me to leave Bamburgh. She wanted me to get out while I still could, before I got caught up in the ring too. But when I came back to see her last week, I realised that was the wrong thing to do. Things have gotten worse. I should never have left her. And now I just want to help her get out."

"Why have things got worse? What's happened? Why are you so determined to get her out now all of a sudden?"

Bobby hesitates. "The thieves in the ring, they've got her keeping their records. Book-keeping, like. You know, as she did in her shop."

Nathan nods faintly.

"She keeps a box safe in her tenement with some of the takings in it."

"Things that people in the ring steal?"

"Aye. It's all pooled together, like. Ma keeps records of what's come in, and from who. It all gets distributed between the ring members. The leaders like to make out as if it's all a fair game. But do you think they share it out even?" He snorts. "I hate that they make Ma keep all the takings under her roof. It's not safe. Anyone could come for it. Especially now."

"Why?" Nathan pushes. "What do you mean, especially now?"

Bobby shakes his head. Shrugs again, folding his arms across his chest. "It's like I said, things change. That's all. Nothing more." He turns to look out the window; an attempt to end the conversation.

Nathan grits his teeth. "Bobby," he says, trying to rein in his frustration, "what are you not telling me?"

"Nothing." After a moment, he sighs resignedly. Turns away from the window to face Nathan's expectant look. "Fine," he says. "Things are worse now because he's left her. Or rather, he's disappeared. And now she's on her own."

Nathan's chest tightens. "Who's disappeared?"

"Calum," Bobby says finally. "Ma's husband."

CHAPTER ELEVEN

Nathan feels a violent, falling sensation in his stomach. "Julia has a husband?"

"Aye. They met in Scotland. Not so long after we left Lindisfarne." Bobby is deliberate in not meeting his eyes.

For a long time, Nathan says nothing. He feels utterly foolish, sitting here agonising over the last conversation he and Julia had had. Agonising over what he might say to her now. What she might say to him. Because of course she has a husband. Ten years have passed since they have seen each other, and Julia is vibrant, intelligent, striking. Of course another man has claimed her.

Nathan feels cold and hollow. "Interesting that you did not share any of this with me before I agreed to help you."

Bobby nods, absorbing his anger. But then he dares to say, "Does it make a difference?"

Nathan lets out his breath. He pounds on the wall of the coach, urging Lewis to draw the horses to a halt. He leaps out before they come to a complete stop. Bobby climbs out behind him.

"Of course it makes a difference," Nathan says tightly. He paces through the mud on the side of the road. "I cannot bring another man's wife to stay in my house."

"Ma said Calum disappeared a few weeks ago," Bobby tells him. "She said something passed between them, but she wouldn't tell me what. Whatever it was, it made him angry enough to leave."

Nathan eyes him. "Leave. For good?"

"I don't know," Bobby admits. He folds his hands behind his head. "Ma hasn't heard from him. She doesn't know if he's coming back. But that's the thing. She's on her own now. Keeping that damn box safe under her roof. And that makes her a target."

Nathan stops pacing. He leans back against the coach, lifting his face to the sky. The rain is cold against his cheeks. Anger bubbles inside him at this man, this faceless stranger, who had married Julia and left her to her own devices, at the mercy of a band of thieves.

"Mr Blake," Bobby says, yanking him from his thoughts. "I'm sorry I didn't tell you about Calum before. But I'm desperate for your help." He digs his hands into the pockets of his coat, shoulders rounding. "I can't leave Ma alone in the tenement. She refuses to let me stay with her because she doesn't want me caught up in the ring. And if she tries to leave without having anywhere safe to go, I'm afraid the thieves will catch her. Punish her."

Emotion in Bobby's voice. Fear for his mother.

Nathan rubs a hand across his eyes. *Of course it makes a difference*, he had said. No. That was wrong. Because this has always been about helping Julia. Getting her to safety. For a moment, he had tried to make it something else. But it is far too late for that. Right now, Julia is in trouble—and what choice does he have but to help her?

He pulls open the door of the wagon and climbs back onto the bench. "Get in," he tells Bobby. "We need to hurry if we're to make it back before the tide."

⁂

When she hears the stairs leading up to her tenement creak, Julia's first reaction is fear.

No, not fear. She doesn't allow herself to call it that. Alertness.

Her body feels taut and breathless, her heart overbeating, fearing thieves. She tries to guess by the intensity of the creaks who might be on the other side of the door.

Calum, perhaps, is the most likely candidate. Or the least likely. Julia has no thought of whether she will ever see her husband again. Nor is she sure if the thought of Calum returning home ought to make her more or less afraid. Alert. When he'd blustered out of here three weeks ago, she had never seen him so angry.

There's a soft tap at the door. "Ma?"

At the sound of Bobby's voice, relief makes her shoulders sag. She throws open the door and pulls her son into her arms. He's far too transient a figure in her life these days, as he traipses around the nearby villages doing itinerant farm work. Still, it's better than him staying here, waiting for the thieving ring to entrap him as it has her. It was why she had insisted on him leaving in the first place.

He glances around the tenement, taking in the bed in the

corner with its blankets heaped at the bottom, the half-drunk teacup and empty plate on the table, the underclothes drying on the pulley above the fireplace. Rain has soaked through the cloth window, leaving a pool of water on the floorboards.

"Has Calum come back?" Bobby asks, voice low.

Julia shakes her head. "I've not heard a word from him."

Her son has a slightly frantic look in his eyes. He stands close, towering over her. "Are you safe?" he asks. "Has there been any trouble?"

"Of course I'm safe." It feels like a lie. She is unharmed, yes, but Julia knows there is no guarantee things will stay that way. The box safe of takings beneath the bed has always made her feel like a target. She knows the thieves tucked in away in every corner of this town are not above stealing from their own ring. And if any of them discover she is here on her own, she is sure it will make them even more likely to do so.

Julia has kept to herself since Calum's disappearance; has told no one but those closest to her about his leaving—half out of a need for safety, and half out of a need to avoid the shame. But she is certain that news of her husband's disappearance will have filtered through the ring by now. After all, it's been three weeks since anyone has seen him.

But she does not want her son to worry for her. She suspects, however, that she is far too late in wishing that. Bobby had been frantic when he had returned from North Sunderland last week to find Calum gone and her alone. She hates that that worry is there. She ought to be the one fretting after him, not the other way around.

Bobby glances over his shoulder towards the door. "Pack your things, Ma."

Julia sighs. "I can't leave, Bobby. I've told you that before.

I can't just walk away from the ring. The last time someone was caught trying to leave, the ringleaders put a bullet in his chest."

"Calum left," Bobby says—as if she needs reminding.

"And I've no idea where he is. No idea if he's dead or alive. There's every chance he's been caught too." And if her husband is dead, well, she cannot even think about that. Dead because he had left on account of his anger at her. "Do you not think I would leave if I could?" Irritation rises in her voice. "I can't try to run with nowhere to go."

"You do have somewhere to go, Ma. We're going to Lindisfarne. To Highfield House."

Julia's stomach dives. She has not heard that name spoken in a decade. But it has always been on the edge of her thoughts, a memory that refuses to fade.

She cannot make sense of what Bobby is saying. Are they to hide out in the house? Squirrel themselves away in the attic like her brothers did during the Rising? Surely he cannot think this is the way forward. "What are you talking about? Is the house empty?" Julia realises her heart is racing.

"The house isn't empty." Bobby looks down. "But I went to Mr Blake. I—"

"Please tell me you're lying." Julia inhales sharply, a flush of dread heating her face.

"It's all right, Ma. He wants to help you."

She turns away, scrubbing her hands across her eyes. A wellspring of embarrassment bubbles up inside her. The thought of Nathan knowing anything of where she has ended up… "No," she says. "Absolutely not. I couldn't."

"Yes you can, Ma. You have to."

"There is no way, Bobby. Absolutely no way. Not after…"

Julia fades out. Shakes her head. "There is no way." Leaving Nathan Blake was the hardest thing she has ever had to do. The hardest—but also the simplest. In the wake of all that had happened, it had been far too clear there was no way forward for them.

"Wait here," Bobby says.

"Where are you—"

He disappears out of the tenement, his footsteps pounding down the staircase. Julia curls a hand around the top of a chair. Her entire body is blazing, heart knocking hard against her ribs. She can't quite untangle the storm of mixed feelings she has towards her son right now.

The stairs creak again beneath the rhythmic thud of footsteps. The door scrapes open against the floorboards. Nathan Blake steps into her tenement.

Julia stumbles backwards, her spine pressing hard against the wall. She wants to turn away. Hide herself. Hide from the shame. But she feels physically unable. Nathan is both the last and only person she wants to see.

He stands close to the door, hands folded in front of him, and she can tell he too is feeling the supreme awkwardness of this. He says, "Please come to the house, Julia."

He meets her eyes for a long second, and she feels almost painfully exposed beneath his gaze. Nathan is well dressed, polished, in a light-grey justacorps, deepened slightly at the shoulders with rain. The dark waves of his hair are unpowdered, and tied back neatly with a length of black ribbon. He looks as though he has found success, satisfaction. Happiness? The look in his blue eyes is too complicated for her to know the answer to that. At the sight of him, she is just as skittish as she was a decade ago. Everything and nothing has changed.

She cannot bear to be a burden to him. Not again. Not anymore. "No. Thank you. I could never ask that of you." She hates how cold and formal she sounds. Wishes very desperately that her underskirts were not hanging from the ceiling.

"You're not asking it of me," says Nathan. "I'm asking it of you." He clears his throat. "Bobby told me about the thieving ring. And I want to help you get out." She hears the thinness in his voice; the strain of being around her. Some distant, unbidden part of her is relieved she still has an effect on him. It's the most useless of thoughts, and she shoves it away quickly.

"There's a wagon waiting at the top of the street," Nathan continues. "It will take us less than a minute to reach it." He shifts slightly, the floorboards creaking beneath his weight. "No one need have any idea where you are. How would they know? And Highfield House is secure. The tunnel entrance has been filled in. Even if anyone sees you leave Bamburgh, you'll be safe there." He swallows visibly. "Far safer than you will be here, at least."

Julia looks down. How many times had she crept into Highfield House through that passage, sneaking food and water to her brothers in the attic? But in spite of all this blazing humiliation, she can't deny the appeal of secure walls around her.

"He's right, Ma," Bobby puts in. "You'll be far safer at the house than here on your own."

"There's room enough there for you and Bobby," Nathan says. "And there's room enough for you and I to…" He clears his throat again. "Well. You never need even see me if you don't wish it."

Julia dares a glance at him. Is that what he believes she wants? For the two of them to avoid one another? Certainly, it must be what he wants. How could he wish for anything else?

And what is it that makes her nod in agreement? Is it the desperate desire not to wake in the night from fear? The hope of getting away from the ring before Bobby is entangled too? Or just the pull of Nathan Blake?

She cannot dwell on her reasons.

"Good," Nathan says. He rubs a hand across the back of his neck. "Pack what you need. I shall be waiting by the coach when you're ready."

CHAPTER TWELVE

Julia yanks her underclothes from the pulley and shoves them into her duffel bag. Knocks her comb from the side table in an overflow of nervous energy. "How much does he know?" she asks Bobby, grabbing the comb and shoving it into her bag. "Did you tell him about... Does he know that I..."

"He knows about Calum, Ma. If that's what you're asking." Bobby takes her elbow in an attempt to calm her. "It's all right."

Julia feels the heat in her cheeks intensify. She is not sure what's worse: Nathan knowing she had married another man, or Nathan knowing her husband had seen fit to leave her.

She kneels and pulls the box safe out from beneath the bed. Fishes out the key from inside her bodice and unlocks the lid. The safe is half full of petty takings: coin pouches and pocket watches, hat pins and brooches. Loose pages of notes she keeps in case her books are ever stolen or damaged: records of who had procured what, from where, and when.

Keeping records for the ring was never something she had wanted to do. But she had found out quickly that what she wanted was of little concern to anyone. She had the book-keeping knowledge, the experience. She was valuable to these thieves, many of whom could barely read or count. And, as she had found out some months after arriving here, her own mother had had connections to this ring in the years before her death. Somehow, that made Julia trustworthy among these people. For better or for worse.

She begins to rifle through the safe. The last of her own money is hidden away in here too. A few coins, and pieces of jewellery that had once lined the shelves of her curiosity shop. She has never told Calum about them. Perhaps a part of her had foreseen something like this. Foreseen the moment when her husband realised she was never meant to be a wife. Without them, she is penniless.

There's a loud knock at the door as Julia is reaching deeper into the box, hunting for the pouch containing her own treasures. Bobby opens the door a crack.

"Who are you?" barks the woman on the other side. "Where's Julia?"

Julia recognises the voice of Lizzie Barrett, the older woman who lives in the tenement below her. "It's all right, Bobby," she says. "Let her in."

Bobby hesitates for a moment, then steps back, letting Lizzie inside. Her neighbour is draped in an oversized striped neckerchief and patched brown skirt, a moth-eaten shawl knotted around her shoulders. Grey-streaked hair hangs loose down her back, partially obscuring the large round birthmark on her cheek. She gestures to Bobby with a flick of her head. "Who's this?"

"No one," Julia says quickly. "It doesn't matter." She trusts Lizzie, yes. The older woman has always been kind to her. Had guided her through the maze of the ring, having been caught in the enterprise for most of her life. She had met Bobby, here at the tenement, in the days before Julia had sent him off to North Sunderland. But despite her trust for Lizzie, Julia is glad her neighbour has not recognised her son. She needs to keep him as disconnected from the ring as possible.

"He here about Calum?" Lizzie asks, eyes drawn downward to the open safe on the floor beside the bed.

"No." Julia stands, shifting to hide the half-packed bag sitting on the mattress. Perhaps when it comes down to it, her trust for Lizzie is not as solid as she believed it to be. "What do you want?" she asks the older woman. "Why are you here?"

Lizzie looks at her dubiously. "Came to see how you were faring," she says. "And to tell you there was word of Calum up north."

Julia's heart jolts. "What?"

"Mr Cameron says he saw him in Edinburgh. Says Calum was being real slippery about what he was doing up there. But he mentioned he was planning to head south again soon."

"I see." Julia sinks onto the bed. So her husband is alive. And there's certainly relief there, though it's rooted mostly in her own guilt. Can she really leave now, with the knowledge that Calum is as close as Edinburgh? That he is planning to head south? What would he do if he returned and found the tenement empty? What if he went looking for her and somehow found her beneath Nathan Blake's roof?

Lizzie looks past Julia to the bag on the bed. "You

leaving?"

"Aye," says Bobby, before Julia can speak. "She is." He looks at his mother pointedly.

Lizzie hesitates, gnawing on a grimy thumbnail. She glances again at Bobby, then turns back to Julia. "Have you somewhere safe to go? You know O'Donnell and the others don't like people just walking away."

"I'm well aware. It's all right. I've somewhere to go. And a wagon waiting outside." Somewhere safe? She hopes so, for Nathan's sake more than anyone's. The last thing she wants is to bring more trouble to his life.

"All right," Lizzie says finally. "It's a good idea, I'd say. Keep yourself hidden until that rogue husband of yours decides to show himself again."

Julia nods. "I'm sure I can count on you to keep quiet about my leaving?"

"Of course." Lizzie nods down at the safe. "What are you planning to do with that? Not take it with you, I hope."

"Of course not. Do you think I'd be so foolish?"

Lizzie gives her a crooked smile. "I'd hope not." Before Julia can react, she swoops down and slams the lid. Heaves up the box and tucks it under her arm. "I'll keep an eye on it. Make sure no one untoward gets their hands to it." She holds her palm out flat towards Julia. "You got the key?"

Julia hesitates, eying the box. She needs her coins, those pieces of jewellery. Without them, she has nothing. Dare she tell Lizzie she has her own money in there? Does the trust between the two women extend far enough for Lizzie to believe her? Or will Lizzie try and gain a little favour by turning Julia over to the ringleaders for pilfering from the safe? She doesn't know. But it's a risk she cannot take. She takes the key from the table and presses it into Lizzie's palm. Feels something sink in her stomach.

Lizzie steps forward and tosses her free arm around Julia. Gives her a quick squeeze. "Take care then." And Julia watches sickly as she carries the box out the door and disappears into the darkness of the hallway.

Bobby strides down the street towards the coach, a faded blue duffel bag tucked beneath his arm.

"Where's your mother?" Nathan asks. "Has she changed her mind about coming?"

Bobby opens the coach door and tosses the bag inside. "Nah. She's just fetching Minerva."

"Minerva?" Nathan swallows. "Her daughter?" he asks stiffly.

Bobby's lips quirk. "Her cat."

"Oh. Yes. Of course." He had forgotten about Julia's cat. Cannot quite determine if this is a better or worse outcome than her having mothered Calum's daughter. "It's still alive then."

"Aye." Bobby smirks. "Still alive." He glances over his shoulder, then nods towards the coach. "Best we get in rather than waiting for her out here. Less suspicious."

"Is it really that bad?" Nathan asks, voice low. "Is there really a chance someone will try to stop her from leaving? Surely she must have cause to leave the village from time to time."

"Aye. But her husband disappearing like he did will have set the ringleaders on alert. They'll be expecting Ma to leave.

And they'll not want that. Not given everything she knows about the ring—who's leading it, what they do, where to find them…"

"I see."

Nathan hears footsteps behind him as he is climbing into the carriage. Turns to see Julia striding down the street in a dark green cloak and black woollen bonnet, a bulbous ginger cat beneath her arm. The bulk of her fiery hair has been shoved beneath her hat, a few stray curls escaping out the sides. She accepts Bobby's hand and climbs into the coach. Tucks her grey woollen skirts around her legs. When, Nathan wonders, had she stopped dressing in yellows and blues and pinks that clashed so brilliantly with her flaming hair? It feels like she has become accustomed to hiding herself. Doing her best to disappear into the background.

Sitting opposite her, he feels painfully breathless. Briefly considers climbing into the box seat beside Lewis for the journey back to Holy Island. The height of cowardice, he knows. But cowardice feels preferable to this.

The cat inspects him with shrewd gold eyes, then turns away in disinterest. Nathan raps on the carriage wall and it begins to rattle over the cobbles, away from the colourless corridor at the back of Church Wynd.

As they turn into the main street, he hears a sharp inhalation from Julia. She presses herself hard against the wall of the wagon, hiding herself from the window.

"Who is it, Ma?" Bobby asks, glancing out into the street.

Julia tugs him back, out of sight. "Just someone from the ring. I don't want him to see me leaving." Her voice is low, and Nathan hears the shame in it. Can tell she does not want him to hear her.

"I don't think we've been followed," Bobby says finally, as the road opens out onto rain-drenched grassland, leaving the village behind.

Julia sinks back against the wall of the carriage. She pulls the cat to her chest and closes her eyes for a moment.

The sight of her here, so close that he could touch her, has stolen Nathan's ability to speak. Has reminded him of how things could have been.

No, perhaps *could have been* is wrong. Because really, is there any other way things could have gone but the way they did? *Ought to have been*—this is closer. *Wishes they had been.*

Julia does not say a word to him either. As the carriage trundles along the coast road, she is acutely focused on Bobby, asking him question after question, about his work and his lodgings and the stain on his coat—Nathan can tell she is deliberately avoiding so much as glancing in his direction.

He has thought often about how things might have been different if he had gone after Julia ten years ago. If he had convinced her not to leave Lindisfarne. Asked her to stay with him. Each time he considers it, he reaches the conclusion that doing so was an impossibility. But right now, he cannot seem to remember the reasons for letting her go.

Yes, a lack of trust. Their inability to be truthful with each other. Her brothers hiding in his attic. Government spies at Highfield House. A dead man in her cellar and blood on her hands.

In the dim light of the past, all those secrets seem meaningless. But he knows he cannot be that foolish. Cannot let himself forget.

He shakes the thoughts away. All of this *is* meaningless.

Or at least pointless. Because Julia has a husband. He dares to glance at her. Her expression is almost impossibly weighted: guilt, shame, regret—he sees it all. Finds himself wishing he could take it away. But even if he knew the right words to say, he feels physically incapable of opening his mouth.

"Thank you," she says to him.

And it's all he can manage to nod.

CHAPTER THIRTEEN

When the wagon jolts off the sand onto Holy Island, Julia feels an unexpected swell of joy.

It had been with no small amount of reluctance that she had left the island; had spent so many years swearing that this would be home forever. But in the midst of the Rising, staying had not been an option. Her brother Hugh had killed Joseph Holland, the government spy, and the two of them had disposed of his body in the ocean beyond the Farnes.

Julia feared that, if she stayed, she would be found out. Surely someone had seen Holland walking into her shop the day of his death. Surely people would begin to ask questions. And surely, if anyone looked too closely at her curiosity shop, they would see the faint rusty bloodstains she had been unable to properly scrub away.

And then, of course, there was Nathan. Even if it weren't for Joseph Holland's death, their parting had made staying on Lindisfarne an impossible thing.

But here on the island, she is buoyed by a sudden

lightness. The sky has begun to clear, and the pink late-afternoon light is making the mudflats glitter. She leans forward, straining to glimpse the village through the carriage window; to catch that achingly familiar silhouette of castle and spire and the ancient stone of the priory.

Holy Island washes aside the stress of the thieving ring, and Calum's disappearance, and of this excruciatingly wordless carriage ride with Nathan. Those stresses, those struggles, she knows will come flooding back in soon, but right now, she allows herself to enjoy being here. Being home. She swallows down a swell of emotion. Hugs Minerva to her chest.

By the time the wagon is rattling over the rugged path carved through the grassland, all that lightness is gone. Highfield House towers from the dunes, inky and solid against the sky. It reminds her of all the duplicity of the past; reminds her of what has always stood between her and Nathan. She thinks of the way she had crept up to the house in the depths of the night, stealing in through the passage in the walls to feed her brothers. Thinks of Harriet's husband casting her from the house moments after she had learnt of her brother Michael's death. Thinks of a night spent out on the dunes with Nathan, their eyes turned to the glitter of the sky, to help soften her grief.

Spending even a single night here suddenly feels impossible.

The carriage draws up in front of the house and a young woman steps out to meet them. Theodora, Julia assumes. She's grown lithe and elegant, dressed in neat sky-blue skirts and an embroidered stomacher, long blonde hair pinned back from her face. She has a far more open and welcoming expression than her father.

Bobby leaps out of the wagon first, offering Julia his hand. She climbs out hesitantly.

"Oh!" Theodora rushes forward to scratch Minerva's ears. "You brought your cat. How wonderful." She looks up at Julia. "Bobby and I are so glad you're here."

Nathan climbs out after them. His eyes dart between his daughter and the cat, then he looks hurriedly downwards. "I'm sorry, but I'd best get back upstairs," he says. "I've a lot of work to do." He vanishes into the house, not waiting for a response.

Theodora watches after him for a moment, then turns back to Julia. "You'll have to excuse Papa," she says. "He doesn't have too many house guests these days. It seems his manners have fallen by the wayside." There's an airy, joking tone to her voice, the bright smile not leaving her face. But Julia can sense the uncertainty, the concern, beneath her words.

Theodora leads her up the staircase to a small guestroom at the end of the hallway, with a window overlooking the ocean. The washbin has been filled and a fire is simmering in the grate. She has clearly been expected.

Theodora holds out her arms for the cat. "Can I take her downstairs? Find a treat for her in the kitchen?"

Julia smiles faintly. "I don't think your father will like her roaming the house. He's not fond of cats."

Theodora waves a dismissive hand. "He's not. But we should definitely not let that stop us." She scoops Minerva from Julia's arms. Nuzzles the cat's pink nose with her own. "Let's go to the kitchen," she tells Minerva in a sing-song voice. "Let's see what we can find for you, shall we?"

Julia thanks Theodora and sets her bag on the chair in the corner of the room. She will not unpack it. Will not make herself at home. Because being here can only be the most fleeting of solutions. All those reasons why she had to leave Lindisfarne ten years ago feel just as pressing and present as they have always been. Besides, there is every chance Calum will be back in Bamburgh soon. And then she will return to her old life as the ring's record keeper. Will do her best to temper her husband's anger.

She peers out the window. The embankment is blissfully empty; just grey sheets of water rolling steadily towards the shore. The discomfort and shame of being here in Nathan's life is almost overwhelming. But for the first time in months, the fear—alertness—she feels in the thieving ring's orbit is gone.

Unbidden, Julia finds herself wondering whereabouts in the house Nathan is. She remembers his study had been up here on the second floor. Is he just a few doors down the hallway, locked away with his ledgers?

Once, she had allowed herself to imagine becoming the mistress of this house. How distant and dreamlike those thoughts feel now.

A knock at the door and Bobby pokes his head inside. "Are you settled?" he asks.

Julia smiles wryly. "I'm not sure 'settled' is the right word."

"Don't worry about your money," says Bobby. "It will be all right. We'll find a way to get to it."

Julia says nothing. How exactly it will be all right, she cannot even begin to imagine. If Calum fails to return, and if she fails to get her money out of the safe, she will be completely penniless. But she has no intention of entangling Bobby in this any more than he already is.

He steps into the room, closing the door behind him. "I'm really glad you're here, Ma. I hated the thought of you alone in that place."

Julia pulls him into her arms and kisses his bristly cheek. His coat is still damp and fragrant from the rain. "I wish you didn't worry for me so. You know I can take care of myself. I always have."

Bobby nods noncommittally. "There's supper waiting for us downstairs."

Julia hesitates. Her stomach is groaning with hunger, but the thought of sitting across the table from Nathan is unbearable. She shakes her head. "I don't think—"

"Thea says her da will take his supper up in his study," Bobby cuts in. "You and I can eat with her downstairs. And then I'll leave you to get a good night's rest."

"You're not staying here?"

"Nah. I'm going back to my lodgings. I don't think Mr Blake is too fond of me. He thought I was trying to get up Thea's skirts."

Julia rubs her eyes. "And were you?"

Bobby chuckles. "Course not. We both just wanted to convince him to come and get you."

She manages a faint smile. "Good. Because that's a complication I really don't need." She draws in her breath and smooths her skirts. "All right," she says finally. "I suppose I could use a little supper."

As she follows Bobby down the hallway, past rows of closed doors, Julia realises she is holding her breath. But for all the stress and unease that being here brings, she is grateful for a night within the security of these walls, where the Bamburgh thieving ring cannot find her.

"So you put two cards down," says Tom, "and then you add them up, and then you turn over three—no, four more and add them up…"

"No, that's not right," Noah tells him. "You put three cards down, then choose one to get rid of, then you turn over three more and add them up." He deals the cards around the table. "I think that's right…"

Finn has no idea what game they're supposed to playing. Is fairly certain Tom and Noah have no idea either. He chuckles. Counts the eight cards in his hand and puts one back into the pile. "Where'd you learn this game?"

"My papa taught me," says Tom, casting his two—or three—cards down on the table.

Noah says, "I learnt it from Thea. But she might have made it up."

Finn catches Eva's eye across the table and smiles.

Most of the time, he is able to see that his fears of Noah leaving are founded on nothing but his own uncertainties and guilt. After all, this cottage is a far different place to what it had been when he had run away. Back then, in the wake of his mother's death, it had been a place of arguments and anger—all, no doubt because he and his da were so damn similar.

These days, it's far closer to the place he remembers when his mother was alive: a place of bedtime stories and warm, civilised conversation. He wishes he could remember more of the tales his ma had told him when he was a boy, curled up in that bed where his sons sleep now. Wishes he remembered more than snatches of her lilting Gaelic.

Oidhche mhath.

Tha goal agam ort.

Archie kneels up on his chair and spreads his cards out on the table for everyone to see, the sleeves of his nightshirt hanging down over his hands. "What does seven plus five equal?"

"You can count that yourself," says Eva.

She's come to parenthood much more naturally than him, Finn thinks, with her innate warmth and caring, fiercely maternal before she ever had a child. He still feels like he's stumbling through the whole thing. Still, they've been blessed enough to see two of their children through the deadly first five years. And while the loss of their first daughter is a thorn he knows will never leave them, it has made him fiercely grateful for the three they have. Fiercely grateful their lost child had not claimed her mother's life too. Finn knows far too many who have not been so lucky.

"Auntie Eva," Tom says suddenly, "did you and my mother play cards? When you were girls, I mean?"

Something flickers across Eva's eyes. It's not the first time Tom has asked about his mother, and Finn can tell how uncomfortable Eva is with the questions. Far more so now, he assumes, that Harriet has returned to their lives.

"Sometimes," she says. Finn can hear the forced lightness in her voice. "She was very good at Piquet. Always used to beat me." She clears her throat. "Your turn, Archie. Which cards are you going to put down?" She leans over, helping him sift through his hand. "You have to put two cards down and then choose another one… or, um… Noah, explain the rules again for your brother."

Tom is still leaning forward, as though hoping for another snippet of information. Edwin might have asked Nathan and Eva not to mention Harriet, but he had clearly failed to account for his son's curiosity about his mother.

"Da," Noah says suddenly, "it's stopped raining. We should light the basket. There might be ships out there." There's a new seriousness in his eyes—has been there since the wreck.

He's at the door before Finn even has his boots on, Eva calling after him to remember his coat. Tom follows them down the stairs. Noah is already rattling the barrow over the rocks towards the coal shed.

The darkness has fallen thick and hard, a hint of the long winter stretched out before them. The light from inside the cottage spills out across black rain-slicked rocks, lighting the path from the coal shed to the beacon. The bedsheets on the washing line beside the shed seem to glow in the darkness, catching the breeze and billowing like sailcloth.

One of the slate tiles has slipped from the roof, Finn notices. It's lying in shards at his feet. He picks the pieces up and flings them into the sea.

He leaves the boys to lower and stoke the basket. Picks his way out across the rocks to a stray nine-pin Noah and Tom have forgotten to collect. Thanks to the boys' nine-pins escapades, one ball has already been condemned to the ocean. A second is sitting at the bottom of the rockpool, waiting for some brave soul to jump in and collect it. Finn has lost count of how many times he's suggested nine-pins might not be such a good outdoor game.

The stray pin is lying on a flat stretch of rock not far from the jetty. Right where Finn had found his father's body, a decade and a half ago, when he had returned to Longstone after seventeen years of running in the wake of Oliver Blake's death. He'd abandoned his father for Henry Ward's ship, without a word. Left him to die alone on the island.

Sometimes—often—he walks past that unassuming rock without a thought to that most shameful piece of his past. Other times, like now, he inexplicably gets caught in the memory.

A burst of light as the beacon flares to life. Finn watches as Tom and Noah heave on the chain, sending the light into the sky.

"I can't see any ships," Noah reports, trudging out to the end of the jetty and panning his gaze across the ocean. "I'm glad no one came out here when the light wasn't lit."

And perhaps his concerns about his son leaving Longstone are unfounded—yes, more often than not, Finn can see this. But he's no more certain that he wants Noah to spend his life on the rim of this island, with his eyes turned out to the sea.

***

Nathan has heard the footsteps, the voices. Knows Theodora spent the evening at the dining table with Julia and Bobby. A scene from an alternative life.

He knows it's the height of rudeness to have tucked himself away in his study with his soup on a tray on his desk. Also knows Theodora is going to hound him for it in the morning. But he cannot bring himself to leave the safety of this room.

His heart is a steady drumbeat against his ribs, the numbers on the ledger in front of him an incoherent mess. He has long given up on trying to get any real work done. With Julia in the house, it feels like a complete impossibility. He feels constantly breathless, overwhelmed by her nearness.

Julia has always been able to bypass his fear of human contact, get closer to him than almost anyone, at least since his late wife Sarah. But he cannot think of that. She is only here for her safety. Nothing more. It cannot be anything more.

He attempts a mouthful of soup, turned cold now from having sat untouched for so long. He pushes the bowl away. What is he to do? Stay locked away in here until Julia is sleeping? Spend the night in his desk chair? If he was going to squirrel himself away like this, he might have had the presence of mind to do it in his bedchamber.

And what tomorrow? He knows he will have to face her at some point. But right now, he cannot think further than the next moment ahead. And that moment is most certainly going to involve him locking himself away with a bowl of cold soup and doing his best not to think of Julia.

There's a soft knock at the door and Theodora pokes her head into the room. "You've been working in here for an awfully long time."

Nathan forces a smile. "Up to my neck in accounts, I'm afraid."

"I see." He can tell she is not even close to believing him.

He squeezes the bridge of his nose, trying to ward off a headache. "I'm sorry, I should not have left it to you to see to it that our guests were taken care of."

"They're fine." Theodora drags the chair from the corner of the room and sets it in front of his desk. Perches on the edge. "Everything is fine."

Nathan sits his quill back in its pot. Leans back in his desk chair. "So," he says, "did you break the window casing on purpose just to get Bobby here?"

Thea gives a short laugh. "Do you really think I would do such a thing?"

Nathan smiles. "Honestly, I would not put it past you."

"I didn't break the window casing. I just brought it to your attention. It was broken for days before you noticed it."

"I see. And there's nothing between you and Bobby then?"

She laughs airily. "Of course not." She twines a loose strand of hair around her finger. "Bobby didn't really fix Mrs Emmett's roof though. I just made that part up. Made a more convincing story."

Nathan closes his ledger, shaking his head with a chuckle. "How did I end up with you, Theodora?"

"Through a brilliant stroke of luck." She bends to catch his eye, her smile fading. "Are you all right, Papa?"

He nods. Hates that she worries for him. That protective instinct he has towards her—he knows it goes both ways. "I'm all right," he assures her. "I'm sorry for behaving like such a coward tonight. I promise I'll do better tomorrow."

Theodora doesn't return his smile. "Was it the wrong thing to do?" she asks. "Having Bobby bring his ma here? I never meant to hurt you."

Nathan reaches across the desk and gives her wrist a quick squeeze. "It was the right thing to do, Thea. Julia wasn't safe in Bamburgh."

Theodora opens her mouth to speak again, then seems to change her mind. She nods towards the telescope set up by the window. "Is it clear enough to see anything?"

Nathan slides around on his chair. He looks out through the window then presses his eye to the lens of the telescope, guides the shaft up through the cloud bank until it catches the faint glitter of Polaris and its snaking constellation. He shifts his chair away, nodding for Thea to look through the eyepiece.

"The North Star is just visible," he says.

Theodora smiles as she lowers her eye to lens. "The star of guidance. How fitting." A reminder—not that he needed one—that his daughter is well aware of the internal chaos Julia's arrival has caused in him.

And though the night sky has long had the ability to calm his thoughts and make his troubles fade, tonight the star of guidance is offering little in the way of answers.

Theodora leaves and the house falls quiet. Nathan gets to his feet, deciding now is the opportune time to escape to his bedroom. A flash of movement in the dark outside the window catches his eye. He looks down; sees her.

Julia has her dark cloak wrapped around her body, her coppery curls loose and tangled on her shoulders. He watches her walk across the embankment in shadow. Watches her sit on the edge of the beach.

He knows how much she had loved this island. Knows how much it had pained her to leave. He has wished, many times over the years, that he had been the one to leave—though he knows Julia could not stay here while questions about Joseph Holland's death were swirling.

He watches her for several long moments, the small figure of her almost lost against the darkness. Catches a glimpse of that life that could have been. And he hopes that being back here has brought her a little peace.

CHAPTER FOURTEEN

Getting her money from the box safe in Lizzie's tenement involves, as a first step, leaving the safety of this bedroom. Facing the risk of seeing Nathan. Right now, that feels far more terrifying that anything the thieving ring might dish up.

Julia glances out the window. The tide is high; if she is to make it Bamburgh this morning, she will need a boat to do so. She had seen a small sloop beached on the curve of the embankment when she had arrived at the house yesterday. Suspects it belongs to one of the workers—the coachman, perhaps? She has a hard time imagining it might be Nathan's. For a man who lives on the edge of the sea, he is painfully awkward on the water. Perhaps she can convince the coachman to sail her across to the mainland—or let her take his boat, in any case.

She pulls on her cloak and bonnet and opens the bedroom door a crack. The house is quiet, but she can hear Theodora chattering away to Minerva downstairs. Hears a muffled cough come from a few doors down. Nathan's study.

Julia hovers outside it for a moment, debating whether to knock. To wish him good morning. To thank him for the tea and toast he had had Mrs Brodie bring to her door. It would be the decent thing to do, after all.

But then she thinks of how quickly he had leapt from the carriage yesterday and bolted up to the safety of his study. And she makes her way down the staircase, without looking back.

She steps out of the house into a damp white morning. After the rain of yesterday, the dunes are still wet and fragrant, weak threads of sunlight straining through the clouds. Julia eyes the embankment. The sloop is gone.

She curses under her breath. Weighs her options. Wait here for either the boat to return or the tide to fall, or head for the village and its sea of familiar faces. She had had a number of friends on the island before she had left. Yes, she had been looked down upon by much of the village for mothering a child out of wedlock. But there were also people she had been close to: Alice Emmett, who ran the dame school; Molly Granville, whose father had fished with Julia's. The Macauleys, too, had always shown her kindness, on account of her father's staunch Jacobite beliefs. Will she be welcomed back to the village? Or treated with suspicion for the way she had so hurriedly disappeared?

Julia has no idea—all she knows is that she needs to get her money from the safe as quickly as possible. If she doesn't hurry, there's every chance her belongings will be divided up amongst the ring members when the takings are next dispersed.

She gathers her skirts in her fists and strides down the narrow path that cuts across the middle of the island. Wind careens across the ridges of the dunes, whipping her skirts around her legs. She is almost grateful for her urgency; for the excuse not to stop and walk the too-familiar lanes of the village. Grateful not to pass the cottage she had grown up in, no doubt filled with another family now. Grateful for an excuse to avoid her curiosity shop. An excuse not to peek inside, see what remains of her old life. What remains of Joseph Holland's blood, tainting the cellar stairs.

Did anyone ever suspect she was involved in his disappearance? She knows most of the islanders are Jacobites. And there were rumours circling about Holland spying for the government in the months before his death. There are many people on the island who would have made likely suspects if anyone ever went digging into his disappearance. But none of that makes this any easier to carry.

She reaches the anchorage. The village is far busier than she had hoped, with handcarts rattling over the cobbles and the streets alive with chatter. Market day, she realises; though most of the herring boats seem to have already left on the high tide. Instinctively, unconsciously, she has pulled the hood of her cloak up over her bonnet, hiding as much of her face as possible. Once upon a time, she had known everyone on this island. And while she suspects that, after ten years, that is no longer the case, she is sure there are still far too many familiar faces here for what she is about to do.

She hides herself behind one of the fishing huts that stands crookedly on the sand. There are still a handful of fishermen milling about the pier—men who had sailed with her brothers and father, no doubt. A woman walks past with a basket pressed to her hip. Julia lowers her eyes to hide her face. Does not want to recognise, or be recognised.

The fishermen climb into a dinghy roped to the jetty, and row out to a larger boat moored in the middle of the anchorage. She waits impatiently for them to climb aboard. Waits for them to rope the dinghy to the stern of the boat. For them to disappear around the point.

When the anchorage is quiet, she hurries out onto the pier. Unties the mooring rope of the first small sloop she comes across. She leaps into it and begins to row before her common sense can catch up with her.

She keeps her eyes pinned on the jetty, making sure she has not been followed. Perhaps she ought to have done this the right way: waited patiently at the anchorage until she found someone willing to ferry her over to the mainland. Somehow, that feels even riskier than stealing the boat—she has no thought of how the villagers will react when they see her, and she needs to get her belongings from Lizzie's tenement as quickly as she can. Besides, there's something mildly ironic about abiding by the law on her way to break into someone's house. One day soon, Julia tells herself, she will leave all this thievery and law-breaking behind.

When she is clear of the anchorage, she unfurls the mainsail and lets the wind carry her over the storm-cloud sea. It has been years since she has sailed; years since she has even been on the water, but the feel of the rope sliding through her hands, the boat rising and falling beneath her, turning at her command, is steadying, somehow. A part of herself she had forgotten. It reminds her, suddenly, of all she had been, done, achieved, in those distant years of her old life. Before she had given up and made herself a wife.

Julia has no thought of whether, after that had passed between them, Calum still considers her his wife, his responsibility. Really, she will not blame him if he doesn't. Calum MacNeill is a proud man, a man of God. He had seen it as his duty to care for her, and for several years, he had done a good job of it. Theirs had never been a marriage full of passion, but nor had it always been unhappy. In the early years as Calum's wife, Julia had felt respected, protected. Had experienced a security she had never known before.

That pleasant, agreeable partnership is in the past now, she is certain. But she has no thought of whether her marriage is too. She doubts it. Calum is not the kind of man to abandon his wife. He would not want that stain on his character. Or perhaps she has it wrong. Perhaps *she* is the stain on his character. Perhaps putting as much distance as possible between the two of them is all Calum can think of to do. His actions would certainly suggest as much. Leaving the ring, even in the middle of the night, as he had done, had been impossibly risky. An all-too-glaring reminder of how furious he had been at her.

After she had left Holy Island, had closed up her curiosity shop and sent her brother Hugh off to die on the battlefields of Lancashire, Julia had taken Bobby north. Over the border to seek work in Edinburgh. Had hoped the Scottish roots of both her parents might anchor her somehow. Moor her after all she had lost, all she had given up—willingly or otherwise.

She had found kitchen work at a manor house on the outskirts of the city, scrubbing dishes and wiping tables, with Bobby assisting in the stables.

And then there was Calum MacNeill, who had come to the house to install new locks on the doors and windows. He and Julia had got to talking when she had brought him bread and cheese for noonshine, and they had found an easy and unexpected connection. When he had finished the job and moved on, Calum had taken Julia and Bobby with him.

In the wake of Nathan Blake and the hollow that leaving him had carved inside her, Julia had had no intention of marrying. But after running her own shop for four years, being a wealthy couple's employee was a bitter pill to swallow. Julia knew that, without the security of a husband, her life would be an endless dredge of counting pennies and scrubbing pans. She'd had far too much of struggling. Of counting pennies. Of craving security.

She had no illusions that she was anything more to Calum than a necessity. He was well past thirty, with no children to pass his locksmith business or his small West Port cottage onto. For Julia, the security being a wife brought was a fair enough exchange for being Calum's necessity. Their marriage was a business-like affair, a thing of handshakes and platonic conversations, but she had always done far better at business than love.

Her new husband was passionately anti-Jacobite. They had married and set up their home in Scotland in the aftermath of the Rising. The cause had split Calum's family down the middle—like Julia, he had lost brothers on the battlefields, had lost friends and family members on account of his pro-government beliefs. He and Julia had bonded over their shared losses, their shared anger at the Jacobite cause. And she had done her best to put the past behind her.

But Calum had been unable to let go of his anger. When he had discovered the Jacobite links of one of his wealthy clients, he had used his position as locksmith to break into the man's private offices and steal a raft of sensitive political documents. And though Calum had once fought passionately as a militiaman for King George's cause, he'd veered too far from the law for the authorities to turn a blind eye.

Two years ago, with redcoats on their tail, Calum and Julia had had no choice but to flee their home. He knew people, Calum had told her, as they had crossed the border back into England. People in Bamburgh who could offer them protection. A place to hide. For the second time in her life, Julia found herself fleeing, with all her belongings crammed hurriedly into trunks.

"Protection in exchange for what?" she asked. In her experience, nothing was ever given for free.

"In exchange for nothing," Calum told her. "Just consider it an act of decency."

She'd believed him at first; had chosen to believe him. Chosen to believe there was nothing untoward about his sudden habit of returning home late at night, or his insubstantial answers to her questions. A mistress, she assumed, and couldn't find the will to care.

Julia had done her best to make their tenement—far smaller than their cottage in West Port—liveable and pleasant, keeping the floor swept and the table laid, and coal simmering in the grate. Had made an effort to befriend Lizzie, who lived in the tenement below. She would make the most of this, she told herself. Would not overthink what Calum might have involved himself in. Would not let herself consider how close she was to Holy Island, and the life she had left behind.

An afternoon spent in Lizzie's tenement had changed everything. Over refilled whisky glasses, Julia had found herself opening up, saying too much. Loose words of Lindisfarne, of her curiosity shop, of her lost and faraway brothers. Michael, Angus, Hugh.

"You're Mairi's daughter," said Lizzie. "Aye, she used to talk about you and your brothers a lot. Used to bring you along with her when you were tiny." She leant across the table and topped up Julia's glass. "She was one of us, you know."

Julia barely remembered her mother. She was seven when Mairi died, and her memories of her had become frayed and faded. "One of us?" she repeated. "What do you mean?"

"Part of the ring," Lizzie said, too easily. She raised her dark eyebrows. "Or has your husband not told you what he's doing here?"

Lizzie laid it all out for her then: a band of thieves formed in the final years of last century, following the Glorious Revolution. Founded by men and women resentful of the Jacobite cause. Still today, rigidly anti-Jacobite. Their hands in everything from pickpocketing to embezzlement.

And though she remembered little of who her mother was, Julia knew exactly who her father had been: a cold, resentful man, made that way by the failures of the Jacobite cause and the bloodshed of Dunkeld. It made perfect sense that Mairi might have involved herself in such a thing. An outlet for her anger, her frustration, her pain.

It also made perfect sense that it was among people like this that Calum had chosen to hide. Anger at her husband swelled inside her. How long had he imagined he might be able to keep all this a secret?

The next day, Julia sent Bobby away. Told him to make his way south; look for work in North Sunderland or Newcastle. She had always wanted him to have a better life than she had had. Had fought for it with every fibre of her being. She would not let all that hard work be undone by letting him get caught up in the thieving ring.

Julia knows she is entirely to blame for the collapse of her marriage; for her husband's anger and subsequent disappearance. But in reality, there were fractures from the beginning, wrought by her pain at leaving her old life; the impossibility of forgetting Nathan. Fissures widened by her inability to give Calum a child. A bitter irony, she knows, that she had fallen pregnant with Bobby after barely so much as looking at his father, and yet she and her husband had spent years failing to conceive. After a while, they had just stopped trying.

Julia leans on the tiller, watching the shadow of the mainland sharpen. Tries to focus on the task ahead.

This stay at Highfield House can only be the most temporary reprieve. But going back to the tenement without her husband cannot be an option. Bobby is right—it's not safe. She has made it out without being caught, and now Calum has left—possibly forever—the threads tying her to the thieving ring have been frayed. She has a faint glimpse of an escape. A life on the right side of the law. And she must turn that faint chance into something more. If she can just get her money from the safe in Lizzie's tenement, perhaps she can make for the anonymity of London. Perhaps even find her brother. It has been years since she has seen Angus. Her missing him is a deep ache inside her.

And if Calum sees fit to return? If he has not been captured and killed by the ring for fleeing? If, somehow, he manages to track her down on the way to London? Well, she can tell him she had no choice but to leave. Will tell him his disappearance had put her in far too much danger, alone in the tenement with the box safe beneath her roof. She will concoct a story—not so far from the truth—of men pounding on the door and waving pistols beneath her nose. Even in his anger for her, even in his rage for the lies she had told, she knows he will never be able to argue.

If she is to go, to take this chance, it must be soon. Because Calum will not be able to argue if he catches her fleeing to London.

But she does not dare imagine what he will do if he catches her on Lindisfarne, beneath the roof of the man she has not for a minute stopped loving.

CHAPTER FIFTEEN

"And so," Theodora pauses for breath as she and Eva stride over the dunes towards the house, "Aunt Harriet is gone, but Bobby's ma is there, and her cat, and quite honestly, I don't think Papa knows what to make of the whole thing."

"Goodness," says Eva, "I really am missing all the excitement."

"You are."

Eva smiles. "After the few days we've had, I'm rather glad to hear it." Though she doesn't want to admit it, a part of her is relieved that Harriet has left the house. She had made this reluctant journey over to Lindisfarne to see her; had detoured to the market as a form of procrastination rather than any real need to buy anything. She can't help but be grateful for the reprieve. Around her sister, she has felt almost painfully on edge.

She wishes she and Harriet could put the past behind them. Though they've never been close, they'd once had a far warmer, more caring sisterhood than the stilted thing they'd stumbled through when Harriet had washed up on Longstone.

But moving forward has not felt possible. Not with Harriet so full of secrets. Eva is aware of the hypocrisy; knows things with her sister would not have fallen apart so spectacularly if she had not tried to keep the truth of Finn and Oliver a secret.

But for all of this, she cannot shake her worry. She wants to believe Harriet is telling the truth about not trying to take her own life. Wants to think the men who saw her trying to jump from the ship were mistaken. But if she allows herself to believe that, is she pushing the worst of realities aside?

She is relieved that Harriet being on the ship does not seem to have found its way into common knowledge—especially with Tom here. Eva knows all too well how much this town loves to gossip. At the market this morning, the villagers had been full of questions for her, seeking to fill in the gaps in the stories that have no doubt been spreading in the five days since the wreck. How many survivors? How many dead? Had any boats come from the mainland, or had Finn gone out to the wreck alone? No mention of Harriet. They'd been full of praise too—kind words that Eva had been unsure how to reply to. She and Finn have been gossiped about for so long that anything else feels unnatural. Sidelong glances feel far simpler to deal with than *do take some of these sweetmeats for the children, Mrs Murray,* and *I hope you enjoyed the seedcake I sent over.*

A part of her wonders why. Why is she finding it so difficult to accept the village's thanks?

Another part of her knows exactly why. Knows that, if the village knew the truth about the deaths of Oliver and Donald

Macauley, there would be no heartfelt thanks. No sweetmeats. No seedcake.

Eva tightens the shawl keeping Maggie strapped to her back and calls to the boys, who are lingering by the rockpools. Three sets of footsteps hammer past her.

"How's your father?" Eva asks Theodora, trying to pull her thoughts back from the channel of guilt they so often manage to veer down. Nathan has never spoken to her openly about Julia, but Eva knows their broken relations had cut him deeply. After Julia had left, Nathan had been withdrawn and painfully quiet. Fixated on his work. It had taken Eva months to chisel out even a fraction of the story. And now, for Julia to be at Highfield House—while she is married to another man? Eva hopes Nathan knows what he's getting himself into.

Thea's smile fades. "I think it's harder on him than he'll admit to me. But I know he wouldn't think of doing anything but helping her."

Eva nods. She knows Theodora is right. "I hope he doesn't mind us calling on him. It sounds like he has more than enough to manage at the moment."

"Oh, don't worry about that." Theodora grabs her skirts in her fist as she rounds a mud puddle in the middle of the path. "He loves when you call on him. Besides, it's good for him. Stops him from turning into a grumpy old man before his time."

Eva laughs.

"Thea!" Tom calls suddenly, waving to them from rocky edge of the headland. "Is this where the Lady in the Dunes appears?"

"No," says Noah, "it's over here by the stream. Isn't that

right?"

Theodora grins. "Actually, you'll usually see her right over there on the embankment, waiting for a ship that never comes." Her voice grows more theatrical. "Or sometimes you'll just see her wandering lost on the dunes. Just before it gets dark."

Eva elbows her. "That's enough. Last time you told them this story, Archie didn't sleep for a week."

Theodora smiles to herself. "Sorry." She doesn't sound sorry.

"I saw her once," Noah announces, bellowing at them from the edge of the stream. "Right over there on the beach. Waiting for a ship to come."

"You did not," Tom barks back.

"Yes I did. How would you know?"

"I saw her too," Archie volunteers.

Noah gives his cousin a broad grin. "See? Told you."

Theodora's private smile widens. She tries and fails to look away before Eva catches it.

The boys reach the house first and ram the knocker into the door, the sound thundering out across the dunes. Mrs Brodie opens the door and the children barrel inside. Eva hears herself rattle out some well-worn line about taking off their muddy boots before they go into the parlour.

When she and Theodora reach the house, Nathan is making his way downstairs, brought out of his study, no doubt, by the apocalyptic roar of the doorknocker. Thea ushers the boys down the hallway to search for the cat as Eva swings Maggie around to her front and unties the shawl. Sets her daughter down to totter off after the boys.

"Sorry for the chaos," she tells Nathan, kicking the pile of boots out of the middle of the doorway. "I hear you had quite a day yesterday. Is Julia here?"

"No." Nathan has a slightly bewildered look about him. "She's not. She's... I don't know where she is. I told her I'd give her her distance."

Eva tries to meet his eyes. "Please be careful, Nathan," she says gently. "I don't want you to be hurt by her again. I know last time was—"

"If you're here to see Harriet, you're too late," he says, blundering past her comment. "She left for the Beal lodging house yesterday morning."

"I know. Thea told me. I thought to come and see you anyway. See how you were faring with... well. Everything."

"I'm fine," Nathan says. "Why would I not be?"

Eva sighs inwardly. She can needle him for a more honest answer later. "We ought to go and see Harriet," she says. "I'm worried for her."

"Mm." He sounds as hesitant as she feels.

Eva hears a burst of Tom's laughter floating out from the parlour. Lowers her voice. "He was asking about her again last night."

"What did you say?"

"I just answered his question. Told him Harriet and I used to play cards when we were girls. Didn't make me feel any less awful about it, carrying on the lie that his mother is dead, when she was right under his nose just a day ago."

"I know." Nathan's glance flickers towards the parlour. "He's asked me about her before too. I hardly knew what to tell him. But you know this is what Edwin wants."

"I really don't think this is the situation Edwin anticipated, do you?" Eva sighs. Looks up at her brother. "Will you come to Beal with me? Make sure Harriet is safe? I'm worried it will only be a matter of time before she disappears again."

Nathan hesitates. "Do you really think she cares to see us? She made it perfectly clear she doesn't want to be in my company." Poorly hidden anger in his voice. "She could hardly leave the house quick enough."

"Let me go." Theodora appears in the entrance hall. Glances between them. "I can ask Aunt Harriet how she's faring. Make sure she's all right."

Eva feels a tug of guilt.

"What's this about, Thea?" Nathan asks. "You've been on edge since Harriet arrived. And now you want to call on her?"

Theodora hesitates, mulling over her response. "The Lady in the Dunes," she says finally. "Aunt Harriet is the Lady in the Dunes."

Eva raises her eyebrows, but Nathan just says, "I see."

Thea twines a stray strand of hair around her finger. "I'm curious about her is all. I'd like to get to know her a little better. To… help my writing."

Nathan shrugs. "Far be it from me to stifle your creativity."

"Good." A satisfied smile appears on Theodora's face. "I'll call on her this afternoon. Once the tide's gone down. Save you both the journey." And she disappears into the parlour before either of them can argue.

Nathan shakes his head as he watches after her. "I've learnt to ask as few questions as possible."

Eva snorts. "Especially if it gives you an excuse not to call on Harriet." The knot of guilt in her chest tightens. "You and I really are completely pathetic, aren't we."

Nathan returns her wry smile. "Incredibly so."

Julia moors the boat in the shadow of Bamburgh Castle, splashing through the shallow water onto the beach. She is grateful for the rain that has begun to fall—hopefully it will keep people off the streets. Prevent anyone from seeing her.

Her eyes dart as she walks into the village, seeking to avoid any familiar faces from the thieving ring. The end of her shawl unravels as she walks and she knots it at her throat in irritation. Her feet squelch in waterlogged shoes. Her body is blazing, palms stinging after relearning the feel of the sloop's ropes against her skin.

This cramped and cobbled village has always been familiar to her, just a few miles from Lindisfarne. She knows now there has been thievery woven into the fabric of the place for her entire life. Since the early days of the Rising, Bamburgh has been known as a Jacobite town—it makes sense, she supposes, that those with a hatred for the cause might have planted themselves here, to try and tear things down from the inside.

These days, when she walks these streets, she does not think of childhood adventures of sailing over here with her brothers, or of bringing Bobby here as a boy so he could admire the great sprawl of the castle. Does not even think of the miserable cottage her father had set himself up in after he had fled Lindisfarne, unable to shoulder the shame of his bastard grandson and unmarried daughter. These days, all she thinks of is alertness; of watching, waiting—for capture or collapse.

Julia lets herself into the tenement house, praying she has not been seen. Instead of going upstairs to her and Calum's quarters, she takes the downstairs passage toward Lizzie's lodgings. The hallway is dark and damp; smells of earth and woodsmoke and soured meat. Julia sees no one, but hears the clatter of pans coming from a tenement at the end of the passage. She presses an ear against the door of Lizzie's lodgings. Hears the faint clop of footsteps. She kneels on the flagstones and peeks beneath the door. A swell of patched grey skirts moves across the room.

Julia debates whether to knock. Decides against it. If she is to get her belongings out of the safe, there is every chance she will have to take them without Lizzie's knowledge. She does not want her to know she is here.

She slips out the door at the end of the hallway. A dark mop of hair is poking out from behind the wash house at the back of the building. Julia's stomach plunges.

"Bobby!" she hisses, tramping through the mud towards him.

His eyes widen and he tugs her down to crouch behind the wall beside her. "Why are you here, Ma?"

"Why are *you* here?" His words from last night rattle through her head: *Don't worry about your money. It will be all right. We'll find a way to get to it.* Dread roils inside her. She nods towards Lizzie's window. "You're trying to break in?"

She regrets not reminding Lizzie who Bobby was when she had seen him yesterday. If she catches him out here—and believes him a stranger—there is no telling what she will do. What in hell was he thinking, charging off like this to play the hero?

Bobby looks indignant. "I'm trying to get your money back. Lizzie's in there now, but if she leaves I can be in and out in a second."

"You are not breaking into her house," Julia snaps.

"Why not? How else do you plan to get your money?"

Julia grits her teeth. "It's my problem, Bobby. I will take care of it."

"How?"

Rain soaks through her shawl and runs down the back of her neck. "I don't know yet."

"If you won't let me break in, why don't we just go and ask her for your money back? Show her the book-keeping records. I thought she was your friend. Don't you think she'll believe you when you tell her the money's yours?"

"I don't know," Julia admits. "I can't take that risk. Lizzie won't want to be held responsible for anything that goes missing on her watch. I don't think she'll just let me take something from the safe."

"This is madness," Bobby says. "Stay here. I'm going to go and speak to her." He gets to his feet and strides towards the door.

Julia lurches after him, grabbing at his arm. "Don't. If she—"

The back door of the tenement house flies open, knocking Bobby backwards. Lizzie blusters out, greying hair blowing around her cheeks, a pistol in her hand.

Julia darts in front of him. "It's all right, Lizzie. He's my son. You remember Bobby, aye?"

Lizzie narrows her eyes, looks at them warily. Doesn't lower the pistol. "What you both doing out here?"

"I was looking for Ma," Bobby says quickly. "She weren't upstairs and someone told me she might be out in the wash house."

Lizzie glances into the empty wash house, the pistol

wavering. Julia reaches out and touches the nose of it, pushing it gently downwards. "Will you put that thing away, Lizzie? Please?"

Lizzie tucks the pistol into her apron, but pins suspicious eyes on Julia. "What are you doing back here? You know it's not safe."

"I know," she says quickly. "I left in a hurry yesterday. Forgot some things. I saw Bobby out here when I was going on my way." She clenches her hand around her son's wrist. "We'll be off now. Please don't tell anyone you saw us."

Lizzie eyes them, considering. "Go on then," she says finally. Glares at Bobby. "Watch yourself, lad. Stop prowling around beneath people's windows. You're lucky I didn't blow your damn eyes out."

CHAPTER SIXTEEN

The lodging house has been getting steadily busier as the morning has stretched into afternoon. Three more women have appeared toting travelling trunks and saddle bags; Harriet has spent the last few hours planted on the side of the bed closest to the door, a silent marking of her territory. The only thing she hates more than sharing travelling beds with strangers is being stuck in the middle of travelling beds with strangers—and she figures she would like to be as close as possible to an escape route if the man with the missing finger decides to show himself.

Two of the women, both older than Harriet, with matching clouds of grey hair, are chatting loudly to one another about the food in some Newcastle tavern—Harriet cannot tell if they are friends, or if they'd simply met here at the lodging house. The third woman, miraculously, is sleeping through the whole exchange. Harriet keeps her eyes down. Tries to focus on her sketching. Unbidden, it's the man with the missing finger that has appeared on the page today. She had had no intention of committing his image to memory. She is no portrait artist; that had been Isabelle's domain. And in a way, she hates that he has taken over her notebook, with his hellish black beard and close-set eyes. But there is something faintly calming about drawing her pursuer; identifying him, shaping him like this. Somehow, it gives her back a scrap of the power he has taken from her.

The older woman—Peggy, she has gathered from the dialogue being hurled across the room—pulls on her boots. "I'm starved," she announces. Looks to the other woman. "Food?"

"Aye, I'm famished."

"What about you, Leonardo?"

Harriet smirks. "No thank you. I'll stay here." Really, her stomach is groaning. There's little more she would like to do right now than go downstairs and eat. But it still feels too risky. Far too few days have passed for her to be certain she has not been followed here.

"You sure?" Peggy tugs the notebook out from under Harriet's pencil. Looks down at the sketch of the bearded man. "Who's this, then? A lover?"

"No" she says. "Nothing like that?"

"The man you wish was your lover?" She holds the book up, displaying the page to the other woman.

Harriet says, "It's the man who's trying to kill me."

Peggy lowers the page. "Bloody hell." Tosses the book back on the bed. "That why you don't want to come downstairs?"

Well, thinks Harriet, there are a lot of reasons. Beginning with the fact that this woman is painfully irritating. But nodding feels like the simplest answer. The quickest way to get these people out of here.

"Well then." Peggy grabs her hand and tugs her off the bed. "You'd best come with me and Martha. You need to eat. And safety in numbers and all that."

Harriet begins to protest, but it doesn't stop Peggy from sweeping her down the staircase into the public house.

It's busier downstairs than Harriet had expected; she's faintly relieved to see three other tables of guests. Rain is tapping steadily against the misty windows, a puddle of water beginning to seep beneath the door. A sorry-looking fire is spitting in the grate, most of the travellers still wrapped in coats and hats. Harriet wishes she had thought to bring her cloak.

"Here." Peggy guides Harriet and Martha towards a table in the back corner of the room. "We'll be hidden here. With a good view of the door. Easy access to the stairs in case we need to make a quick exit."

Harriet smiles faintly. "Thank you." There's something steadying about following Peggy's brusque orders. Since she had set out into the world on her own, it's a rare day that she allows herself to be directed, even when it comes to something as simple as where to sit or what to eat. There's something strangely blissful about relinquishing control.

She sits opposite Martha while Peggy disappears to the bar to order their food. Harriet feels Martha inspecting her, taking her in with shrewd blue eyes. Can practically feel her considering whether sitting here with a woman someone is trying to kill is an inordinately bad decision.

"I don't know for certain he's trying to kill me," Harriet blurts. She feels her cheeks redden, as Martha's thin grey eyebrows rise. "I'm sorry. I assumed you were wondering…"

"I wasn't, actually," Martha says. "I was thinking about the wreck."

Harriet swallows. "The wreck?"

"I heard there was a shipwreck out near here a few days ago. Some people were talking about it on the coach. I heard the lightkeeper pulled the survivors off the reef. Him and his wife kept them all at their cottage until the rescue boats came."

"Is that so?" Harriet can't quite make sense of why Martha's words are needling her so much. She knows all too well that Finn and Eva had saved her life—and the lives of many others. Doesn't stop her from being irritated by it.

More than that, she doesn't like the knowledge that people were talking about the wreck on Martha's coach. It feels too dangerous. How far has the news spread? Does anyone know she is here?

Peggy returns to the table with three tankards, dumping them unceremoniously on the table. Harriet brings one to her lips, gulping down a mouthful of lukewarm ale. It manages to take a scrap of the tension from her shoulders.

"Who is he?" Peggy asks, sliding onto the chair beside her. "And what did you do to make him want to kill you?"

Martha gives Peggy a smirk that tells Harriet she does not believe her story.

"I didn't do anything," Harriet says anyway. "And I don't know who he is. He's just... after me." The words feel pathetic. Weak. She hates that she has been reduced to this.

She wants to say more. After days of secrecy under Eva and Nathan's roofs, there is something almost liberating about sharing even these tiny pieces of the story. Peggy and Martha may well judge her, doubt her, but tomorrow morning they will be gone, and what they think of her will be of no consequence.

She wants to tell them of the way the bearded man had first appeared on the closing night of Lord Allbridge's exhibit, when she had displayed her paintings of Lindisfarne. Wants to tell them of the way he had followed her out of the Allbridges' manor house and right up to her carriage. She had approached him then, assuming him just an overenthusiastic admirer of her work. Had begun to grow suspicious when he had walked away from her without a word. All the way back to her rented rooms that night, she had been unable to shake the feeling she was being followed.

After that, he had appeared to her on several more occasions—on her way to a student's house; while returning from a dressmaker; in the middle of Leadenhall Market. And then that terrifying night when she had woken to hear someone prising open the ground-floor window of her lodgings. Just as the lock had sprung open, she'd heard a man's voice calling out to the intruder; heard a pistol shot splintering the sky.

Three days later, she had climbed aboard the *Cygnus* to escape London, only to find the bearded man had followed her aboard.

She tells Peggy and Martha none of this. Knows it is too dangerous. These women are strangers. Harriet has no idea if she can trust them.

Peggy takes a long gulp of her ale. "Why don't you just take care of him?"

"You mean, kill him?"

She nods.

"I couldn't do that."

"Why not? Sounds as though he deserves it."

Harriet lets out a long breath. Allows herself, for a moment, to imagine she is capable of such a thing. Would it feel liberating? Or would it be a weight she would never be free of? She thinks of all the men who had been sent to the gallows because of her. No part of that has ever felt liberating.

And yet, the bearded man has forced her from her unconstrained London life; the life she had crafted from nothing. To have had it stolen from her like this, without a scrap of explanation, feels like a cause for retribution.

Three bowls of stew land on the table in front of them. Though the meat is gristly and dark, Harriet swallows it down quickly. The idea of killing the bearded man seems to have only increased her appetite. She is not sure what, exactly, that says about her, but she is fairly certain that whatever it is, she is aware of it already.

The door creaks open and Harriet whirls towards the sound, heart jolting. It is not the bearded man.

Theodora shakes the rain from her hood and glances around the tavern, a faintly bewildered look on her face. She heads towards the counter, changing course when she catches sight of Harriet at the table in the corner. Theodora glances between Martha and Peggy, then looks back at her aunt. "May we speak a moment?"

Harriet nods hesitantly, surprised to see her. She doesn't like it. The last thing she wants is to put Nathan's daughter in danger. She slides off her chair, ushering Thea away from the table. She's been sent here by her father, no doubt. Probably to find out why her troublesome aunt had tried to fling herself off a ship.

"You didn't need to leave the house," Theodora blurts,

before Harriet can speak.

She frowns, taken aback by Thea's outburst. "It's all right. It's best this way."

Theodora hesitates. Looks at Harriet, then glances away. Harriet can tell she is unnerved by her. After a moment, Theodora says, "Did you leave because of me?"

"Why would I leave because of you?" The moment Harriet asks the question, she knows the answer. And a for a horrible, fleeting moment, she is back in the parlour at Highfield House, holding a pillow to her husband's face, feeling a million dark, conflicting thoughts batter through her head. Has she ever been at a lower point in her life than that day she had thought to kill her own husband? She cannot think of many.

Theodora toys with the edge of her damp cloak. "I've never told anyone what I saw that day. And I never will. I swear it."

Harriet is grateful. Manages a shameful thanks. Briefly, she considers giving her an explanation—*a terrible point in my life; I never intended to really do it*—but she knows there are no words that will make what Theodora saw any less dreadful. Does not even know if those words are true.

"Does your father know you're here?" she asks instead.

"Yes. But he doesn't know why I wished to speak to you. I just made something up about one of my stories. Well, no, I didn't make it up, but I said that I…" She shakes her head slightly, flustered under Harriet's questioning. Her cheeks flush and she swallows heavily. "Are you safe?" she asks. "Are you well?" And this, Harriet knows, is why Nathan has agreed to his daughter being here in this miserable tavern; this is Theodora's task. To determine if her aunt is safe and well and not the kind of person to throw herself into the ocean.

The corner of Harriet's lips turn up. "Did you father tell you to ask you that? Or was it Eva?"

Theodora gives a tiny smile. "Both."

Harriet puts a hand to Thea's shoulder, ushering her towards the door. "How did you get here?"

"I walked."

"Then you'd best be on your way. Unless you fancy swimming back." It's the worst of excuses. Even through the foggy, rain-streaked windows of the lodging house, Harriet can tell the tide has completely drained away. But she does not want Theodora here for a moment longer than she needs to be. She cannot take that risk.

Thea doesn't argue. Allows Harriet to walk her to the door. There's a new lightness to her, Harriet notes, now she has learnt she was not to blame for her aunt absconding from the house. This family, Harriet notes, has always been painfully good at shouldering blame.

Thea pauses in the doorway. "You're certain you'll not come back to the house?"

"I'm certain," says Harriet. "I'm better off here. Truly. But thank you."

"What was that about?" Peggy demands, when Harriet gets back to the table. "If you got a house to stay at, what you doing in this place?"

Harriet raises her eyebrows.

"I got the hearing of a wolf," Peggy grins. "Serves me well from time to time."

"I can't stay at the house," Harriet says shortly. "Not when I've got someone after me." She swallows down a mouthful of stew. It's beginning to grow cold. She feels a tug of guilt at putting the other women in the dormitory in the same danger. "Perhaps I ought to ask for a private room. In case he—"

"If that bastard shows his face in our room tonight, I'll take him down before you even know what's happened," Peggy announces. "Got a pistol between my treasures."

Harriet covers a faint laugh. What would it be like, she finds herself wondering, to be the kind of woman who carried a pistol in her underclothes? The thought brings her an unexpected surge of power. She'd like to see the look on the bearded man's face if she pulled a pistol out from inside her stays.

Martha snorts. "Lucky you." She cocks her head toward the innkeeper. "The bastard made me turn mine in at the door."

Peggy grins. "Should have kept it somewhere he wouldn't go looking."

CHAPTER SEVENTEEN

Julia sits shivering in the boat she had stolen, blowing on her hands in an attempt to keep warm. The sloop rocks on the silver water out beyond the Lindisfarne anchorage. The sun is leaving golden pools on the horizon, the last of the light refusing to drain away. The air smells bitingly cold. The first snow of the season will be here soon, she thinks. A time for making wishes.

"You don't have to be here," she tells Bobby, for at least the fourth time. "Why don't I take you back to your lodgings? Once it's dark I'll just tie the boat up where I found it and be on my way."

"No. I'll see you back to the house. Just in case we've been followed."

The insistence in his voice is beginning to annoy her—his worry for her starting to become less endearing and more patronising.

"You shouldn't have come to Bamburgh today," he says. "If you hadn't, I'd have got your money from Lizzie's safe already."

Julia snorts. "If I hadn't come to Bamburgh today, Lizzie would have put a bullet between your eyes."

Bobby doesn't speak. Just folds his arms across his chest, a deep frown creasing the bridge of his nose. With this pinched expression on his face, he looks infuriatingly like his father. "I've a little money of my own we can use," he says finally. "Won't get us as far as London, but it'll get us clear of Northumberland. Out the way of the thieving ring. If we used that, you wouldn't need your money from the safe."

"No." Julia's response is instinctive. Fleeing with nothing but Bobby's pennies is bound to lead to trouble. Besides, the money her son has earned is supposed to be for him to build his own life. One free of the thieving ring, and the Jacobite cause, and all the other things his mother has dragged him into over the past eighteen years.

"But Ma, I—"

"I said no." Julia shifts awkwardly on the bench, tugging her cloak tighter around her. "I've money in the safe. Enough to start afresh if Calum decides not to come back. I just need to get to it."

"And how do you plan to do that?"

She tries to swallow her irritation. "Sunday morning Lizzie will be out of the tenement at church," she says tightly. "She never misses a service. I can go back for the money then. Alone." It's a flimsy plan, but far more solid than anything else she's come up with since finding herself at Highfield House.

Bobby doesn't respond. Just huffs again and turns to look out over the ink-black water. Julia can tell he's annoyed with her. Good. She's annoyed with him too.

She stares out across the leathery sea, watching the black interruptions of seals out past Saint Cuthbert's Island. "It's dark enough," she says finally. "Let's take the boat back."

Refusing Bobby's offer to take the oars, she guides the sloop carefully towards the mouth of the anchorage, peering over her shoulder into the darkness. She sees the street lamps pooling their light on the cobbles; lanterns flickering in windows. But the wharf is dark. She pulls the boat back to the jetty. Snares it to the mooring post and rushes up the beach.

Head down, hood up, she begins to walk, turning right towards the castle and the coast path. The dark is thickening and she would rather keep to the lamplit streets than attempt a lightless trudge along the edge of the island. But she does not want to risk anyone seeing her, on her way back from returning a stolen boat.

Bobby jogs to keep up with her. "I'll see you back to the house," he says again.

Julia doesn't bother to argue.

They walk in silence for a long time, picking their way through the disappearing light, watching as the dunes roll into blackness. A few faint stars peek out from between the clouds, a sliced moon trying to light their way. Julia stumbles over the uneven ground, sloshes through an unseen stream. Hears the distant knock of deer hooves, the rhythmic burble of owls. She is almost relieved when the lights of Highfield House finally lift the darkness.

She leaves Bobby at the edge of the path leading up to the house. "Wait here," she tells him. "I'll fetch you a lamp to find your way back." She knocks tentatively on the front door. Hears a rapid volley of footsteps, then the door flies open. At the sight of Nathan, Julia's heart skips. She had been expecting the housekeeper.

He is without a jacket or cravat, his shirtsleeves rolled to his elbows and the top button of his simple blue waistcoat undone. Coils of dark hair have come loose from his queue and tickle the top of his shoulders. "I thought you had left." He swallows. "And forgotten your cat."

Julia can't help but smile. "No, I… I had some errands to run, is all." It's the flimsiest of excuses, she knows. What kind of questionable errands would have her creeping about the place in the darkness?

For long moments, neither of them speak. Julia inches backwards, out of the puddle of light cast by the lamp hanging above the door. Tries to hide her mud-caked skirts in the shadows. Her feet are frozen inside her wet shoes.

The aroma of roasting meat drifts in from the kitchen, making her stomach groan loudly. She cringes, feeling colour rush to her cheeks.

"I apologise if I made you feel unwelcome," Nathan says. "If you felt the need to stay out of the house tonight."

A sudden urge comes up on her to pull him close. Press her head to his shoulder and inhale the rosewater scent of him she has conjured up in her mind so many times in the last ten years. She pushes the thought away. "You've nothing in the world to apologise for," she says, a faint waver in her voice. "I'm very grateful for all of this." She clears her throat. Takes another step away from him. "Could you spare a lantern for Bobby to take back to the village?"

"Of course." Nathan takes the lamp from the hook in the entrance hall. Steps outside and passes it to Bobby. "You know there's a bed for you here if you need it," he tells him.

"Thank you, Mr Blake. But I'm quite all right in my lodgings." Bobby takes the lamp. Murmurs a strained goodbye to Julia. She watches after him as the light disappears into the dunes. Tries to let her annoyance at him dissipate. She knows, after all, that he just wants what's best for her. Just as she does for him.

She can tell Nathan is still behind her. His presence feels weighted, magnetic. She draws in her courage and turns to face him.

He holds her gaze for a long second. "Are you safe?"

"Yes," she says, too quickly. "Of course."

He hesitates for a moment, as though debating whether to push the issue. Whether to seek a more honest response. Finally, he nods. Clasps his hands in front of him. Unclasps them again. "Very well. If there's anything you need…"

Julia nods. "Thank you."

He flashes her a short smile that doesn't quite reach his eyes. Turns to leave.

"Nathan," she says suddenly.

He looks back to face her. "Yes?"

"Was there ever any suspicion? About… the way Joseph Holland died?"

He doesn't look surprised at the question. "There was talk," he admits. "After Holland disappeared, everyone came to assume he was a government spy. But no one ever suspected you or your brother were involved in his death. At least not to the best of my knowledge."

"Even though I left the island so quickly after his disappearance?"

"I think…" He shakes his head. "Rather, I *know* people came to suspect there was something between you and me that… well. That fell apart." He looks down, away from her eyes. "I did not deny it. I allowed people to believe that was the sole reason behind you leaving." There's a rigidity to his voice, a formality. The words come out devoid of emotion— betrayed only by the rapid rise and fall of his chest.

Julia's throat tightens. "And my shop?" she asks. "The blood on the stairs?"

"There's an apothecary there now."

Minerva stalks into the entrance hall on silent paws. Circles Julia's legs. "Have you been inside?"

"Once or twice. There's blood on the stairs if you know to look. I suspect you and I are the only ones who know to look."

She dares a small smile. "I'm glad of it." Catches herself quickly. "Not that it matters, of course." She scoops Minerva from the floor. Holds her against the place her heart is thumping. "It's hardly as though staying on the island has ever been an option."

CHAPTER EIGHTEEN

"I want him to come here tonight," Harriet says suddenly.

The dormitory is dark, the bar downstairs quiet. Soft snoring is coming from the two women in the opposite bed, intermittent rain tapping against the windows. Harriet has been lying awake, staring into the blackness for hours. Can tell by Peggy's breathing that she's awake too.

"I want him to come here tonight so you can take care of him."

Peggy shifts to face her, making the mattress sag. In the faint light shining beneath the door from the lamp in the hallway, Harriet can just make out her storm cloud of hair. Her wild, determined eyes. "Why don't you take care of him the next time you see him?"

Harriet sighs, rolling onto her back. It's not like she hasn't thought about killing the man with the beard. She's thought about it a lot, although it's always been some vague, intangible concept, rather than anything solid to be acted upon. She'd never have the strength to do something so dangerous. So final. Strength—is that even the right word to use when it comes to killing someone? Anonymously sending men to the gallows is far more her style. "I couldn't," she says.

"Why not?"

Harriet is silent for a moment. Why not? Because she does not want to take a life. But hasn't he taken hers? He's forced her to flee London, leaving behind her commissions, her friends, her students and sponsors. Though she has spent a decade working and fighting and struggling to make her dreams a reality, in so many ways, she still feels weak. Still feels, sometimes, that she is caught in the same current of life she had been as Edwin's wife. Tossed and towed by rips she never meant to get caught in. Yes, she had found the courage to break free from her marriage. But she had let society tell her to leave Isabelle. Had let the man with the beard force her from her home.

"I don't have a weapon," she says.

"Ought to get yourself one."

"Where from, exactly? We're miles from any gunsmith." Harriet can hardly believe she is even having this conversation.

Peggy tosses the blankets off them and slides out of bed. "Come with me. We're going to find a way to get rid of this bastard."

Harriet doesn't move. But something stops her pulling the covers back over her body.

Peggy tugs her boots on over bare feet. "Come on," she hisses.

Harriet finds herself obeying. She pulls on her shoes and shawl and follows Peggy into the dark hallway. "Where are we going, exactly?"

"Innkeeper took everyone's weapons at the door," Peggy whispers as they tiptoe down the creaking stairs. "He must be keeping them somewhere."

"And you don't think they'll be locked up?"

"Probably. Maybe we can break in."

This feels like a terrible idea. "Break in to where?"

Peggy shrugs. Doesn't answer.

They reach the dark tavern. The remains of the fire are glowing in the grate, and the room still holds a thick warmth, along with a heady smell of old stew and ale. A mouse scuttles across the flagstones at the sound of their footsteps. Disappears into the kitchen.

Peggy runs her hand along the top of the mantel until her fingers land on the tinderbox. She lights the candlestick sitting beside it. Pans it around behind the bar.

The pale light falls over rows of barrels and bottles, and a trough filled with dirty tankards. A wooden locker is tucked in against the wall. "There," Peggy says. She hurries towards it. "I bet this is where he's keeping the weapons." She rattles the lid. Hands the candle to Harriet. "Hold this. The damn thing's locked."

Of course it is, Harriet wants to say. She glances edgily towards the staircase.

She stands over Peggy while the older woman crouches by the chest and jams the prong of a fork into the lock. Wiggles it around. Harriet can tell she has no idea what she's doing.

Peggy gets to her feet with a grunt. Tosses the fork back onto the bar. "I don't think that's going to work."

"Let's go back upstairs," Harriet whispers, gripping her shawl tighter around her body. "We're going to get caught down here. And the last thing I need is for the innkeeper to throw me into the street. Besides, you don't even know that the weapons are in there."

"Let's try the innkeeper's room," Peggy says, as though Harriet has not even spoken. "You can be sure he'll be keeping a weapon under his pillow. Just in case. Who knows what kind of mad things come through this door?"

Harriet smiles wryly to herself. She's fairly certain she's with one of those mad things right now. Is also fairly certain she's becoming one herself.

A loud creak sounds at the top of the staircase. Instinctively, Harriet crouches, hiding herself behind the bar. She looks wide-eyed at Peggy.

Another creak, followed by the soft thud of footfalls.

"Someone down there?" The innkeeper's voice. Harriet's heart speeds. She can't be thrown out of here. She can't. She already feels as though she has nowhere in the world to go. What was she thinking following this madwoman down here on a misguided search for weapons? Even if they had swung open that storage chest and found it full of pistols, Harriet knows she would never have had the courage to pull the trigger.

Peggy blows out the candle. Gestures with her head towards the door in the corner, leading to what Harriet assumes is the kitchen. The creaking of the stairs grows louder. Closer. Harriet darts into the kitchen behind Peggy.

The room is hung in shadow, the glowing coals in the fireplace picking out a long wooden table, shelves stacked with jars and barrels, a side of meat dangling grimly from a hook on the ceiling. A flicker of light from the innkeeper's candle pans across the doorway.

Harriet drops to her knees beneath the table, tugging

Peggy down to do the same. As the older woman crouches, she knocks a knife sitting on the edge of the table. Sends it clattering to the floor.

Harriet sucks in a breath. Hears the innkeeper's footsteps coming towards the kitchen. This is it, she thinks, she's going to be caught down here on this most foolish of missions, with this most foolish of women, all because of her foolish need to let someone else take the reins of her life for a moment. When has that ever led her anywhere but into that suffocating undertow she has spent so long trying to thrash her way out of?

"Pardon me, sir," Peggy blunders, sickly sweet, getting to her feet as the innkeeper steps into the kitchen. "Thought I left my purse down here when I came for supper tonight."

The innkeeper grabs a hold of her arm, tossing her back into the bar. "Left your purse in my kitchen, did you? Have to try harder than that."

Peggy wavers. Beneath the table, Harriet curls her hands around her knees. Holds her breath.

"All right," Peggy says finally. "Was after a drink to put me sleep. Get bad nightmares you see. A dram of whisky usually does the trick."

"Get out of here." Harriet hears the innkeeper's voice moving towards the staircase. Hears the loud groan of the steps as two pairs of footsteps disappear into the darkness.

Harriet waits huddled under the kitchen table for what she guesses to be close to an hour. Long enough, she hopes, for the innkeeper to have fallen back to sleep. Peggy too, if she's lucky. If the older woman is still awake when she gets back to the dormitory, Harriet knows she'll not manage to hold back the harsh words on the edge of her lips. Especially not given how many mice have been tickling the hem of her nightshift, and how deeply the chill of the kitchen has seeped into her bones.

She creeps upstairs on silent feet. Pushes open the door of the dormitory and slides into bed.

The mattress shifts. "Sorry," says Peggy. "Don't suppose that was the wisest of ideas."

Harriet doesn't speak. She tugs the blankets up to her chin. Shivers. Her feet feel like they've forgotten what it's like to be warm.

Peggy wriggles around again and Harriet is about to bark out an order for her to go the hell to sleep, when she feels something cold and hard nudging her shoulder. A pistol, she realises. "Here," says Peggy. "Take this."

Harriet rolls over to face her. "Where did you get it?"

"It's mine. I want you to have it."

Harriet hesitates. Finds the other woman's eyes in the darkness. "I couldn't."

"Yes you could. You need it more than I do. I don't have some lunatic chasing me."

I couldn't. The thought comes to her again; comes from the part of her that is still afraid, still doubting. Even after all this time. Even after all she has achieved. She allows herself to reach out and touch the cold metal. Feels the weight of it in her palm. Real power, she thinks. Not the imagined kind that comes from sketching the man so his likeness stares up at her every time she opens her damn notebook.

She lies in silence for a long time. "In the morning," she says finally, "will you teach me how to shoot it?"

CHAPTER NINETEEN

Finn curls his hands around the top rung of the wooden ladder and looks out across the roof of the cottage. He'd woken to find several more tiles lying in pieces on the rocks beside the front door. Sees now that others are close to following.

He uses his hands to prise off a slipped tile that seems to be hanging by a thread.

"How bad is it?" he hears Eva call from below. He looks down to see her tying her bonnet beneath her chin.

"Worse than I'd hoped. Better than it could be."

She smiles. "At least that's something. Fixable?"

"Aye. If I can get my hands on enough slate. Could take a while to get the tiles out here. I'll ask around the farm when I go over there next week. See if anyone can help." He climbs down the ladder. "You're going to see Harriet?"

Eva nods, pulling in a breath. "Yes. Before I change my mind. I've set the boys to their schoolwork. Maggie is sleeping." She looks up at the roof again. "Is there anything I can do to help?"

Finn smiles. Nudges her towards the jetty. "Go and see your sister. The roof will still be here when you get back." He chuckles. Kisses her lips. "I hope."

He watches as the skiff pulls away from the island. Tosses the cracked tile into the sea. He hopes the worst of the autumn rain holds off until he has what he needs to fix the roof. With all these gaps in the slate, they're likely to wake one morning and find a lagoon in their living area. Still, this house has stood more than fifty years. He's sure it will stand another fifty yet.

As the thought comes to him, he glances up through the window at his sons, dark heads bent over their texts, quills in hand. This house may stand for another fifty years, but is this really the life he wants for his children? Thanks to Eva, both boys are on their way to being well educated; he has no doubt Maggie will be too. Finn wonders what his parents would think if they knew their grandchildren were studying arithmetic and Latin at that table, where they themselves had counted pennies and re-tarred their boots. Heaven knows these children could have far more from their life than to be marooned out here on Longstone forever. Could have that broader life Finn had once longed for for himself.

For not the first time since he had taken up the role of lightkeeper fifteen years ago, the thought of leaving Longstone flickers at the back of his mind. It's chased away by the thought that always follows it: that he cannot leave this patch of sea dark. The wreck of the *Cygnus* has only solidified how much he and his family are needed out here. In the face of all the recognition and thanks he and Eva are finally getting, are they really to turn away and leave the Farne

Islands lightless?

They won't, of course. He won't. And at the back of his mind, Finn knows the reason is not the children, or the wrecked ship. It's because his being here is what his father would have wanted. Really, that's what this has always been about. He had left Longstone and abandoned his father to die alone; and in the midst of that broader life he had once sought so desperately, he had killed Oliver Blake. And for all of that, Finn knows he needs to pay a penance.

He takes the ladder to the shed and leans it up against the wall beside a mountain of peat. Yanks hard on the door, which has become warped with time and moisture. It squeals loudly against the stone floor as it closes.

As he returns to the house, he sees a small sloop sailing steadily towards the island. He makes his way out to the jetty.

Finn has not thought about the man at the tiller for many years. No, that's not right. For many years, he has done his best not to think about the man at the tiller. And yet somehow, he has never been far from the front of his thoughts. Finn knows Henry Ward has made far too big an impact on his life—for better or worse—for things to ever be otherwise.

He lifts a hand to shade his eyes from the pale sun bouncing off the water. Watches Ward approach. He feels an old, instinctive unease. But perhaps that unease does not need to be here. After all, after his pirate ship had been captured, Ward had told the authorities that Finn was his prisoner. Had saved him from the hangman's noose.

Ward secures the sloop to the jetty without speaking, then climbs out with one large stride. Though he must be past sixty, he still stands rigid, upright, arctic blue eyes spearing

Finn from beneath the brim of his black tricorn hat. His sharp jaw is clean-shaven, a long coil of white hair hanging down his back. He gives a brusque nod of greeting; a weighted gesture. Finn feels a thousand unspoken words pass between them. After a moment, Ward says, "It's good to see you, lad."

Finn is not sure he can say the same. How does he greet this man who has made such a deep impact on his life? Over the three decades he has known Henry Ward, Finn has revered him, been awed by him, felt protected by him in his father's absence. Feared him, hated him, been simultaneously overcome by anger and gratitude towards him. He has never had a chance to thank him for his freedom—indeed, he had expected Ward to die on the gallows after the *Eagle* had been captured.

Since he had learnt, some years ago, of Ward's unexpected survival, Finn has toyed with the idea of hunting him down to give him his thanks for sparing his life. Has always discarded the idea as soon as it arrives. Because how can he thank Ward for the reprieve when his former captain had been the one to force him aboard his ship in the first place? Thanks to Henry Ward, Finn had come painfully close to leaving Eva a widow with their son growing inside her.

Ward's glance drifts past him, and Finn turns to follow his gaze. Three small faces are lined up at the window, their schoolwork apparently forgotten.

"You've made quite a life for yourself out here," says Ward.

"Aye. I have." Finn decides not to tell Ward one of the boys at the window is his grandson. He shifts instinctively, to block Ward's view of the children. "Have you been in Northumberland all this time?" he asks, trying to divert the conversation away from his own life.

"No." Ward turns up the collar of his coat as wind barrels off the sea. "I've only just returned. I have pressing business up here."

The response feels deliberately vague, and Finn cannot deny a hint of curiosity at what Henry Ward's life might look like now. At exactly how he might have escaped the gallows. He supposes that, for a man with connections high up in the government, and the damning information he had had about the Whig party, wrangling his freedom had not been so difficult. But that curiosity is not powerful enough for him to want Ward here, encroaching into this life Finn was sure he would once be denied. "Why are you here?" he asks.

Ward doesn't look surprised at his bluntness. And perhaps he is in no mood for conversation either. Because there's a look of intensity in his eyes that Finn had not caught before.

"I heard news of the wreck of the *Cygnus*," says Ward. "And I need to find my daughter."

CHAPTER TWENTY

Eva knocks tentatively on the door of the dormitory. "Harriet?"

There's a knot in her stomach as the door clicks open. Harriet does not look surprised to see her. Perhaps just surprised it had taken her so long to appear. Eva has spent almost a week trying to work up the courage to face her sister. She wants the truth about what happened on that ship. But she also fears that truth. Is afraid of what Harriet might have tried to do. And why.

Only once in the last ten years has Eva tried to find her sister. She had written to Edwin and several of Harriet's acquaintances in London, asking if anyone had had word from her. Edwin's response had come back clipped and empty; it was more than Eva managed to get back from any of Harriet's friends. She was not sure if they knew nothing, or if they were keeping quiet at Harriet's request. Either way, it was clear enough that she did not want to be found.

Eva wonders if she had given up too easily. If she had let

her anger at Harriet get the better of her. Perhaps she ought to have pushed aside that bitterness and kept looking until she knew her sister was safe. Happy.

She steps inside the dormitory, pulling the door closed behind her. The room is large, filled with two hastily made beds. She and Harriet are the only people inside. "You have this place to yourself?"

Harriet sits back on one of the beds and picks her notebook and pencil up off the side table. "Only because there are so few travellers in these parts." She sketches as she speaks, not looking at Eva. "There were three other women in here last night. They all moved on this morning."

Eva smiles faintly. "I'm glad you didn't see fit to join them."

"Are you?"

"Of course I am. We've barely had a chance to speak since you came back."

Harriet doesn't look up from her notebook. "I thought we'd had plenty of conversation."

Eva stays hovering in the doorway. Swallows down her irritation. "It's a beautiful day." She tries to keep her voice light. "Shall we take a walk?" It feels safer, somehow, to be out in the open than locked in here with Harriet, and the years of resentment that have been simmering between them.

"It's freezing," Harriet says, without looking up.

"Put your cloak on then."

"I'd rather stay here."

Eva presses her lips together, stifling a sigh of annoyance. She unbuttons her cloak and hangs it on the hook beside the door. Comes to sit beside Harriet on the edge of the bed. Eva peers over at her notebook. Recognises the sketched shades of Lindisfarne, the view through the lodging house window.

"It's beautiful," she says.

Harriet closes the book and sets it on the side table. Turns to face her sister expectantly.

"How are you?" Eva asks.

"I'm fine."

"Really?"

Harriet sighs. "Yes, Eva. Really. Do you wish it to be otherwise?"

"Of course not," she says tautly. "I'm just worried for you, is all."

"Why?"

Eva knows the question is designed to irritate her, and she forces herself not to rise to it. "Because I don't know what happened on the *Cygnus*," she says evenly. "If you would just tell us what—"

"What's there to tell? The ship ran aground on the reef. The crew were young and inexperienced. I can promise you, the investigation will show nothing different."

Eva hesitates. Toys with a loose thread on her shortjacket. "And you didn't..."

"Try to drown myself? Of course not." Harriet gets abruptly to her feet. She begins to pace in front of the bed, anger clouding her eyes. "I had my coin pouch with me. With my travel documents in it. You were the one who took them out of my cloak to keep them safe. If I was trying to end things, why would I bother taking my damn travel documents with me?" She shakes her head incredulously. "I can't believe you would even think such a thing." Her voice begins to rise. "Is that really what you imagine my life has become?"

"What else was I supposed to think?" Eva demands. "The

crewmen said they saw you trying to jump from the ship. One of them said he pulled you back—"

Harriet lets out a cry of frustration. She scrubs a hand across her face. When she looks back at Eva, her eyes are hot and glimmering with emotion. "What else did they tell you? Did they tell you about the man who was after me? Who's been after me since London?" Her voice wavers slightly. "The man I got on the ship to try and escape, only to find he'd followed me aboard?"

Eva feels suddenly hot, then cold. "The man at our cottage?" she asks sickly. "The man with the beard? He followed you up here from London?"

"Yes."

"Who is he?"

Harriet goes to stand at the window. She wraps an arm around her middle. Gnaws at a thumbnail. For a long time, she doesn't speak, and Eva suspects she is about to shut down again. But then, in a half-voice: "I don't know. I don't know what he wants with me. I first saw him at an exhibition one of my patrons was holding. After that, he started following me around the city. When he tried to break into my lodgings one night, I knew I had to leave. I thought I could hide away in Northumberland for a while. Let him lose track of me and go back to London when it was safe. I didn't realise he had followed me onto the ship until we were out at sea and it was too late to get off."

Eva lets out a breath. "Have you been to the authorities?"

"Of course I have. They didn't do a thing. I had no proof for them of who he was or what he'd done. Do you have any idea how quickly men like that will disregard a woman without a husband?"

Tentatively, Eva moves to stand behind her sister at the window. "Why did you not tell us all this before?"

No response.

"Did you… do something you were afraid to tell us about?" Eva ventures. "The money in your pouch…"

Harriet whirls around. "What?"

Eva swallows heavily. She shakes her head. Regrets her words. "Never mind. I—"

"You think I stole the money in my pouch? You think that's why this man is after me?" Harriet's eyes are blazing. "I earned every penny of that money," she hisses. "I wrote letter after letter of introduction and I tutored half the young women in London and I stayed up painting every night until my damn eyes gave out. I worked so damn hard for all of it." She shakes her head. "*This* is why I didn't want to tell you anything, Eva. Because of the suspicion. The distrust."

"I'm sorry," Eva says. "And I'm sorry for assuming…" She hates that her sister had thought to keep all this a secret. Hates that she can expect nothing else.

Outside the door, footsteps thump down the hall. When they disappear into the room next door, Eva says quietly, "You tried to get off the ship to escape the man who was after you? Is that why the crewmen saw you trying to jump?"

Harriet leans back against the window and nods faintly. "We were due to land in Edinburgh the morning after the wreck. I knew that once the ship docked, he would come after me, just like he had in London. I knew I'd have no chance of losing him, not when there were so few of us aboard the ship." Her eyes turn downward, fixing on a knot in the floorboards. "When I came out onto the deck that night, I saw how close we were to the Farne Islands. I thought getting off the ship with a buoy was my best chance of escaping." Her voice rattles. "I didn't realise we were not supposed to be that close to the islands. I didn't realise we were off course. Or that the ship was about to be wrecked."

Eva feels an ache in her chest. She can hardly bear to think of how desperate and frightened Harriet must have been to have considered such a thing. "The waters near the Farnes are so dangerous, Harriet. You're so lucky to be alive." She swallows hard. "Or did you choose those waters because you did not wish to be?"

"I chose those waters because I knew you were there!" Harriet's voice wavers and it catches Eva by surprise. She cannot remember the last time she saw her sister cry. "I thought I could make it to the islands with the buoy," she says. "Maybe make it to Longstone." She swipes angrily at a tear as it slides down her cheek. "I could see the firebasket." She turns away. "In any case…" Coughs down her tears. "I'd rather die by the sea than at the hands of a man."

For a long time, Eva doesn't speak. She wants to believe all this. As horrifying as it is to hear this man has been following her sister, it's a better outcome than Harriet wanting to end her own life. She dares to take a step towards her. "What can we do to help you?"

"Nothing."

"Harriet—"

"There's been no sign of him since the wreck," she cuts in. "I don't think he knows I'm here." She gives a murmur of humourless laughter. Wipes her eyes with the back of her hand. "Seems like my plan of throwing myself into the water worked. In a roundabout way."

For a moment, Eva doesn't speak. "What will you do? Stay

here in Northumberland?"

"I don't know what I will do," Harriet admits. "But no, I'll not stay here. This isn't where I belong. Coming here was a mistake."

Eva tries not the let the hurt show on her face. Is Harriet completely oblivious to the sting of her words? Or does she just not care?

She tries to let her anger slide. After all, she can hardly begin to imagine the fear Harriet must have gone through— not just on the ship, but in the days and weeks beforehand. And then to wake up at their cottage to find herself in her son's presence…

Eva knows seeing Thomas had cut Harriet deeply. Also knows she will never admit it. She thinks of all the questions Tom has asked her and Nathan. Thinks of that look in his eyes as he sought scraps of information about his mother. Thinks of everything she has kept from him. Half-truths that had hurt to tell.

She sinks onto the edge of the bed. "I've been thinking about Tom," she says stiffly. "And I wondered if you might… care to spend a little more time with him. If you wish it, I can—"

"No," Harriet says quickly. "No."

"Are you sure? It's not too late. He—"

"Not too late?" Harriet repeats, laughing incredulously. "He thinks his mother is dead. I am not going to upturn that for him. I am not going to put him through the same kind of upheaval I went through when I learnt who my father was."

"Do you not think he might wish to know you?"

"The mother who abandoned him?" Harriet says bitterly. "No, Eva, I don't think he might wish to know me. Do you?"

She shakes her head. "He is better off without me. He always has been."

"Do you really believe that? Or is that just what you tell yourself to excuse your leaving him?" Eva's own bitter words surprise her. Words she has been holding in for longer than she has been aware of them.

"Why are you even asking me this?" Harriet hisses. "I thought you were under strict instructions from Edwin never to even speak my name around my son."

"Well," Eva says shortly, "I don't imagine this was quite the situation Edwin had in mind when he made that request. I can only imagine how I would feel if I were face to face with my own son and couldn't speak openly to him."

"I'm not you, Eva. And I don't want Thomas in my life."

"And what about what he might want?" Eva feels her anger pulsing beneath the surface. The response feels so cold, so unfeeling. Inhuman. "It's all about you, isn't it, Harriet. It's always all about you. No thought to anyone else, even your own son." She gets to her feet. "You were sleeping in my children's bedroom, and you did not even think to ask me a single thing about them. Not even their names. You were at our cottage for two days and you didn't ask any of us a single thing about our lives. I would have thought that after ten years, even you might have had a little curiosity about someone other than yourself."

"I almost died," Harriet hisses. "I was hardly thinking clearly."

"No," Eva says. "You're never thinking clearly. You're never thinking about anyone but yourself. How could you just leave without a word to any of us?" She hears old, unresolved anger bubbling up in her voice. "How could you cause us to worry like that? On top of everything else we were going through back then?" She had not intended to take this abrupt dive into the past. Had come here only to ask about Harriet's safety. At least that was what she had told herself.

But none of this is in the past, she realises. It has not been washed away by time, or by all Harriet has just told her. It is all right here between them, as if it had happened yesterday.

"Could you not even have managed a single letter?" Eva pushes. "Anything to let us know you were safe? Offer any word of explanation…"

"An explanation for what?" Harriet shoots. "For why I left?" She laughs coldly. "Believe me, Eva, you of all people do not want an explanation for that."

"What is that supposed to mean?"

"I would have thought you were glad I left," Harriet says, avoiding the question. "Given what I knew about Finn and Oliver." And here is Harriet's own unresolved anger, Eva realises. Rage at her sister for marrying the man who killed their brother. For trying to keep it a secret.

"I'm sorry," she says, swallowing hard. "I ought to have told you about… all that."

Harriet smiles wryly. "You cannot even say it, can you."

Eva looks down, avoiding Harriet's eyes. Feels a knot tighten in her stomach.

"Do you and your husband ever speak of it?" Harriet presses, coming to stand close. "Do your children know? Will you ever tell them?"

Eva pushes past her suddenly, striding across the room to put space between them. "I told you I was sorry." Her voice rattles. "I never should have kept it a secret from you."

Harriet snorts. "You're only sorry I found out about it.

You would have kept it a secret forever if you could have. Anything to keep from disrupting your perfect life."

"A perfect life?" Eva repeats. "Is that what you think I have? You've always been the first to tell me just how pathetic our little cottage is. The first to list all the reasons why I would never be happy there." She shakes her head. "Is that what this is about, Harriet? You're angry at me because I'm happy and you're not?"

Harriet stumbles backwards as though the accusation is a physical blow. She gathers herself quickly. "Please," she snorts, "I would choose my life over yours a million times over."

In a way, Eva is glad for this outpouring of anger. It feels like a release of something held far too tightly for far too long. Not just the past ten years, but for Harriet's entire life. Her sister has always been this: selfish, angry, lost in her own world. Abigail had always made excuses for her. Why? Because she was the youngest? Because she wasn't Samuel's daughter? Because she was so precious, born in the wake of Oliver's death?

Harriet, with her impossible beauty, and her prodigious talent. Too young, too flighty, too lost in her own world. Always one excuse after another.

Harriet turns to face her, blue eyes icy. "I would have liked to reconcile with you and Nathan," she says bitterly. "But the first thing you did was blather on to one another about how much you distrusted me."

"The first thing we did was save your life," Eva snaps.

"Yes. You and your husband are heroes." Harriet turns to give her a thin smile. "I wonder what everyone would think if they knew the truth about Oliver's death. Or Donald

Macauley's."

And it comes from nowhere: an old fear, one that had been buried deep. The same fear Eva had felt towards her eldest brother. Innate and unplaceable. She has no idea why Harriet's words have sparked it, or how her sister has been able to dredge it up from so deep within her.

She only sees now that what she ought to have recognised from the beginning: that this could only end here, with anger and bitterness and not a hint of resolution.

Eva snatches her cloak from the hook and throws it over her shoulders. And she leaves the dormitory without looking back.

Harriet stands leaning up against the wall for a long time after Eva leaves, her body hot with anger.

You're angry at me because I'm happy and you're not?

The accusation feels impossibly brutal.

Somewhere inside, Harriet knows this is what this has always been about. Eva was supposed to be the dreary, rigid sister, the one who lived a tiresome life in the confines of all that was expected of her. She was supposed to watch from the corner while her sister made a name for herself painting the skies.

Eva was not supposed to be the one who defied convention and married for love and had the villagers fall at her feet for saving her lost and broken sister from a shipwreck. She was not supposed to represent everything Harriet knows she will never have. Can never have.

Worst of all, is that, in spite of all this, in spite of all her failures and imperfections, Harriet *had* found something close to happiness. Had found pride in the life she had built for herself, had found joy in seeing her dreams of being an artist come to life. Happiness—or at least some watered-down form of it.

But all that has been stolen from her by this nameless black-bearded man, and she has no understanding of why. Now she has nothing but the bleakest unhappiness and a pistol in her pocket, with nothing close to the courage to use it.

She watches through the window as Eva's boat shifts steadily towards the horizon. Lets the curtain fall.

She paces back and forth across the dormitory, rage simmering inside her.

Harriet hates that she had not fought back against the marriage Nathan had laid out for her, as her sister had. Hates that she had blindly married Edwin, had allowed herself to be walled into a life in which she had felt no choice but to abandon her child. She hates that she is incapable of loving a husband as Eva does. And she hates that she had not had the courage to keep Isabelle in her life.

She knows these were all choices she could have made. But none of them had felt even remotely possible. She hates that dour, colourless Eva was the one brave enough to build a life that has made her happy. Most of all, Harriet hates that she cannot manage any more self-loathing, so the only place she can lump all this hatred is on her sister. Heroic, lightkeeping Eva, who has Donald Macauley's blood on her hands.

Harriet knows it will do no good to wish this part of her did not exist. That bitterness, that angry jealousy simmering inside her, sometimes hidden, sometimes pushed aside, is always there. She cannot remember a time she was without it.

Right now, all she wants is retribution. Wants her sister to hurt, as she herself is hurting. *You're angry at me because I'm happy and you're not?*

Harriet reaches for her notebook. Tears a page from the back and stares down at the blank paper, her pencil hovering inches from the page. Rage pulses, hot and guilty.

This is justice, isn't it? Eva and Finn have both taken lives. Both evaded punishment for their crimes. Instead, they have been rewarded with these accolades. Yes, she thinks. Justice.

Harriet writes the letter, doing her best not to think; not to feel.

CHAPTER TWENTY-ONE

Harriet marches down the stairs. Do not think; do not feel. She strides through the public house and hands the letter to the innkeeper.

Don't think; don't feel.

"I need this delivered. And I need a coach out of this place."

The innkeeper takes the letter. "Tuppence to deliver this," he tells her. "Next coach out of here is in two days. London via Newcastle."

"Two days?" Harriet says tautly. "Are you certain? There's nothing before then?"

He chuckles. "Fairly certain, aye. You'll just have to make do with our fine hospitality for a little longer yet."

She grits her teeth. She had hoped to be out of this damn place by tomorrow morning at the latest. Leave all this mess behind her. At least, she thinks, the coach is going in the right direction. Back to London, and not dragging her up into the heathen wilds of Scotland.

Is it dangerous to go back to London? Perhaps. But the last she had heard from the bearded man, he had been carted up to Berwick. If he has gone north, best that she goes south.

The innkeeper nods down at the letter. "You want this delivered or not?"

Harriet huffs at his impatience. "I suppose I'll have to wait two days for that to be sent as well?"

The innkeeper gives her an insincere smile. "Lucky for you, it'll make it over to Lindisfarne tomorrow morning."

Lucky for you.

Really, she thinks, it would be lucky for her if she was far from this place by the time the letter reaches its destination. Should she wait until she leaves to send the thing?

No. Do it now. Before she loses her nerve.

She digs into her coin pouch and hands the innkeeper the money.

As she is turning to go back upstairs, Harriet hears someone call her name. An unfamiliar voice. No, it's not unfamiliar. It's a voice that's deeply known to her—just unexpected. She knows before she turns around that it's her father.

Ward is standing beside a chair in the corner of the tavern, his coat and hat tossed across the table. Has he been down here waiting for her to show herself? How in hell does he know she is here? She has not seen or heard from him in ten years.

His being here does not make sense. Does not feel real.

At the sight of Henry Ward, Harriet's thoughts are back on that cold and clear night when she had sent the authorities after his pirate ship. They are back in Wapping, as she stands at Execution Dock with her eyes on the hangman's noose, waiting to watch her father die. The sight of his face brings all that guilt surging to the fore.

And it's all she can do to rush back to the safety of her room.

From his precarious perch on the roof of the cottage, Finn sees the misshapen sail heading straight for Longstone. Feels that old unease at the sight of Martin Macauley. He climbs down the ladder and looks out towards the water. Today, Martin is alone. And there's a look in his eyes that suggests this visit is about far more than a bag of apples and seedcake from the villagers.

Finn looks over at the boys. The three of them are teetering around the edges of the rockpools, inspecting the lobster pots. "Inside, lads," he says. "Quickly now."

Macauley's cutter thuds against the jetty. He climbs from the boat. Stands inches from Finn. "I need to speak with your wife."

"She's not here," Finn lies. "You can speak with me."

Macauley shoves a crumpled piece of paper into his hand. "What is this?"

"A letter," says Macauley. "That I found most interesting." He narrows his eyes on Finn. "If you can't read it, I've come to know the contents quite well. I can recite them for you if you like."

"That's not necessary." Finn opens the page. Looks down at lines of small, coiled pencil strokes; the neatness of the handwriting betraying the brutality of the words. A letter to Martin Macauley. Outlining the circumstances of his father's death. Brusque and matter-of-fact words: *German Ocean* and *blow to the head* and *Eva Blake*.

Who had Macauley asked to read him the letter, he wonders? Who else knows about this? He screws up the page. "These are all lies."

"For what purpose?"

Finn hears Maggie squalling inside the cottage. He prays Eva doesn't see Macauley. Prays she stays occupied with their daughter. When she had returned from seeing Harriet yesterday, Eva been wound up and on edge, wild with rage, and yet convinced her sister wasn't safe. The last thing she needs is to hear all this. He knows how much she has feared the truth of Donald Macauley's death coming out.

"If this were true," Finn says to Macauley, "why would whoever wrote this wait ten years to tell you? Your father was lost at sea. They found his boat."

"Aye. Floating out near Longstone."

"And why would you think Eva had anything to do with that? She was living at Highfield when your father disappeared."

Macauley stares him down. "Eva was on Longstone the night my father disappeared. I saw you bringing her home the next morning."

Finn folds his arms. "What, the day you tried to kill me with your hunting musket?"

Macauley snorts. "If I wanted to kill you, you'd be dead."

Finn shoves the letter into his pocket. "Look," he says finally. "I know there's always been bad blood between your family and mine. But that's between you and me. Leave Eva out of this."

Macauley chuckles. "And just forget everything that's in

that letter?"

Finn hesitates. "What do you want?" he asks finally. The question is an admission of sorts; yes, he realises that. At least, as much of an admission as Macauley is ever going to get from him. But he needs to know where this is going to lead.

Macauley takes a step back, eyes narrowing. What's that look on his face? Indecision? He's come here on a whim, Finn realises. Come here in a burst of anger—likely the moment he heard the contents of that letter. Has not considered at all what he plans to do with this information. He steps into his boat, looks back at Finn. "Just tell her I know."

CHAPTER TWENTY-TWO

Eva dreams about her dead brother. Oliver is faceless, wordless—but she knows it's him from the fear that consumes her. She dreams of Oliver and she dreams of Harriet, and she dreams of Donald Macauley. Dreams that this time it's her plunging downwards into dark water, never to resurface.

She sits up in bed with a racing heart, and the relief of being awake is sloughed away quickly by the harshness of reality.

Just tell her I know.

There's a pale dawn light reaching through the gap in the curtains. Finn is sleeping lightly beside her, his skin fragrant with woodsmoke. She guesses he has just come to bed. Eva reaches out to lift the curtains; sees the last glow of the firebasket simmering in the grate. Tendrils of pale blue mist are coiling off the sea, hiding the rest of the world.

Just tell her I know.

Martin Macauley's words have been circling through her

head since Finn had—all too reluctantly—relayed their conversation last night. She wonders if he would have told her any of it if she had not caught sight of Macauley leaving the island.

She shuffles across the bed, curling up against Finn's warm body. She wants to wake him; is craving his company. She won't of course—sleep is far too precious a thing, especially these days. He'll wake soon enough when the boys come barreling out here with bright eyes; will do his best to squeeze in a few more hours' sleep in the children's bedroom. Keeping the light had been manageable with one child, challenging with two. Life is utter chaos with three.

And how could she want anything but this chaos? How can she regret what happened to Donald Macauley when his death had led her to Longstone? If he had not forced her into his boat that day; if he had not rowed her out into the ocean and raised his musket on her—and if she had not swung that oar and knocked him into the sea—she would never have found her way to this island. She would not have her husband. Would not have her children. She would have lived a stilted, loveless life as Matthew Walton's wife.

Donald Macauley's life for her sons' and daughter's. Donald Macauley's life for her happiness. How can she have regrets?

And yet, the guilt is searing. Always has been. She has struggled for ten years to force it to the back of her thoughts. Has searched for some sense of absolution each night she has set the firebasket burning. Each night she has foregone sleep to keep the Farne Islands illuminated.

"He has no proof of anything," Finn had told her last night. "As far as he knows, this is nothing more than gossip."

There's a part of her that wants to speak openly to Martin Macauley. Tell him everything; answer his every question. She wants to rid herself of this weight of guilt, and let whatever is to come of it come. But perhaps Finn is right; perhaps right now Macauley has his doubts, his own uncertainties—if not of her guilt, then at least of what to do with this new knowledge. If she stands face to face with him and tells him how she knocked his father into the sea—and thought to hide the truth for a decade—there is no telling what he might do.

Finn rolls over and wraps an arm around her in his sleep, and she runs her finger over the coarse skin on his knuckles. Chaos, she thinks, but this is the ordered, beautiful chaos they have built together. A life of lobster pots and made-up card games, clothes that smell of woodsmoke and sea. A life that has held the deepest grief and the most profound and dizzying happiness. Right now, it feels completely precarious. And sitting here, doing nothing, waiting for Macauley to act feels foolish.

Feels as though she has built a life on foundations of sand and now she is standing back, watching, waiting for the tide to rise.

―――――◆―――――

Sometimes, Nathan is able to forget everything that had happened between Eva and Donald Macauley.

When he thinks back to those stormy months during the Jacobite Rising, it's his own weighted memories that come to the fore: the ball in Edwin's side and his long, incomplete recovery; the inevitable choice to let Julia walk away; the heat of the pistol in his hand as he had cast John Graveney's body onto the dunes. There is little room for Donald Macauley amongst all that chaotic memory. Yes, Nathan can still conjure up rage at the man if he allows himself to. After all, he had tried to kill his sister. But Macauley has been long forgotten, by most of Lindisfarne. And in the end, her desperate night on Longstone had led Eva to happiness.

In the end—no. There is no end. Not yet at least.

Nathan looks across the tea table at his sister. She is perched on the edge of the settle, turning a cup edgily around in her palms. Her eyes are underlined with shadows of sleeplessness.

"Have you any idea who told Macauley?" Nathan asks. "Or why?"

Eva shakes her head stiffly. She glances down at her two youngest children, who are petting Julia's cat beside the fire. Minerva lies stretched out on the hearth, patient as the children prod at her ears. "I can't imagine why anyone would see fit to tell him after so long." Her response does not feel entirely honest. Feels like a lie to cover a truth she does not wish to disturb. And yes, Nathan understands. Because this he knows: two women have returned to Lindisfarne now, when talk of Donald Macauley's death has resurfaced. Two women who both know the truth of how the man died.

He can think of no possible reason why either Harriet or Julia would do this to Eva. But he cannot ignore the coincidence. Which is worse, he wonders? For him to have brought Julia back into their lives and for her to have told Martin Macauley about his father's death? Or for Harriet to have done this to her own sister?

He does not speak of it out loud. Can tell this is a conversation Eva cannot bring herself to have. But knows he needs to speak with Julia. A proper conversation, not a few stumbled sentences in the doorway. He needs to find out if there is any possibility she might have been the one to go to Martin Macauley. He cannot imagine what she would stand to gain from doing so. But Nathan knows Julia's life has complications in it now that he cannot even begin to comprehend. Perhaps it always has.

That evening, he finds some hidden reserve of courage and knocks on the guestroom door. He hates that Julia feels the need to lock herself away in her room like this. Not that he can blame her. He's hardly been a picture of hospitality. Nonetheless, he's relieved that she is here tonight, instead of out running whatever questionable errands saw her and Bobby blundering over the dunes in the dark the night before last.

Surprise on her face when she pulls open the door and sees him.

"Will you join me for supper?" he asks, blurting the words out before he can change his mind. His heart quickens at her nearness. Though she is still in her grey woollen skirts, she is wearing a neckerchief splashed with pinks and blues and yellows today, her fiery hair spilling loose down her back. She makes Nathan think of blazes, and sunlight, and sea-thrift and orchids exploding across the dunes.

Her lips part. "Are you sure that's what you want?"

"Yes," he says. "It is."

She swallows. "I… All right. If you're certain." The cat stalks out of her bedroom and disappears down the staircase. "Shall I tidy myself? Pin my hair, or…"

Nathan manages a faint smile. "There's no need for that.

I'd just like your company." The words spill out thoughtlessly. This is not supposed to be about enjoying her company. It's supposed to be about determining if she was the one to go to Martin Macauley.

Julia follows him downstairs into the dining room. Candles are lit in the centre of the long table, bread plates and wine glasses already filled. Julia takes in the two place settings. "Theodora won't be eating with us?"

"No. I've asked her to take her supper upstairs. She's more than happy to be up in her room writing."

"I see."

Is she suspicious of this? Nathan knows he could have spoken to Julia about Martin Macauley anywhere: a quick aside in the hallway, or outside the house, in bright, searing daylight. Instead, he had chosen this private, candlelit table, just so he might catch a glimpse of that life he had let pass him by.

He pulls out a chair for Julia, then slips into the seat at the head of the table. Tries to order his thoughts. "I'm sorry for being so distant these past few days," he begins. "I'm not usually quite so rude."

"I know you're not." Julia shakes her head. "There's nothing to be sorry for. This is hardly the easiest situation. Our children have a lot to answer for." She lifts her wine glass and takes a shallow sip.

Nathan smiles. He appreciates her bluntness. "They do. But I'm glad you're here. Glad you're safe."

Julia turns as Mrs Brodie enters, carrying two plates filled with roast meat and potatoes. She sets them down on the table then disappears, pulling the door closed behind her. For several moments, they eat without speaking, forks clinking against the plates and steam curling silver in the candlelight.

"I imagine you have questions," Julia says finally.

Nathan puts down his fork. "Only if you wish to answer them."

"What do you wish to know?"

Tread carefully, he thinks. He cannot ask her the things he wants to ask her. Because really, the things he wants to ask her have nothing to do with Martin Macauley and his father's death. No. He wants to ask Julia if she has been happy, and if she regretted leaving Holy Island. Whether she has thought of him at all in the last ten years. *Tread carefully.*

"The thieving ring," he says instead. "How much do you know about it?"

Julia turns her wine glass around by the stem. "It's been in place since last century. It began with women stealing from Jacobite fundraisers because they lost their husbands to the rebellion in '89. My mother was one of them," she says. "Not that I knew that at first."

Nathan raises his eyebrows. "Your mother?"

She nods. "I was surprised at first. I never imagined her as a thief. But it makes perfect sense that she'd want to rebel against the Jacobites after what the cause did to my father. It didn't make her a widow, but it may as well have, for all the care Elias showed her after he returned from Dunkeld."

"How did you get involved with them?" Nathan asks.

Julia lowers her eyes. "Calum is passionately against the Jacobite cause. He was a militiaman during the Rising. But he went too far. Stole from one of his clients when he found out he had Jacobite connections. We had to leave our home in Edinburgh and go to Bamburgh to seek the ring's protection."

Nathan catches the faint colouring of her cheeks. She takes a hurried mouthful of wine.

"Is that why you married him?" he asks carefully. "Because you wanted to rebel against the Jacobite cause too? For taking your brothers?"

"Rebel against the Jacobite cause? Do you not think I had enough of that madness during the Rising?" She shakes her head. Looks down for a moment, then back up to meet his eyes. "I married Calum because I was too proud to scrub dishes for the rest of my life. If I didn't want to do that, marriage was my only option."

Nathan feels an apology on the edge of his lips. Perhaps marriage was her only option, but it ought to have been to him. All too easy to say that now, he knows. It had not felt possible to look past their differences ten years ago, when Joseph Holland's blood had stained the steps to Julia's cellar.

He knows they would not have had a good life together. How many times had they looked one another in the eye and lied? They would have been forever questioning. Forever doubting. Distrusting. He knows that. But seeing her here, her green eyes shining in the candlelight, and her curls falling loose over her shoulders with the casualness of a woman at home, those reasons feel far too flimsy.

He dares to ask, "Do you love him?"

Julia looks down. She slices her meat, but doesn't eat.

"I'm sorry," Nathan says. "That was too forward of me. I—"

"I care for him," she says. "But no, I don't love him."

Nathan wishes her answer didn't bring him quite so much satisfaction. A strange thing, he thinks, that Julia might be so open and honest with him now. Where would they be if they had managed a little more of that ten years ago?

"He's not..." She fades out, then tries again. "He's not a bad man. He's always treated Bobby and me well."

"He left you alone with the thieving ring." The words fall out before Nathan can stop them.

"Yes," Julia says. Doesn't look at him. "He did. Not that I can blame him."

"What happened?" Nathan asks. "What did you do to make him leave?"

She runs a finger around the rim of her wine glass. "I lied to him. When we first met. I told him I'd been married to Bobby's father. Widowed. I knew Calum wouldn't have me as his wife if he knew I'd had a child outside of wedlock. It would have offended him. Disgusted him." She sighs. "The lie was good enough when we were up in Scotland. But down here... Too many people knew my father. Knew why he'd cut his ties with me. I've never seen Calum as angry as he was when he found out the truth. He went on and on about all the shame I've brought him and his family name."

Nathan doesn't speak. Doesn't trust himself to say the right thing. He dares to ask the question that has been circling through his head most violently since Julia had stepped inside his house: "Do you think he will come back?"

"My neighbour's friend saw him in Edinburgh," she tells him. "Calum was talking about heading south. There's a chance he's on his way back to Bamburgh."

"I see." The words come out sounding too thin. Before he can speak again, Julia says:

"You've made a good life for yourself here, I can tell."

It's a blatant attempt to divert the conversation away from her husband, and Nathan is all too willing to oblige. "I have," he admits. "Business is good, and I think I've finally regained the trust of the villagers." He chuckles. "I don't think our family name is spoken with quite so much disdain as it once was."

Julia smiles. "You must be a very hard-working man."

He laughs. "Indeed."

"Theodora seems to love it here too."

"She does. She's very inspired by the place. She loves the folk tales from this part of the world. Has she told you her story about the lady in the dunes yet?"

"Not yet. I shall have to ask her." Julia shifts in her chair so she is facing him squarely. "Didn't I tell you, this is where your home is? Some part of you has always been Northumbrian."

"You may be right. There is something about the place that I can't help but love." Nathan smiles. "You'll be pleased to know I'm even learning to sail. I thought it was long overdue." He chuckles at the look of open surprise on Julia's face.

"I never thought I'd see the day," she grins.

"Lewis is teaching me," he tells her. "The man has the patience of a saint. I've nearly run us aground on more than one occasion and he still insists on taking me out for more lessons."

Julia brings a forkful of potato to her mouth, her eyes not leaving Nathan's. "Well," she says, "you are quite full of surprises. The next thing I know, I'll come home to find you with Minerva on your lap." She swallows heavily. Looks down. "Come *back*, rather. I didn't mean…"

Nathan just smiles, all too willing to overlook her misstep. "Let's not get carried away. I'm certain that cat can see right into my soul."

Julia laughs. "Oh she can," she says. "And she can read your every thought."

Nathan chuckles. "And what does Calum think of the cat?"

"He loves her."

"Of course he does."

Julia gives him a crooked smile. Peers at him over the top of her wine glass. "It's good to see you," she says finally.

"It's good to see you too." Nathan feels something shift in his chest. This feels easy. Too easy. And far too dangerous.

Somewhere in the back of his mind, he acknowledges that finding out who had written to Martin Macauley was just an excuse to put aside his unease and his guilt and the shadow of Calum, and sit down with Julia and hear about her life. Nathan has known this from the beginning.

And if he acknowledges this, he must also acknowledge the other, more brutal truth. That Harriet was the one who had told Macauley what had happened to his father. A brutal truth, yes. But not a difficult one to believe. Harriet has always had it in her to do something of this magnitude.

Nathan does not understand why she had done it. But when has he ever understood anything about his youngest sister?

Right now, he does not want to think about Harriet. Not now, when he is sitting face to face with Julia, with this lightness in the air and this warmth in his chest.

She takes another mouthful of meat, her free hand resting on the table beside her bread plate. Her fingers are inches from his.

It would be easy, he thinks. Easy to place his hand over

hers. Feel her fingers twined with his own. Perhaps, easier than it has ever been for him. This desperate need to be close to her, after so many years, it washes aside his fear of physical closeness. Outweighs it. The need to feel his skin against hers is almost overwhelming.

The crunch of footfalls sounds outside the window. Julia sucks in a breath and pushes her chair back abruptly, making it squeal against the flagstones. She hurries to the glass and peeks through the gap in the curtains.

Her panicked reaction catches Nathan by surprise. He comes to stand beside her; looks out onto the dark roll of the dunes. "It was just a roe deer," he says. "They often come close to the house."

Julia looks unconvinced. Nathan thinks of the way she had sat so rigid in the coach out of Bamburgh. Thinks of the way she had pressed herself against the carriage wall, desperate not to be seen.

She rushes out of the dining room towards the front door. Opens it a crack and peeks out, a bluster of cold air billowing inside.

Nathan takes a lamp from the hallway and follows her out of the house. "No one from the ring has come for you," he says. "No one knows you're here."

"You don't know that." There's a hard look in her eyes now. A fierce alertness.

In spite of himself, his heart is quickening. It has been a long time since he has been alert to people creeping around Highfield House. He's taken back, suddenly, to a time when this house had felt anything but safe. Anything but home. A time he does not want to return to.

He pans the lamp over the embankment, then steps out

onto the dunes and circles the dark bulk of the house, Julia at his shoulder. The flimsy light of his lantern is swallowed by the empty island. But he sees no movement, no sign of any figure.

"Roe deer," he says again.

Julia glances at him, eyes hard in the lamplight. "Or thieves. I heard footsteps. It did not sound like a deer."

Nathan decides not to press the issue. He puts a soft hand to her shoulder, leading her back into the house. Feels his fingertips pulsing at the touch. "Well," he says, "if there are people from the ring out here, you're far safer inside." He pulls the door closed, turns the key. Hangs the lamp back on its hook, its beam passing over the painted eyes of an ancestor staring down from the wall. Julia wraps her arms around herself, her hair blown wild by the wind.

Nathan wishes he could take away some of her anxiety. Wishes he could take them back to that easy warmth of the dining room. He can't, of course. Because that easy warmth was never meant to last. Pretending otherwise will do neither of them any good. "What do you intend to do?" he asks instead. "Will you go back to Calum if he returns to Bamburgh?"

"Yes," she says after a long silence. "I have to. He's my husband."

Nathan tries not to let his anger show on his face. Anger at Calum for leaving her. For marrying her in the first place. Anger at himself for letting her go. "And if he doesn't return? What will you do then? How long do you intend to wait?"

Really, he does not want to speak about what is next for her, because he knows that what is next will be her leaving his house, his life—no doubt, forever. He wants to keep talking about Thea's folktales and Julia's cat and his shore-hugging sailing lessons. But he also wants her to see a way out. Wants her to see a life in which she does not panic at every sound in the night.

"I need to go back to Bamburgh," she says. "I've some money of my own in a box safe. If Calum doesn't return soon, I can use it to get to London." She picks at her thumbnail. "The safe has ended up in the home of one of the other thieves. I need to get to it without her knowing about it."

"Is that what you and Bobby were doing when you were out the other night?"

Julia's cheeks flush in the lamplight. "It's what we were trying to do. Bobby went off like a half-cocked madman trying to break into Lizzie's tenement right beneath her nose. He's lucky she didn't take his damn head off." She leans up against the banister. "Lizzie will be out of the house at church on Sunday morning. I'll have a much better chance of getting to the box safe then. Especially if I leave my cavalier of a son behind."

Nathan wants to argue. Wants to tell Julia she has no cause to be breaking into the homes of thieves. Wants to tell her he will give her whatever she needs. But he knows he is far too late for that. And so he does the only thing he can do from here. Says, "I will come with you."

CHAPTER TWENTY-THREE

It's late—those dream-blurred hours between midnight and dawn. Long hours at this time of year; days are short and nights endless.

The light of the firebasket reaches in through the unshuttered window, casting long shadows over the cottage. Eva is sitting at the table with a pile of the children's clothes in front of her, head bent over her sewing. Finn sits opposite her, twining the frayed edges of the lobster pot ropes. He has barely got more than one-word answers out of her all night. The hiss of the lamp on the table between them punctuates their wordlessness.

Finally, Eva looks up. "I'm not going to sleep tonight," she says. "I'll stay up and watch the light. You get some rest."

Finn reaches across the table, takes her hand. "I don't need to sleep yet. And you ought to try."

It's rare for the two of them to be alone, awake, in the quiet like this. He's missed it. But he knows it's Eva's fears that are keeping her from sleeping.

Since Martin Macauley had paid them a visit two days ago, she has only left Longstone to take Thomas back to Highfield House—to endless pleas and protesting from both Tom and Noah—convinced she is unable to keep him safe here on Longstone. As for their own children, she has hardly let them out of her sight. Has spent far too long standing at the window, waiting for Macauley to reappear and enact his retribution.

She has phases of this, Finn has come to know. This intense awareness—sleeplessness, alertness, periods of violent concern. Those surreal, dazed weeks when they'd first become parents. The murmured prayers and fuming pots when an influenza outbreak had torn across the county. And yes, those long-ago nights with Henry Ward's ship on the horizon. Just as he had been unable to take away his wife's fears then, Finn knows he can do little to stop her agonising over Martin Macauley now. Not that that will stop him from trying.

He tightens his grip on her fingers. "He's not going to act on this, Evie."

She raises her eyebrows. "Not going to act? How can you say that?"

In truth, Eva has not been the only one preoccupied by Macauley since he'd appeared on Longstone yesterday. Finn's thoughts have been circling around and around the issue. How can they do anything but?

And this is the conclusion he has reached. "If Martin does a thing to harm you, people are going to start asking what his father did to you." He releases Eva's hand and she goes back to her sewing, the needle darting furiously in and out of the cloth. "Everyone knows you weren't spying for the government during the Rising. If word gets out that Donald tried to kill you, think how badly that'll reflect on him and his son. Besides, surely Martin must have some doubt over this letter. It's been years. How does he know for sure it's telling the truth?"

"It is telling the truth," Eva says stiffly.

"Macauley doesn't know that. And he doesn't need to. Let him have his suspicions. They can't hurt us."

Eva sighs, tying off her sewing and yanking violently at the thread. "I wish I had your faith in the matter."

"Then let me have faith in the matter for the both of us."

She manages a pale smile. Reaches for the next piece of clothing.

Finn wonders if she's going to speak of it. Or if she's going to pretend she doesn't know it was her own sister who has done this to her. Finn is under no illusions. And neither is Eva—he is sure of it. There are only a handful of people who know the truth of how Donald Macauley died. And for this letter to have appeared the day after Eva had fought so bitterly with Harriet?

Finn had been reluctant to show her the letter in the first place. Would likely have thrown it in the fire and never spoken of it if Eva had not seen Macauley leaving the island. He had hoped that seeing those words—in her sister's handwriting—would make the truth undeniable. But Eva is continuing to deny.

He wishes she would confront the reality of who her sister is. Wishes she would stop trying to make their relationship into anything other than the poisonous knot it has always been. Harriet has been taking up space in Eva's thoughts for the past ten years. Probably for her entire life.

Finn says, "I assume you've not spoken to Harriet lately."

Eva looks at him for a long second. She knows the conversation he is trying to guide her towards, he has no doubt. "No," she says shortly. "You know I've not left the island since I took Tom back to the house."

"And do you mean to—"

"I want to speak to Martin Macauley," she says suddenly. "I want to tell him the truth."

Finn's stomach tightens. "Why? Why on earth would you want to do that?"

She stands up and begins to pace. "I can't bear the guilt. And I can't bear the uncertainty of waiting to see what he intends to do to me. To us."

"So instead you'll just hand yourself over to him? Tell him everything and let whatever is to come of it come?" It's the worst of ideas—he hates every piece of it. He and Eva have had to fight so hard for this peaceful, uninterrupted life. The letter Harriet had written to Macauley has knocked that peaceful life off its axis; Eva confessing to everything will shatter it completely.

He gets up from the table. Takes her shoulders gently. "You have nothing to feel guilty for," he says. "Donald Macauley was trying to kill you. All you were doing was trying to save your own life."

She looks at him squarely, and Finn can tell she is thinking of Oliver. Thinking of the utter frailty of these words— because was that not exactly what he had been trying to do the night he had killed Eva's brother? Trying to save his own life? That has not saved him from years of guilt and regret. He knows it will not save Eva either.

He wraps his arms around her. Presses his nose into her

hair. Feels the faint tremor of her body.

"Do you truly believe he is not going to act on this?" she asks, her voice muffled against his chest.

"Yes," says Finn. "I do." And he believes this with conviction. "Digging into the truth of what happened will reflect far worse on Martin's father than it will on you. He's not going to want to pry. He's not going to want the truth of this to become public knowledge." He steps back slightly. Looks her in the eye. "Please, Evie," he says, "just leave him be. Let him have his doubts. Confronting him on this won't achieve a thing."

Eva slides out of his arms and goes back to her sewing, not speaking.

"Eva," he pushes. "Please tell me you'll not go to Macauley."

She nods faintly. "I'll not go to Macauley." But her words are far from convincing.

CHAPTER TWENTY-FOUR

Nathan cannot quite determine which particular detour in his life has led to him sitting in this coach beside Julia, rattling his way towards the Bamburgh thieving ring. He was under the mistaken impression that he'd left all this cavalier madness behind years ago.

"We ought to have sailed over," Julia says, peering out the window at the grey pall of the ocean. "It would have brought me great joy to see you at the tiller of Lewis's sloop." She's had an intense seriousness about her all morning, but now a faint glimmer appears in her eye.

"That would not have allowed for a quick getaway," Nathan says with a smile. "Believe me."

Lewis draws the carriage to a halt at the edge of the village. Nathan climbs out, offering Julia his hand. "Wait for us here," he tells his coachman. "We'll not be long. I hope."

Julia is already striding into the snarls of the village. Nathan jogs after her.

"You don't have to be here," she says, looking back over

her shoulder at him. "I'd hate for this to reflect badly on you. I know you've worked hard to build a good name for your family again."

"I'm already here, Julia," he says. "There's no need to have this conversation again." He puts a thoughtless hand to the small of her back. "Let's just get your money and leave as quickly as possible."

She nods. Keeps hurrying towards Church Wynd with her head down and her hood pulled high. There's a heaviness to the air this morning; the sky is vivid white and smells of rain. Despite the chill in the air, Nathan is hot and breathless by the time they reach Julia's tenement building.

Her glance shifts upwards to take in the second-storey windows. "Wait here," she says tautly. "I need to go upstairs for a moment."

"Why? I thought you wanted to get in and out of Lizzie's lodgings as quickly as possible."

"I do. But…"

Something sinks inside him. "But you need to see if Calum has returned."

She nods faintly, not looking at him.

Nathan swallows hard. Bites back angry words intended for her husband. "Of course. I shall wait for you across the street." He forces himself to keep his voice even. "And if you don't come back, I'll…"

"I will come back," Julia promises. Her fingers brush his gloved hand, so softly he is not certain he didn't imagine it. "Even if Calum is there, I will come back to tell you. I'll not leave without saying goodbye."

Nathan nods. He turns away, unable to watch as she opens the front door and makes her way up to her tenement. He hates every part of it: this squalid, teetering building, this town overrun with thieves, Julia's bastard of a husband who had seen fit to leave her alone in the midst of all this.

He thinks of the unease in her eyes as they had searched around the house last night for what Nathan was certain was just a deer. He thinks of her fear they had been followed the day he had first brought her to the house. And he thinks of following her upstairs to make sure she is not in danger.

He cannot do it, of course. Because there's a chance her husband might have finally decided to show himself. And if Calum is upstairs in their tenement, then Nathan crashing through the door on some ill-advised rescue mission is the last thing Julia needs.

He begins to pace the street, shoes sucking through the mud, arms folded across his chest. He's making himself a suspicious character, he supposes, but he has too much nervous energy to stay still and hide like he probably ought to be doing.

He is dreading Julia coming down here to tell him Calum has returned—and yet isn't that what's best for her? For her husband to have returned? For her to no longer be alone?

It doesn't feel like what is best.

Nathan reminds himself that her staying at Highfield House was never an option. Cannot be an option. As much as he had loved her company last night, he knows that having her at the house is no good for either of them. It can lead nowhere but to that same cold devastation he had felt when she had disappeared from his life a decade ago.

Julia reappears at the doorway of the tenement house and waves him over.

"Has Calum returned?" he dares to ask.

"No." She avoids his eyes. Whispers, "What time is it?"

Nathan checks his pocket watch. Forces himself to keep his expression neutral. "Almost nine."

"All right. Lizzie ought to be at church by now. We need to hurry." She leads him around the side of the building and squints through the gap in a cloth window on the ground floor beside the wash house. "I don't see anyone inside," she reports.

She reaches into her pocket and produces a small fishing knife. How long has she been carrying that for? It reminds Nathan of the blade Oliver used to carry around—the blade that had been pressed to his own skin on far too many occasions. The sight of Julia using it to carefully cut the window open makes something tighten in his chest. He hates that this is where she has ended up. And he hates that he has had no choice but to follow her here.

She pushes aside the cloth and hoists herself up on the windowsill. Gathers her skirts in her fist and wriggles through the narrow space.

Nathan closes his eyes for a moment. Julia is right—the last thing he wants to do is make a bad name for himself and his family again. But there is also no way he can leave her to do this alone. He heaves himself up onto the sill and clambers inside.

Lizzie's tenement is small and dark, with a wooden table in the centre of the room and a straw sleeping pallet pushed up against one wall. The bricks above the fireplace are blackened, the faint glow of the coals suggesting Lizzie has just left—or plans to return soon.

Julia goes straight to the flagstones beside the hearth. Begins to trace the shapes of them with her knife. "Lizzie said her ma used to keep the takings under the stones of the hearth when she was a child," she explains. "I thought maybe she might do the same. Makes a good hiding place, I suppose." She moves from one stone to the next, tracing, prying. Nathan hovers over her, eyes darting edgily towards the door.

Julia groans in frustration and gets to her feet. "None of them are loose." She turns in a slow circle. "Where else could she be keeping it?"

She lifts the blankets of Lizzie's sleeping pallet, peeks behind the cannisters on the shelves. When she lifts a pile of what look to be discarded underskirts, she lets out soft cry of elation. Dumps the wooden box safe on the table and rattles the lid. "Locked," she says matter-of-factly. She turns the box over and digs the blade of her knife beneath the lid, sliding it over to the edge of the table. "I need you to help me," she tells Nathan. "Push down on the lid with all your strength. Lever it open. I'll hold the box steady."

There's a fierce determination to her now. It's a side of her Nathan has never seen—but not, he imagines, a new side. He joins her at the table.

He does not want to break into a safe belonging to a ring of thieves, any more than he had wanted to break into Lizzie's tenement. But he cannot help but feel responsible for this, at least in part. He had let Julia go. And this is the life she had found in exchange.

He pushes down hard on the handle of the knife and the lid pops open with a loud splintering sound. Instead of the metallic rattle of coins he was expecting, there's a dull thud as a small cloth bag drops to the floor. Julia kneels to inspect it. Curses under her breath.

"Look at this." She holds the bag up under his nose. It's

filled to the brim with oats. "Damn Lizzie."

"Is it the wrong box?" Nathan asks.

"No. This is definitely the one I gave her. She's taken everything out of it. Moved all the money."

"Stolen it?"

Julia begins to pace, eyes darting. "She wouldn't have risked that. She's been caught in this ring for most of her life. She'd know better than to steal the takings. She'd know what the repercussions would be."

"Maybe she's escaped?"

Julia glances around the room, tapping her chin in thought. "I don't think so. Her belongings are still here. Her clothes. Her comb. Her food. And she left the fire lit." She looks back at the empty box. "Maybe she was using this as a decoy. You know, in case anyone came to steal it. They'd take this safe instead of the one with the actual valuables in it." She shoves the box back beneath the pile of underskirts. "We have to keep looking."

Nathan wants to tell her to stop. Stop tearing Lizzie's home apart. Stop digging herself deeper and deeper into the mess of this ring.

You're out, he wants to tell her. *You got out. Don't force your way back in.*

Instead, he finds himself rifling through the wood pile and peering beneath the sleeping pallet. Lifting the lids from pots and pans.

"Julia," he says. "Look."

She comes to stand beside him and peers down into the soup pot at a second smaller wooden box. She grabs it. Dumps it on the table and hacks at the lock again.

She pulls at the lid as it breaks open, exhaling in relief as she pulls out a pearl necklace.

"Your things?" Nathan asks.

She nods.

And why does he feel such a pull of disappointment?

At the click and scrape of the front door of the tenement building, they both turn towards the sound. Julia drops the necklace back into the box and shoves the lid back on.

"Come on," she hisses, snatching his wrist without warning and sending a rush of energy searing up his arm. "We need to leave."

CHAPTER TWENTY-FIVE

Julia darts towards the door of Lizzie's tenement, tugging Nathan out behind her. They turn down the lightless tunnel of the hallway as the footsteps grow louder. Julia slows to a walk so as not to attract attention, and climbs steadily up the stairs to her tenement. Nathan follows close behind, unable to help a glance over his shoulder. He hears footsteps from down below. Sees nothing but the shadows of the stairwell.

Julia unlocks the door of her lodgings and sets the safe on the table. She sinks back against the door, staring down at the box with its broken lid. "Hell," she hisses, "what am I going to do? Lizzie's going to see the torn window and she's going to realise the safe is gone."

"She'll not know it was you who took it."

Julia exhales sharply. "Except that she saw Bobby prowling around her window the other day looking suspicious as all hell."

Nathan takes a step towards her. Stifles the urge to pull her close. Before he can speak, the stairs creak loudly. Julia whirls away from him, looking towards the sound. Fear in her eyes—and yes, Nathan feels it too. He knows she is expecting her husband. He also knows that Calum finding her here with another man will be far worse for her than him finding her with a box safe stolen from inside Lizzie's soup pot.

"Mrs MacNeill? Are you in there?"

The fear in Julia's eyes intensifies. "It's O'Donnell," she hisses. "One of the ringleaders."

And it's blind impulse that makes Nathan snatch the safe from the table. Blind impulse that makes him dart into the empty bed-closet and yank the door closed behind him.

He hears Julia's footsteps tap across the tenement. Hears the click of the front door. "Mr O'Donnell," she says. "Mr Briggs. Can I help you?" Her voice sounds thin, taut. Sounds like someone else.

"We're looking for your husband," says one of the men. "He wasn't at church again today. As I suspect you well know."

The men are inside the tenement now, Nathan can tell. He presses a hand to his mouth to silence his breathing. Clutches the safe to his chest.

"I don't know where he is," Julia admits. "I've not seen him in more than three weeks."

Nathan understands the danger this admission has just put her in. Now, the ringleaders know she is without the protection of her husband—just another reason, he thinks, why she needs to get out of this place and never return.

"I see. And you've not heard word from him?"

"No," she says stiffly. "I haven't."

There's a moment of silence, and Nathan can almost sense the men sifting through Julia's words, trying to determine the truth beneath. The floorboards creak as footsteps come towards the bed-closet. Nathan holds his breath.

Finally, one of the men says, "You'll be sure to let us know if you hear from him." His words are spoken simply enough, but Nathan can hear the threat beneath.

"Of course," says Julia.

"And we shall see you at the end of the week for the allocation."

"Yes. You shall."

Footsteps clop towards the door, and as he hears the latch click closed, Nathan lets out his breath.

Julia throws the door of the bed-closet open. She lurches for him, then seems to remember herself and pulls away at the last moment. Her eyes glisten with unshed tears. "Thank you," she says. "I'm so sorry to have dragged you into this mess."

A coil of coppery hair falls across her eye and Nathan stifles the urge to touch it. "Get your things from the safe," he says gently. "Lewis is waiting for us in the square."

Julia shakes her head. "It's not that simple. Now the ringleaders know Calum is gone, they'll be watching me. Waiting to see if I try to leave too. Besides..." She glances at the box still clutched to Nathan's chest. "What am I to do with that? I can't just leave it here. If Lizzie finds it in my tenement—"

"So take it with you," Nathan says.

Julia's eyes widen. "Do you have any idea of how much trouble that would cause?"

"You said yourself, they are already going to suspect you of stealing it," he says, voice low. "And you can't keep it here."

Julia lifts the edge of the cloth window and peers down into the street. "The ringleaders will be keeping a lookout for me. Even if I wanted to, there's no way I could get the safe back to the wagon without them seeing."

"They're not keeping a lookout for me," Nathan says. Before he can change his mind, he unbuttons his coat and slides it off his shoulders. Slings it over his arm to hide the box from view. "I'll go to the carriage. Wait a while before you follow. Let the ringleaders think you're just going for a walk in the square, or to the market, perhaps." He is on his way to the door before Julia can protest. "Lewis and I will be waiting."

CHAPTER TWENTY-SIX

When Julia finally makes it to the carriage, the panicked look in her eyes has not abated. She accepts Nathan's hand and tucks herself hurriedly onto the bench seat, pressing her back against the wall of the coach to keep herself hidden.

Nathan raps loudly on the wall, urging Lewis to leave.

Julia sets the basket she has brought with her on the floor beside her feet. A few loose potatoes and carrots are rolling around in the bottom of it—Nathan is not sure if she had actually made a detour to the market, or if this is just part of her ruse to keep the ringleaders away.

For a long time, her gaze lingers on the safe sitting on the bench between them. "I ought to get rid of it," she says finally. "Throw it in the ocean or something."

Nathan doesn't respond. He can think of far more useful things to do with a safe full of jewellery and coin—fund a life away from Calum MacNeill, to begin with. But he feels fairly certain his suggestion will not be welcome.

Julia produces a bag of coins from the safe and carefully

counts out a sum. She shoves the coins into her own purse, along with the pearl necklace. "All I wanted was what belongs to me," she says distantly. "I never intended to become a thief."

But Nathan is only half listening. His attention is snared suddenly by a small brass box sitting at the bottom of the safe.

The memory comes from nowhere, flying at him with ferocity. He has seen this box before. Has held it in his hands. It's an instinctive piece of knowledge, a memory so deeply ingrained it had kept itself hidden for the past thirty years.

I've a new game, said his brother. *It's called Plundering.*

Oliver sending him to their mother's nightstand to fetch this box. Nathan handing it over for his brother to hide in the priest hole.

And this tiny, tarnished brass box, it contains the Jacobite letter Henry Ward had once been so determined to lay his hands on. Nathan is suddenly certain.

He reaches down and grabs the box. Exhales. All these years, all that searching, and this piece of knowledge has been hiding within him all along. That precious letter that had once caused him so much trouble—he had held it in his hands as a young boy.

Oliver had had Nathan steal this box for him from their mother's nightstand. What had he done with it then? How has it ended up here in the possession of the Bamburgh thieving ring? Nathan can only guess at answers, of course. But he feels as though he has returned to the beginning of a vast, far-reaching circle.

The box is far smaller than he had imagined it to be when he had been searching the house for it. Its lock is broken and the lid swings open easily. Nathan pulls out the folded page inside. It is faded and soft with years.

He reads the words slowly, carefully.

We ought to meet urgently, Henry...

*A morsel of information to whet your appetite: Lord Haver,
prominent Whig party politician, is harbouring Jacobite tendencies...*

Meaningless now—Lord Haver has been in his grave for
several years, after slinking away from politics and
disappearing into obscurity. But how valuable this must have
been all those years ago, when the rebellions and Risings were
finding their feet. Nathan is not surprised Henry Ward and
his crewmen had been so determined to get their hands to the
damn thing.

"What's that?" Julia asks, setting down her coin pouch.
"I've not seen that brass box before. It must have been
among the takings Lizzie was guarding."

"It's Henry Ward's letter."

Julia frowns. "The one you were looking for when you
first returned to Lindisfarne?"

He nods.

She leans over, peering down at the faded page. "Why is it
here?"

"I've no idea."

It feels implausible that he might be holding such a thing
in his hands. But also, in a strange kind of way, it feels as
though he has been led here. Feels as though he was supposed
to find this. Find Julia again.

No. No, no, no. Julia is another man's wife. He cannot
look past that. He had had his chance with Julia, and he had
not taken it.

She points. "What's that?" There is a second folded page
in the brass box, Nathan realises. It has been hurriedly stuffed

into the bottom.

He takes it out carefully. Turns it over in his hands. Henry Ward's name is written on the front in his mother's handwriting, the ink faded with years. The seal is unbroken. Ward had never read this letter.

Nathan snaps open the seal. The sight of his mother's words scrawled across the page makes something ache in his chest.

Dear Henry,

I hardly have a thought of where to begin. There is so much I need to tell you. I wish we could speak of these things face to face, but I fear that will never be. I must leave Lindisfarne, for reasons I will explain, and I do not know when, if ever, you intend to return to the island.

And so, where to begin? My heart is pounding as I write, at imagining your response to everything I am to tell you. I have not been entirely truthful with you—and I suppose this is as fine a place to begin as any. As you know, I have been stealing funds from the Jacobite cause, and I allowed you to believe I was doing so out of financial necessity. This was an easier story to speak than the truth: that I was coerced into such actions by a thieving ring entangled in the Jacobite movement. The thought of telling you this made me feel unbearably foolish—far less shameful to be a penniless widow than to admit I was naïve enough to fall into a thieving ring's trap.

The tale is too tangled to tell you everything here—I will simply say that your letter full of Jacobite secrets and its little brass box have been of great interest to the Bamburgh thieving ring, thanks in no small part to the actions of my late son. This is just one reason why I must leave Lindisfarne for the relative safety of London.

And as I am speaking of my dear late son, I must tell you how much I regret sending you from the house the night of Oliver's death. I know I let you believe I held you responsible for all that happened. But I know who my son was, and I know placing blame will do no good. The past cannot be changed. I only hope you can forgive me for sending you away.

The night Oliver died, you told me there was a place for me in your future. I pray you still feel this way, after everything that has happened, and everything I have told you here. For what I must next tell you is this: you are to be a father, Henry. I hold my breath as I write this, in anticipation of your reaction. I hope that, with this knowledge, this is a future you still wish to be a part of.

I understand the gravity of all I am asking you. To have a life outside of your ship. To raise another man's children alongside your own. And if this not a future you wish to be a part of, I will understand. But as this letter is my attempt to unburden myself of all my secrets, I want you to know that I love you.

If you feel as I do, you will find me in London, at the address penned below. I hope and pray we will see each other again.

Ever yours,

Abigail

Nathan releases a slow breath as he stares down at the page. He feels the weight of it, the complete upturning of everything he thought he knew about those years.

For a decade, he has not questioned his belief that Abigail had fled Lindisfarne to keep Ward from finding out about his daughter. Had been certain his mother had hauled him and Eva through the rising water of the Pilgrims' Way so she might keep her secrets intact. But Nathan sees now that he has cobbled together the pieces to make an image that does not reflect reality. And in his clumsy reconstruction of the past, he has let Harriet believe she was a shameful secret. The mistake that had caused them to flee.

Other truths here too, just as powerful. *Coerced by the thieving ring… Just one reason why I must leave Lindisfarne…*

Nathan has made an uncomfortable peace with the knowledge that his mother had been thieving from the Jacobite cause. Henry Ward had told him as much, back when they had been searching for the letter. But here, in her own words, her own handwriting, is the proof that she had not been stealing for her own purposes. Here is the proof that, just like Julia and Mairi Mitchell, his own mother had been entangled in this cursed thieving ring. *Just one reason why I must leave Lindisfarne…*

He feels an odd sense of things unravelling.

Julia peers over at him. "What is it, Nathan? What have you found?"

He clears his throat. "I'll have Lewis take you back to the house," he says. "Have Mrs Brodie prepare you something to eat if you wish."

She frowns. "Where are you going?"

"I'm going to the lodging house in Beal." He tucks the box into the pocket of his coat. "I need to find Harriet."

CHAPTER TWENTY-SEVEN

Harriet knows she has stayed here in Northumberland far too long. Has been far too destructive. With the benefit of hindsight—or whatever it can be called when she is still stuck right in the middle of all this—she sees what an inordinately stupid idea it was to have come up here in the first place. How could she have imagined it would end any other way than with her counting down the minutes until the coach comes to take her away?

She is sitting in the corner of the public house with a bowl of lukewarm porridge in front of her, the pistol Peggy had given her heavy in her pocket. Head lowered, doing her best to hide herself. This morning she is the only person in the public house besides the innkeeper, who keeps shooting bemused glances at her from behind the counter.

She hates being down here in the wilds of the tavern where anyone could find her; she had fought her hunger for as long as she could. But she knows she needs to eat something before she gets on the coach in a few hours' time.

Yesterday, she'd only had half a bowl of stew, forced down in a single breath before she'd hurried back up to the safety of the dormitory. Now her father has reappeared, she has two people to try and keep her distance from.

She can't determine who she is more afraid of seeing: Henry Ward, or the bearded man. It does not feel coincidental that they are both here. Harriet has come to learn that nothing about her father is coincidental.

She has no thought of how Ward even knew she was in Northumberland. The last time they had spoken, her father had told her he did not want her in his life. Had believed that was what Abigail had wanted. In return, Harriet had reported his pirate ship to the militia. Almost sent her own father to the gallows.

She forces down a mouthful of porridge, her stomach churning and tight.

With her eyes down, she sees movement on the edge of her vision. Sees a dark-coated man approaching her table. She holds her breath as she looks up, but it is not the man with the missing finger, or her father.

Nathan takes off his black felt hat as he cuts a deliberate line towards the table. He must know, surely, that she had been the one to tell Martin Macauley that Eva had killed his father. But his expression gives nothing away. "I'm glad I found you, Harriet," he says. "There's something I need to show you."

For a long time, they sit opposite each other, not speaking, the brass box on the table between them. Harriet stares down at the letter in her hand, her heart knocking hard.

She had spent the first nineteen years of her life believing she was Samuel Blake's daughter. Has spent the last ten years believing a lie about what her mother had felt for Henry Ward. Believing herself a shameful mistake. The consequence of a bad decision.

She has no thought of how this letter came to be among a thieving ring in Bamburgh. Nor does she have any thought of why, if her mother had loved her father, she had grown up believing she was Samuel's child. They are questions Harriet knows she will never have the answers to. Abigail has been in her grave for fifteen years.

Harriet keeps staring down at the page. She does not want to look at her brother, for fear he will see the emotion in her eyes. She can feel him watching her as he sits silently on the chair opposite.

Harriet feels a deep, aching sense of loss for what might have been. But something more than that too—something far more steadying. Something far closer to peace. Somehow, in spite of all the lies, and all the mistakes, this new knowledge comes close to being enough.

Finally, she lowers the page, pushing her bowl of porridge away with the back of her hand. Still, she cannot look at Nathan.

"Are you all right?" he asks.

She nods, not trusting herself to speak.

There is so much she wants to ask her brother. So much she needs to know. What, if anything, does he remember about Ward coming to the house? How had Abigail had behaved around him? Had their mother truly loved her father?

Harriet desperately hopes this is the case. She wants to believe everything Abigail had tried to tell Ward in this letter—and yes, she realises, she does believe it. As unmooring as it is, she lets herself accept this new truth.

And it changes things. Though Abigail has long passed, and her father is a figure she can never have back in her life after everything that has happened, this knowledge, it makes her see herself in a new light. She is not the result of a night her mother had regretted. She was not a secret Abigail had never wanted Ward to know about. The truth of that is right here in faded, thirty-year-old ink: *You are to be a father, Henry* and *I want you to know that I love you.*

Harriet wants to speak openly to her brother about all of this. Wants to release the weight of it by speaking it aloud. But she cannot bring herself to open her mouth. She does not know how to do this—to be open. The thought of that vulnerability is terrifying.

Nathan clears his throat, and Harriet is afraid he is going to speak of these things—ask questions that have answers she does not know how to put into words. But he says, "I don't suppose you have any thought of how to find your father? I'm sure this is a letter he would like to read."

Harriet shakes her head. "I don't know how to find him. We've not spoken in ten years." It's not a lie. And though she knows there's every chance Ward might come looking for her again, this letter does not change the fact that she and her father cannot be in one another's lives. This letter, it rewrites many things, but it does not undo the fact that she had tried to send Henry Ward to the hangman.

Nathan nods. Nudges the box towards her. "You ought to keep it," he says. "And if you ever do see him again..."

"I won't," she says. "But thank you."

Nathan is at the door of the lodging house before he changes his mind. He cannot do it, he realises. He cannot leave Harriet to her own devices, however much he might wish to. Especially now, after all she has just learnt.

He turns back and returns to the table. Harriet is still sitting with the letter in her hands, staring down at their mother's words. There's emotion in her eyes, but at the sight of him, she steels herself quickly.

"Eva told me about the man pursuing you on the ship," Nathan says. "Has there been any sign of him?"

Harriet shakes her head stiffly. "There's no need to involve yourself in my problems. I can take care of myself."

Nathan sits back down in the chair opposite her. "I'm your brother, Harriet. And whether you believe it or not, I care about you. I want you to be safe."

She sighs. Folds Abigail's letter carefully and slips it back inside the box. "I've not seen him," she says finally. "I don't think he knows I'm here. And I'll be leaving on the coach in a few hours."

"Where will you go?"

She traces a finger over the tarnished brass lid of the box, not looking at him. "I'm not sure yet. Back to London, I hope. If it's safe."

"Why didn't you tell us the truth about why you came up here?" Nathan asks. "Why keep all this to yourself?"

Harriet is silent for a long time, and Nathan doubts he will get an answer. But then she says, "Because I did not want to involve you and Eva in all this mess. When I left London, I had no idea I was going to be followed up here."

"Do you have any thought of why this man is after you?"

She shakes her head. "I don't know who he is. Or what he wants with me. But I didn't want any of you in trouble on my account."

"If that's how you feel, why did you tell Martin Macauley how his father died?" Nathan keeps his voice level.

Harriet is silent for a long time. He can tell she is unsurprised by his accusation. "It's just what I do," she says. "I ruin people's lives. I sent the authorities after my father's ship ten years ago to punish him for not wanting me in his life. His crewmen were sent to the gallows. Finn was almost one of them. And I told Martin Macauley about his father because I wanted to punish Eva for having all the things I will never have."

"What things?" Nathan pushes. "A husband? A family? You had those things, Harriet. You chose to leave them behind."

She shakes her head. "I couldn't expect you to understand."

Nathan waits for her to continue. When she doesn't, he says, "Eva is terrified of what Macauley is going to do to her and her family. She brought Thomas back to the house because she's so afraid of Macauley coming to Longstone to punish her."

Harriet looks down. Swallows visibly but doesn't speak.

Nathan leans back in his chair. There's anger there at her, of course. Wild anger, if he thinks too hard on it. The truth of Donald Macauley's death is one they had managed—rightly or wrongly—to keep buried for a decade. But there's no part of him that is surprised at what Harriet has done. He has long known she has it in her to do something like this; to upturn her sister's life on account of her own pettiness.

But he is not going to let that anger out. Not here, not now that Harriet has finally been open and honest with him. And not now, after learning the truth of what her father had meant to their mother. That knowledge has left him questioning everything he thought he knew about the past. He can only imagine how unbalanced Harriet must feel.

"Are you certain you want to leave?" he asks. "Will you not come back to the house like you first planned to do?"

She smiles faintly. "After all I've done? I don't think so."

"It's your home, Harriet. You're always welcome there, regardless of anything else."

"No," she says. "It's not. And I'm not. But thank you." There's a genuineness in her voice that Nathan rarely hears. "I'll be leaving on the coach in two hours. It's for the best. I think we both know that."

When will we see you again? Nathan wants to ask. But he feels he knows the answer. Knows that, had Harriet not found herself in trouble, she would never have come up here in the first place. Would have been content never to see her family again.

What would their life have looked like if Henry Ward had received that letter? Would they have stayed here in Lindisfarne? Would there still be such a gaping divide between Harriet and the rest of the family?

Nathan knows there's little point dwelling on what might have been. He stands. Looks down at his sister. Can tell from the expression in her eyes that she intends this to be a final goodbye. What will she go back to when she leaves this place, he wonders? He hopes there is someone for her to return to, in whatever shape her life takes now. He swallows down a swell of emotion. Swallows down all the useless phrases like *if you change your mind,* and *you know where to find us.* "Take care," he says instead. And, "I hope you find what you are looking for."

CHAPTER TWENTY-EIGHT

When she hears the front door of Highfield House click open and closed, Julia feels a fluttering in her stomach. She knows it's foolish to let Nathan's return conjure up these feelings. But it does not seem to be something she can control.

She feels a storm of emotions: gratitude at his helping her, guilt over allowing him to become so entangled in the thieving ring, and at the danger she had put him in. And yes, unbidden, the lingering warmth of their supper together last night. There's no future to this, of course—can be no future. But just for now, she will allow herself to enjoy his company.

His footsteps clop towards the parlour. Julia is perched on the edge of the settle, her money on the table in front of her, along with a scrawled page of sums. Calculations of how far these elaborate riches will get her. The total is nothing grand, but nor is it the most dire of prospects.

"I'm glad to see you in here," Nathan says, stepping into the parlour and closing the door behind him. "Glad you're no longer feeling the need to hide yourself away."

Julia returns his smile. "I could say the same for you."

He nods down at the piles of coins she has stacked neatly on the tea table. "Where did you put the safe?"

"Theodora took it. Said she had a good place to hide it."

Nathan smiles wryly. "Inside the priest hole, I imagine."

"I'm sorry, I didn't mean to involve her. She saw the safe when I came inside. I couldn't think of a lie quick enough." She regrets the words the moment they are out—knows in Nathan's eyes she has never been short of a lie.

But he just gives her a faint smile. "It's all right. She would have wrangled the truth out of me sooner or later. I'm sure it will inspire her next story. What will you do with it?" he asks. "Do you really intend to throw it in the ocean?"

"It's the safest thing to do," Julia says. "Dispose of it all, where the thieving ring cannot find it."

Nathan nods. He reaches into his pocket and passes her a folded note. "Here. Mrs Brodie gave me this to give to you. From Bobby, perhaps?"

Julia looks down at her name on the page in her son's messy scrawl. She opens the note. Feels her stomach fall.

"Is everything all right?"

"Yes, of course," she says stiffly. She tucks the note into her pocket. "Did you find Harriet?"

"I did."

"And?"

Nathan sinks into the armchair opposite the settle. Lets out a long breath, his shoulders sagging. "And she's just as difficult as she's ever been. Although I do hope that letter of Mother's might change things for her somewhat. That may be wishful thinking." His eyes drift back to the coins. "Where will you go?" he asks. "Now you have your money?"

Julia can't look at him. She thinks of Bobby's note:

I've just seen Calum in Bamburgh. I told him you'd been staying with an old friend in Berwick and that you need him to collect you. He's gone up there now—should give you time to get back before he does.

And yes, she will tell Nathan the truth of this. Will tell him her husband has returned, and that she must return too. Must face Calum, and hope his anger at her has settled enough to allow them a civil marriage. She cannot imagine that will be so easy, especially when he realises Bobby has led him off to Berwick on some completely fictitious mission.

She knows Calum's return is not a truth that Nathan will want to hear. But she will not let herself lie to him any longer. After all he has done for her, she will give him the honesty she ought to have given him years ago.

But not quite yet. As soon as this conversation is over, she must go upstairs and pack her things, and leave Highfield House for the last time. And so just for now, she will let herself imagine that other life. The one where she takes her hard-fought-for money and builds a life of her own again. Perhaps, in this other life, she also allows herself to take the contents of the stolen safe and reopen her curiosity shop. In this other life, there is no guilt at doing so; no fear of the thieves coming after their takings.

It's not a possibility, of course. Taking the safe is far too dangerous; far too grating against the morals she is trying so hard to cling to. And her scribbled sums tell her that if she were to take her own money and run, she would have the life of a scullery maid over the life of a businesswoman. That is even less appealing than trying to salvage something from the ruins of her marriage.

But to Nathan, she says, "Perhaps I'll follow Bobby down to North Sunderland. See if I can find work there too. Or perhaps go down to London to find my brother."

"Would it not make you sad to leave Northumberland? I know you love it so." No mention of Calum. And so this is the game they are playing: the game where nothing is impossible. The game where they let themselves imagine these prospects are real.

"Yes," Julia says, "it would make me sad to leave." *Perhaps I shall find a way to stay.* The words are on the tip of her tongue—because this is the game they are playing, after all. But she knows from experience that allowing herself to imagine that future will only bring her to her knees. She had given herself permission to believe in it once before, and it had taken every ounce of her strength to pull herself from the despair that had engulfed her when the life she had imagined had not come to pass. She will not put herself through that again. Will not put Nathan through it either.

She scoops the coins from the table and tucks them back into her purse. Says, "But that's the way things have to be."

The afternoon is turning, a raft of blue-grey clouds beginning to gather at the bottom of the sky. It's the kind of weather she would paint; angry colours hurled across the canvas. Make a thing of beauty from all this natural anger.

Today, it doesn't feel beautiful. It just feels foreboding.

Harriet is the only person out here, waiting for the coach by this thin ribbon of road. She finds it hard to believe the carriage won't just rattle right on by her. Up the hill out of the village and disappear. She glances over her shoulder. Sees only rolling grassland and the gnarled black fingers of trees. She shivers, pulling her cloak tighter around her body.

Finally, the coach approaches, four dappled horses trotting steadily down the narrow road, mud spraying from the carriage wheels. Harriet wills it on quicker. She cannot wait to leave this place behind. Her thoughts are charging—full of Thomas and Eva and Martin Macauley. The brass box containing her mother's letter to her father. Every piece of being here feels like a mistake, and yet somehow, she cannot quite find a way to regret it. If she had not come back to Northumberland, she would never have learnt the truth of what her father meant to her mother. She would never have learnt what might once have been.

The coachman tugs on the reins, drawing the horses to a halt. He leaps from the box seat. Looks down at the small cloth bag sitting at Harriet's feet.

"That all the luggage you got with you, ma'am?"

"Yes. Thank you."

He nods. Opens the door of the coach.

He is there as though he has been waiting. As though, somehow, he knew she would be here on this lonely road, with clouds sucking away the light, having fractured all her relationships beyond salvageability.

The man with the missing finger is sitting right by the door, and his grey eyes meet hers squarely. Some distant part of her sees that perhaps he has not been waiting for her at all; had just sought this coach back to London—this coach that has come from Edinburgh, from Berwick, where the survivors of the wreck were taken. But right now, that logic means nothing—not to her, and not to him; this she knows by the sudden look of recognition in his eyes, the upturning of his lips beneath the dark storm of his beard. A look that recognises that, in spite of all the bad luck that has befallen him, things are finally going right.

Harriet does not think. She just runs. Grabs her skirts in her fists and tears down the road, away from the coach, back towards the village.

She hears the coachman call after her. Doesn't look back. Is the bearded man following? Footsteps thunder in her ears—just hers? Or his as well? Surely he must be chasing her. He had trailed her across the capital, and all the way up the country. Had tried to break into her bedchamber. He is not going to let this opportunity slide.

Another shout from the coachman. And then the steady clop of hooves as the carriage pulls away from the village.

Harriet crouches in the narrow gap between two cottages, gulping down her breath. Her lungs are burning, straining against her tightly laced stays.

Where does she go from here? The tide is low—she could make it across to Holy Island. But out on the open sands of the Pilgrims' Way, there is nowhere to hide.

The public house, she supposes, is her best chance. Likely the first place he will look, but there will be other people around—the innkeeper at the very least. Perhaps from there she can get word to her brother. Beg for the help she was too proud to ask for just a few hours ago.

She hurries across the narrow street, eyes darting. Sees movement on the edge of her vision. She tears away, past the jetty, footsteps thudding in her wake. Feels a presence bearing down on her. A hand reaches out, grabbing her arm from behind.

Harriet whirls around. Comes face to face with her father. At the sight of the blatant panic in her eyes, Ward releases his grip on her arm. Harriet cannot make sense of why he is here. He feels like a vision she has conjured up in her guilt-ridden imagination. Instinctively, she breaks into a run again. Past the lodging house, past the jetty, out towards the Pilgrims' Way.

Ward calls her name. Charges after her.

"Goddamn it, Harriet," he barks. "Stop running." And somehow, the intensity of the command makes her obey. She hunches over, gulping down her breath. Finally dares to look up at her father.

"There's a man after me. I—"

"I know," says Henry Ward. "This way. I've a boat." And it's all she can do to follow.

CHAPTER TWENTY-NINE

Harriet sits alone below deck on her father's small sailboat, feeling the vessel careen across the water. She has no idea where they are or where they are going. No idea if she ought to feel safer here on Ward's boat, than being pursued by the man with the missing finger.

The space below deck is cramped and airless, with benches tucked around a narrow, rough-hewn table, and a sleeping pallet rolled up in one corner. It smells of the sea, of whisky and potted meat. Of her father.

After what seems an eternity, Harriet hears a metallic groan and clatter, and the rattle of what she assumes to be the anchor chain. The hatch groans open, letting in a shaft of pale daylight. The ladder creaks and Ward appears from above. He takes off his coat and tosses it over a storage chest in the corner. Slides onto the bench on the opposite side of the table to Harriet.

"Where are we?" she asks.

"Just outside Beadle Bay. I've seen no sign that we've been

followed."

Under her father's gaze, Harriet feels jittery and on edge. Her heart is still thumping after being chased across the village, her shift clinging to sticky skin. "Is this your boat?" she asks. Right now, all the other questions she needs to ask feel far too weighted.

Ward nods. "Not quite as big as the *Eagle*." Smiles. "But it does what I need it to do."

She looks at him for a long second. His face is weathered and worn, and though his eyes are still fiercely blue, there's a weariness to them. A deep exhaustion.

"How did you know where I was?" she asks. "How did you know I was in trouble? Have you been following me?"

He sighs heavily. Rubs a scar on his knuckles. "The man that's after you," he begins, "he's pursuing you because of me. He is the brother of one of my former crewmen who was executed ten years ago."

"What?" Her voice comes out strangled.

"When Mr Lawler learnt I had been spared the hangman when his brother died, he hunted me down. Demanded some form of compensation. I paid him handsomely with what wealth I had that wasn't seized by the crown on my arrest. Several years later, he found me again. Demanded more. More than I was able—or willing—to give."

For long moments, Harriet doesn't speak. The sea clops rhythmically against the hull of the boat. "Why is he after me?" she dares to ask. Could he possibly know she had been the one to send the authorities after Ward's ship? How could he know? Her knuckles whiten as she grips the edge of the bench seat.

"Lawler knows you're my daughter," Ward says. "He

imagines, I presume, that he can get to me through you."

"By kidnapping me?" Harriet swallows hard. "Or killing me?"

Ward is silent for a moment. "I'm not certain."

She thinks of Lawler prising open the window of her bedchamber in London. Thinks of him trailing her across the city. Onto the *Cygnus*. Thinks of the thinly veiled threats he had whispered as he passed her in those narrow, creaking corridors of the ship.

We're not far from Edinburgh now.

See you when we land.

All this had been because of whose child she is?

"I'm not certain how he came to know I'm your father," Ward says, before she can ask. "Lawler knew I'd spent much time on Lindisfarne. Perhaps he made the connection when he saw your paintings of the island. And there's a certain family resemblance…"

"My paintings of the island? How do you even know about those?"

Ward is silent for a moment. There's an uncertainty in his eyes now. The same vulnerability she had seen from him the day they had first met. A vulnerability so far removed from the unyielding façade he presents to the outside world. "I admit I've been following your work in London," he says. "I read about the commissions of a painter using your mother's unmarried name. I suspected it might be you." He smiles faintly. "You're a fine artist. Very fine. You have my mother's talent."

Harriet feels her chest tighten. "Really?" The word comes out strained.

"Yes. She was a landscape artist like yourself. Wished to

push the boundaries of what was expected of her as a female painter."

Inexplicably, Harriet feels tears gathering behind her eyes. Cannot make sense of why, after all she has just learnt, it is this piece of information that has struck her the hardest.

The faint smile disappears from her father's face. "I saw you presenting your work at the Allbridge exhibit," he says. "And I'm afraid Lawler followed me there. I assume that's how he came to know of you."

Harriet knots her fingers. "He came to my lodgings one night," she says. "Tried to break in. It was you who stopped him, wasn't it." Some part of her has known this all along, she realises. Some part of her had recognised her father's voice when he had called out to Lawler to scare him away from her window. It had felt like a truth too difficult to acknowledge.

Ward nods. "I fired a warning shot before he got through your window, but he got away before I could catch him. When I realised he had left on the *Cygnus*, I came up here as quickly as I could. I heard of the wreck when I landed in Edinburgh. I went to Berwick, then to Longstone searching for you. Finn told me you were staying in Beal." He shifts on the bench, leaning forward to meet her eyes. "I'm sorry," he says. "I truly am. The last thing in the world I wished to happen was for you to be put in danger because of me."

Harriet looks down, unable to hold his intense gaze. As frightening as it is to know Lawler is after her to punish Ward, there's something steadying about sharing the strain of this. Of having the support of her father. And perhaps it's this that frightens her more than anything. She is not used to feeling supported. No—she is not used to allowing herself to be supported. Not anymore.

"Why did you follow my work?" she asks. "The last time we spoke, you said you wanted nothing to do with me. Because you thought that was what my mother wanted." Instinctively, her fingers slide into her pocket. Graze the lid of the brass box.

Ward glances down. What is that look on his face? Regret? "I suppose narrowly escaping death changed my outlook somewhat." He keeps rubbing at his knuckles. "I read about the work you had been commissioned to do. When I heard your sponsors were opening their salon to the public, I admit I found it difficult to stay away."

Harriet swallows heavily. "You did not approach me at the Allbridges'."

"No." He manages a wry smile. "Too much of a coward, I suppose. It felt like the wrong thing to do, given I was the one who told you we ought to stay out of one another's lives." He sighs, leaning back against the bulkhead. "I did try to find the will to approach you that night, once or twice... or several times. I suspect that told Lawler all he needed to know."

Harriet feels a deep, hollow discomfort in her stomach. When she had first met her father, she had longed for a connection with him. Had longed to mean something to him. And if she is honest with herself, that desire has never really left her. If he has been following her and her work, he likely knows she has left her husband and son. What must he think of her? She supposes it doesn't matter. Because even after all her father has told her; even after Abigail's letter, how can she have a life with him in it when she had tried to send him to his death? This is what she does: destroys people's lives. Chips away at the foundations of every relationship she has until they crumble and shatter at her feet.

"How did you escape the gallows?" The words come out husky. "Was it because of the information you had about the Jacobite cause? The information in the letter you were trying to find at Nathan's house?"

He nods. "I gave up Lord Haver's name in exchange for my freedom."

Harriet closes her eyes, feeling tears well in her throat. They spill down her cheeks with little warning. She brushes them away hurriedly. "The night your ship was captured," she blurts. "It was all my doing. I sent the authorities after you. I told them there was a pirate vessel leaving the bay." As the words fall into the silence, she feels the ugliness of them, their petty brutality. She hates that she is the kind of person to have done such a thing. Hates that she is *this*.

She dares to look at her father, an apology blazing in her eyes. Does not speak that apology. Doing so feels far too flimsy, far too trite.

Ward leans back on the bench, studying her for a long time with an expression that is impossible to read. After a moment, he says, "Why?"

Fresh tears gather in her throat and she swallows past the pain of them. "I was hurt because you chose to leave. Because you did not want me in your life."

Ward pins his gaze on her, not speaking until she looks up and meets his eyes. "It was never a matter of not wanting you in my life, Harriet. I was only doing what your mother would have wanted."

She closes her eyes. Tightens her fist around the box in her pocket. A part of her is desperate to give it to him. Let him read Abigail's words, thirty years too late.

A bigger part of her is too afraid. Because Abigail's letter will be permission for Henry Ward to seek a life with their daughter in it. It's permission for him to be her father. And the thought of that is far too terrifying. Having her father in her life is just another relationship for her to shatter and destroy.

"I'm sorry," she says. "I was young and foolish and angry. Not that I'm any less foolish now."

Ward gives a short chuckle. Shakes his head. "You sound like the daughter of a man who's made his own lifetime of mistakes."

Harriet looks up at him in surprise. "You're not… Should you not be feeling a little more… furious?"

"What point would there be in that?"

She lets out an incredulous breath. "What *point* would there be?"

Ward takes a tarnished spying glass from the table and turns it around in his hands. "I'm an old man. I don't want to spend what years I have left holding a grudge against my only child."

Fresh tears spill, faster than she can blink them away. This unexpected reprieve is far too difficult to navigate. She wants his anger. Wants that old belief that Abigail had never wanted her to know her father. Those things were easier than this.

No. She doesn't want those things back. She wants the truth of Abigail's letter. *I want you to know I love you.* She wants her father to know that truth too. Wants the courage to tell him.

She swipes at her tears. Draws in a breath in an attempt to steady herself. "What do I do now? How do I rid myself of Mr Lawler?" Perhaps she cannot open up completely; cannot tell her father everything she ought to tell him. But Abigail's letter gives her the strength to ask him this. To seek his advice. His help. "I don't have information to blackmail anyone with. I don't have a safe home to return to. And I've ruined things with my family so badly I can never go back to them." She looks to her father with desperate eyes. "How do I escape this?"

Ward stands. "It's not your plight to escape, Harriet. It's mine."

"It's my fault Lawler lost his brother." And somehow, because of this, it feels only right that he has come after her.

Ward doesn't respond. Just looks down at her, taking her in. What would it have been like, Harriet finds herself wondering, to have grown up with Henry Ward as a father? What would her life have looked like if he had read Abigail's letter thirty years ago, when she had first written it?

"I'll see to it that he doesn't come near you again." There's a resoluteness to his voice. A determinedness.

"How?"

Ward goes to the storage chest and clicks open the lid. Produces a pistol and a handful of shot. "I'm going back to Beal," he says, pulling on his coat. He slides the weapon into his pocket. "I ought to have gone after Lawler earlier. But I wanted to get you to safety."

Harriet swallows hard. "What makes you think you can stop him now if you couldn't in London?"

"This is a far emptier part of the country. A far easier place to... do what is needed. I've no desire to find myself back on the gallows again."

Harriet's stomach turns over. Her father could die for this—could die because of events she herself had set in motion. He needs to see her mother's letter. She cannot let him die without knowing the truth of it. The urge to give it to him, to show him what had been in Abigail's heart is almost overwhelming. But so is the fear of where this could lead.

Ward steps onto the ladder and shoves open the hatch, leaving Harriet down below, fingers curled around the brass box in her pocket.

CHAPTER THIRTY

"Evie." She feels Finn's hand on her shoulder, tugging her out of a dream. Shadows and crashes and water rolling down the walls of their home. "Evie." He shakes her gently and she thrashes, panicked, against him. "It's all right."

She opens her eyes, disoriented and breathless. Muted grey daylight is streaming in through the window. She had closed her eyes for a moment after putting Maggie down in her crib. Had not intended to fall asleep.

She sits up hurriedly, making her head spin. "Where are the children? I was—"

Finn takes her shoulder to steady her. "They're fine," he says. "The lads are outside. Maggie's right here."

Eva turns to look at him. He has their daughter in the crook of his arm, she realises. The sight of Maggie pressed to her father's chest is faintly steadying. But she needs the boys here too.

"They can't be outside." She slides out of bed. "It's not safe."

Finn catches her hand, tugging her back gently. "Eva. Come on. It's all right. They know to keep away from the edges of the island."

"Macauley," she manages. "What if he…"

"Macauley is not going to come for our children," says Finn.

"How do you know that?" Eva goes to the washbin and splashes her face, trying to let the cold water sear away her nightmare. "I didn't mean to fall asleep."

Finn sets Maggie on the floor. Stays sitting on the edge of the bed. "I'm glad you did. You were awake most of the night."

Eva uses the cloth beside the washbin to dry her face. She still feels painfully unsteady. Exhausted to the core. Not just from lack of sleep, but from a lack of peace. From the constant pulse of guilt that has been inside her for a decade. It has grown from a murmur to a roar since Martin Macauley learnt the truth about his father's death.

She needs this to end. She knows she will never be rid of the shame that comes from having killed a man. But she can rid herself of the guilt of keeping secrets.

She tugs on her shoes and strides towards the door, snatching her cloak from the hook on the wall.

Finn scoops Maggie up again and follows Eva out the door. "Where are you going?"

"I need to speak to him." She can see Noah and Archie on their knees at the edge of the rockpool. The clouds at the bottom of the horizon are beginning to thicken, darken. A pulsing surrounds her—in the air or in her chest, she cannot tell.

Finn hurries after her. Lurches for her wrist. "Stop," he

says, voice low. "Think about what you're doing."

She keeps walking. Finn marches over to the rockpool and hands Maggie to Noah. Catches back up to Eva as she steps onto the jetty.

"Since the wreck, we're finally being treated like decent people," he hisses. "We're finally being treated with some respect. Why in hell are you trying to undo that by bringing up the past?"

"Because there's never been any decency about this, Finn!" she cries. "There's been nothing decent about keeping the truth of Donald Macauley's death a secret for ten years. Martin should never have found out through some anonymous letter. He ought to have found out from me."

Finn blows out a breath. "Anonymous letter? So that's what we're doing? We're not even going to acknowledge the fact that that letter came from your own sister?"

Eva turns away. Can't look at him. "You don't know that."

"Yes I do. So do you."

Eva is silent. Perhaps he's right. Perhaps there's a part of her that does know the letter was Harriet's doing. But acknowledging that is far too brutal. She would rather the letter have come from someone nameless, faceless. "It doesn't matter where it came from," she says tautly. "I need to speak with Macauley. I need to explain myself. I cannot keep it all inside anymore."

"And do you think that's something he's going to want to hear? That his father tried to kill you?" Finn takes her hand and tugs her close. His grip on her is firm, possessive. "Let him have his doubts," he says. "Haven't we had enough trouble? Why would you go looking for more of it?"

"I'm not *looking* for trouble. The trouble is already here.

Martin already knows."

The island feels suddenly stifling. Oppressive and constrictive. And for the first time, with her husband's hand snared around her own, she lets herself imagine it: that other life she could have chosen. That ordered, respectful life she was supposed to have had. The life Nathan had laid out for her.

An easier life.

The thought comes to her like a physical blow and she curses herself for even thinking it.

She looks across the island at her children. How could she even for a second have allowed herself to envisage a life they are not a part of?

But the thought is there in the front of her mind now, pulsing and violent. She cannot push it away.

She had not chosen that easier life. She had chosen this one: this challenging, sea-drenched, firelit life. A life of love—intense, consuming love—but a life of guilt and struggling too. Because in this life she has chosen, she had killed Donald Macauley, and tried to keep it a secret. And now she must face the consequences of that decision.

As she reels towards the skiff, Finn grabs her arm, tugging her back. "Please, Eva. Don't." He wraps his hands around her shoulders, looks at her squarely. "I know how you feel. You know I do. I know how it feels to carry the weight of the life you took. But do you really think confronting Macauley is going to make it any easier?"

"You have your absolution," Eva says bitterly. "Oliver's death is not a secret anymore."

She sees something flicker and harden behind Finn's eyes. It has been a long time since they have spoken of her brother.

Years since they have spoken his name.

"Absolution?" Finn repeats. "Is that what you think I have?"

There's an incredulous tone to his voice and it makes Eva's anger rise. "You have far more absolution than I've ever had. Nathan and Harriet both know how Oliver died. You don't need to keep it a secret any longer." She forces herself to keep her voice to an angry hiss. "I need to tell the truth about Macauley's death too. I can't carry it any more. You of all people ought to understand that."

"Eva. Please." His grip on her wrist tightens. "I have never forbidden you from doing anything as your husband. But I am begging you not to do this."

She yanks her arm back and Finn lets his hand fall. "I have to," she says. "I'm sorry. But I have to. I don't have a choice."

CHAPTER THIRTY-ONE

This is the second time Nathan has had to restart the letter to his distributor. It's been a chaos of clumsy wording and spilled ink; he's been far too tangled in thoughts of Julia and Harriet and his mother's involvement in the thieving ring. When the knock at the door comes, he is relieved at the distraction.

Julia steps inside the study, her gaze drawn to the telescope set up at the window. She smiles faintly. "I'm glad you're still using it."

Nathan returns her smile. "It's a fine piece."

She hovers in front of his desk for a long moment, hands clasped in front of her. "Calum is on his way back to Bamburgh," she says.

The words feel like a physical blow. "I see. And are you…"

"I have to go back," she says. "Yes."

He waits, hoping for more. Nothing comes. "Are you certain?" he dares to ask. "You could—"

"I'm certain," Julia says tightly. "Calum is my husband. I cannot just walk away from my marriage. That's not the kind of person I want to be."

"Of course. I'm sorry, I did not mean to suggest..." He fades out, lowers his eyes, not entirely certain of what it is he is trying to say. For several moments, neither of them speak. The window rattles with a loud gust of wind.

Nathan turns his quill around in his fingers. "I know it's no place of mine to ask, but when he returns... will you be safe? Given how angry he was with you when he left?"

Julia stares at her feet, colour rising to her cheeks. "He's never hurt me. And I don't believe he would."

"Even now he knows the truth about Bobby's father?"

"Yes. I trust him. I do. He's not a violent man."

Nathan nods. He's glad of this, of course. He must be glad of it. But there is something galling about Julia's blind trust for her husband when she had never managed such trust for him. He stands. Folds his hands behind his back and clears his throat. "Shall I ask Lewis to take you over?"

"No. It's all right. I can make my own way." Her voice is clipped. Deliberately so, Nathan can tell. Already, she is putting distance between them. Necessary distance, he reminds himself. It's what they ought to have been doing all along.

"Do you have your cat?" he asks.

A faint smile flickers on Julia's lips. "I shall make sure I don't leave her behind. I'd not do that to you."

Nathan tries and fails to return her smile. He takes a step closer to her. Drinks in the sight of her: her gold-flecked eyes, her freckled cheeks, her chaos of coppery curls. He's sure it will be the last time he ever sees her. And the words fall out before he can stop them: "Is this really what you want?"

Julia's lips part. "What I want has nothing to do with anything." He hears the ache in her words. Or perhaps that ache just belongs to him.

And suddenly the words spill out, angry and unbidden. Nathan hears his own voice say, "You can't go back to him."

Julia blinks, eyebrows shooting skyward. "I beg your pardon?"

Words keep tumbling out before he can rein them in. "How can you turn around and walk straight back into the thieving ring?" His voice rises. "How can you go strolling back to the man who left you alone in the midst of all that?"

Julia blows out a breath. "I'm *strolling back* to that man because I'm his wife."

"He abandoned you, Julia."

"No, he didn't. He's on his way home. And I need to be there when he returns." Her green eyes flash. "Besides, what choice do I have?"

"You have a choice," Nathan pushes. "You have all that money in the box safe."

She gives an incredulous laugh. "I am not using stolen money to leave my husband." Shakes her head. "Do you really think I want to be that kind of woman? Don't you think I've had enough of being looked down upon in my life?"

"So you'd rather stay with the man who left you alone with the thieving ring?"

She wraps her arms around her body. Begins to pace as she gnaws on a thumbnail. "You talk like the alternative is so easy, Nathan. I've been out on my own without a husband before, and I never knew if I was going to be able to keep a roof over my head. Never knew if I was going to be able to feed my son. I will not go back to that life again."

"So use the money in the safe."

"I am not using stolen money," she repeats through gritted teeth.

Her stubbornness is infuriating. "Why do you care so much about breaking the law?" he snaps. "It's not like it's ever bothered you before." He regrets the words the moment they are out.

Julia's eyes flash, and for several moments she stands wordless behind his desk, jaw clenched. When she finally speaks, her words are clipped and controlled. "I was dreading leaving you," she says tautly. "I was dreading saying goodbye. I'm grateful to you for making it so easy."

CHAPTER THIRTY-TWO

Julia knocks on Theodora's bedroom door. No answer. She clenches her hands into fists. Anger is coursing through her, and all she wants to do is get the hell out of this house. What was she thinking, coming here in the first place? How was it ever destined to end in anything other than carnage?

Carnage, she supposes, is better than the deep, aching emptiness she anticipated feeling when she left Nathan for the last time. Right now, she never wants to look at him again.

She hovers impatiently outside Theodora's door, Minerva mewling and squirming like a terror beneath her arm. She needs to get inside; get the safe out of the priest hole.

She needs to get out of this house.

Which is worse, she wonders: letting herself into Theodora's bedchamber uninvited? Or leaving the safe under her and Nathan's roof?

She is saved from the decision when Theodora appears on the staircase. At the sight of Julia waiting outside her door, she hurries down the hallway. "Is everything all right?" she asks.

"Yes," Julia says tightly. "I just need to collect the safe from the priest hole."

Theodora glances at Minerva, then catches sight of the duffel bag slung over Julia's shoulder. "Are you leaving?"

"Yes."

Julia is glad Theodora doesn't push the issue. She follows her into the room. Watches as she pushes on the panel of the fireplace, the priest hole swivelling opening beneath her hand. She bends to collect the safe and hands it to Julia.

"Are you sure you want to leave?" Theodora asks. "Is it safe? You're always—"

"I'm sure. Thank you." Julia hugs the box to her chest. With Minerva under her other arm and her duffel bag lolling on her shoulder, the safe feels too heavy, too unwieldy. She can't wait to rid herself of the damn thing. Can't wait to hurl it into the ocean and let every piece of this be forgotten.

She forces a smile. "Thank you for your hospitality, Thea. You've been more than kind."

Theodora says nothing, just gives a short nod, and Julia can tell she has not bought her forced brightness. She can't make herself care. She just needs to get away from this place, away from the memories. Away from Nathan, before he knocks the ground out from beneath her again.

She doesn't look back as she charges from the house. Doesn't dare to look up at the study window to see if Nathan is watching. She just tramps over the dunes, mind on nothing but escaping.

The tide is rising, but there's still only a thin sheen of water covering the Pilgrims' Way. Too shallow for a boat. Too deep for shoes. She charges into it anyway, tightening her grip on

Minerva. What are wet shoes and cold feet if it means she gets far away from Nathan and this cursed island? *Why do you care so much about breaking the law? It's not like it's ever bothered you before.*

She'll wave down a wagon when she gets to the mainland, or walk to Bamburgh if she must. Hopes she makes it back before those potato sack clouds above her head spill open.

Hopes she makes it back before Calum returns from Berwick.

The water is only at her knees in the middle of the steppingstones, but she cannot bear to look at the safe for a minute longer. With a loud cry of frustration, she hurls it into the ocean. The broken lid swings open as it flies through the air, coins and jewellery splattering down into the shallow sea. The half-empty box lands with a weighted splash. It tilts and hovers on the surface for a moment, then disappears into the water.

Eva has not been this close to Martin Macauley's farm since before she had killed his father. Ever since, she has always given the place a wide berth; has taken detours around the village to make the chance of seeing him as remote as possible.

But somehow, standing here outside his gate like this has always felt inevitable. Some part of her has never doubted that one day Martin would come to know the truth of his father's death. Heaven knows there have been times over the past years when the guilt has been so strong she has teetered on the verge of coming here and telling him everything.

She thinks of Finn. Thinks of the anger, the pleading in his eyes when he had tried to stop her from leaving their island.

The emotion of their argument is gathered in her throat, knotting her belly. There's a deep regret in her for going against what he had asked of her. And yes, she knows the danger of what she is about to do.

But she also knows this is the only way forward. She cannot spend any more of her life carrying this weight. She has no thought of what Macauley will do with this information, this confirmation. All she knows is that she has no choice but to confess.

She lets herself through the gate. Trudges through a trough of ankle-deep mud past a gnarled, bare apple tree. Knocks on the door of the farmhouse.

Macauley appears from around the side of the house, carrying a shovel. A worn knitted cap is pulled down to his grey eyebrows, his dark coat patched and riddled with holes. The look he gives Eva is blazing. "Wasn't expecting to see you here."

Her heart thunders against her ribs. "May we speak?"

Macauley steps past her, tossing down the shovel and shouldering the door of the farmhouse. It opens with a shudder and groan. He stands at the doorway, gesturing for her to enter the single room of the cottage. He pulls the door closed behind her. Turns the key in the lock and slides it into his pocket.

The place is just as worn and threadbare as Macauley's boat and jacket, with an icy draft sifting between the beams of the roof, and an earthen floor beginning to turn to mud. One window is boarded up and the door of the sideboard is dangling off its hinges. It makes the cottage on Longstone feel like a palace. Have the Macauleys always been so hard-pressed? Or has Martin fallen to hard times after the death of his father? It's a question Eva cannot bear to follow too far.

He drops into a seat at the table. "Why are you here, Mrs Murray?"

At the look of blatant animosity in Macauley's eyes, panic squeezes her lungs. She thinks of her children; suddenly craves the safety of Longstone. But it is too late for regret.

She hovers by the table for a moment, then sits opposite Macauley. Dares to look him in the eye. "I came to tell you I'm sorry."

A cold smile appears in the corner of his mouth. "That's not why you're here."

Eva lets out a breath. He is right, of course. At least on some level. And the least she can offer him is the truth. She says, "I've come to find out what you are going to do to me."

Macauley leans back in his chair, studying her wordlessly for several long moments. Wind makes the cloth window drum. Sends a frigid draught snaking through the cottage. A tree branch taps steadily against the window frame.

"What do you think I ought to do?" he asks. "A life for a life? Is that a fair trade?"

Eva squeezes her hands together in her lap, fear pulsing inside her. Finn was right—she should never have come. But she *has* come, and now she must see this through. Wherever it takes her. This is what she wanted, she reminds herself. For her guilt to be laid out in the open. For her confession to ease the constriction of it.

"If you wish to kill me, I cannot stop you," she says. "But you do not want that on your conscience. Believe me." She hears her voice waver.

Macauley is silent for a long time. He keeps his eyes down, picking at the splintered edge of the table. When he speaks again, a little of the venom is gone from his voice. "What did he do to you? Why were you out at sea with him? I don't suppose you were there by choice."

"He believed I was spying for the government against the Jacobites. He forced me into his boat and rowed us out to sea. Once we were far enough from shore, he raised his musket and tried to kill me."

"And you defended yourself."

"Yes."

Macauley gives a short, humourless laugh. "He always was a stupid old bastard." He folds his wiry arms across his chest. "The innkeeper in Beal said you were staying at the lodging house the night of Da's death. How d'you get him to lie for you?"

Eva swallows hard. The truth, she knows, could lead to more trouble. But the truth is why she has come here. "The Beal innkeeper is staunchly anti-Jacobite," she says huskily. "We promised the government spies use of Highfield House in exchange for him accounting for me at his lodgings."

Macauley snorts. "Always knew your family were in Geordie's pocket."

"No," Eva says quickly. "No. It's never been like that." She feels a rush of regret. How hard has Nathan worked to regain the villagers' trust? To rebuild their family's good name? "We were never spying for the king. My brother only ever agreed to it to help me. He's never been involved in the government cause. I swear it." She feels as though she is back in that dinghy with Donald Macauley, pleading with him to

241

accept the truth of her family's innocence.

Donald's son eyes her. Does he believe her? It's impossible to tell.

"I'm so sorry," she says. "Truly. I'm so sorry for all of it. And I'm sorry for keeping it a secret. I know it was the wrong thing to do." And they are out now, the words she has imagined speaking for the last ten years. Her absolution? It does not feel like it. Speaking of what happened just makes the past feel so much more present. Her guilt has not eased. It has just become more precarious.

Martin doesn't respond. Doesn't look at her. Just keeps picking at the splinters on the edge of the table. The tree branch knocks and knocks and knocks.

And what now? Does she turn and walk out the door, and hold her breath, praying he does not produce a pistol and shoot her from behind? Is Martin Macauley that kind of man?

Martin Macauley is the son of the man who had tried to kill her on account of rumours.

Martin Macauley had put a bullet in Finn's calf on account of a little stolen coal.

So, yes, she realises sickly. Martin Macauley is the kind of man to produce a pistol and shoot her in the back as she walks out of his cottage.

But she is here now, and the thing is done. And now she has to leave.

She gets to her feet, dizzy with the racing of her heart. She looks down at him for one last moment, waiting for him to speak. When she gets only silence, she turns. Walks towards the door of the farmhouse. Waits, with held breath, for him to unlock the door.

She hears no movement. No click of a pistol. But her pulse

is roaring in her ears, drowning out all other sound.

He will always know, now. And perhaps he will tell others. Perhaps he already has. And this will be her punishment, she thinks. Every time she sees Martin Macauley, she will think of what she did to his father. And she will wonder who else might know of her direst of mistakes. But if this is the weight she must carry, she can manage it. Because the burden of her guilt has been lightened, if only a fraction, by this confession. She will take a fraction. She will take whatever she can get.

"Why are you leaving?" Macauley says suddenly. "You've not got the answer you came for."

Eva swallows. Turns to face him. "What?"

"You came here to find out what I was planning to do to you. And I've not told you."

She squeezes her hands into fists, trying to stop them from shaking. Presses her spine against the door and dares to look into Macauley's eyes. "What are you planning to do to me?"

He looks at her for a long second, and she sees more in him now than she did before. That blatant animosity has become hatred; has become his father's anger. And Eva sees that, just as her guilt has been festering for the last ten years, so too has Martin Macauley's anger at the unanswered questions about his father's death. And now, after so much uncertainty, he finally has a place to put that rage.

His colourless lips part, but he doesn't speak. Just stares her down—a look of blazing anticipation. Then he stands, comes towards her with slow, measured steps. He leans over her, accosting her with the stink of sweat and animals and unwashed skin. Slides the key into the lock and shoves the door open. Cold, damp air punches into the cottage. Eva looks up at Macauley, but he says nothing, leaving her with no choice but to start walking.

She steps from the farmhouse into icy, rain-heavy air. Wonders if perhaps her direst of mistakes was not Donald Macauley's death, but this moment, right here, right now.

CHAPTER THIRTY-THREE

Nathan has a lot of regrets when it comes to Julia. But he is not sure any quite match up to this.

Now she has left, the house feels almost unbearably quiet—perhaps just made that way by the deafening rattle of his thoughts. He hates that he had said such terrible things. Hates that she had left on such terrible terms.

Most of all, he hates the inevitability of it all. Julia was always going to leave. Was always going to go back to Calum. And Nathan was always going to behave like a complete arse about the whole thing, because he couldn't manage anything different.

Clouds are drowning out the last of the sun, the lamp on his desk doing little to lift the long shadows that have fallen across his study.

Theodora and Tom are out turning wild on Saint Cuthbert's Island, and Nathan can hear no sign of Mrs Brodie. He had sent Lewis home to the village not long ago, so he might be saved from travelling once this downpour inevitably hits.

Nathan has stayed planted at his desk in the two hours since Julia left, finally finishing the bungled letter to his distributor and making arrangements for his next trip to Scotland. Throwing himself into his work had seemed like the best way through this. A desperate attempt to distract himself from his own stupidity.

Go after her. It's a thought he's been trying to push away all afternoon. A thought that refuses to be silenced.

Go after her. Go after her. Go. After. Her.

It's almost overwhelming. There can be no future for them, of course. But he feels certain this is the last time Julia will ever be a part of his life. And he cannot bear for his last words to her to be so bitter and hurtful. For all the turmoil Julia has brought him, his feelings for her are undeniably precious. Undeniably rare.

He looks out the window, grateful for the gunmetal tide locking him onto the island. Good. He needs this—this emphatic reminder from the natural world that going after her can achieve nothing.

But his eyes are drawn to the sloop outside the window.

He pushes the thought away as soon as it arrives. The daylight is beginning to fade, and the wind is whipping the sea into choppy grey peaks. He is still far from a confident sailor. Trying to sail over to Bamburgh would be madness.

Of course it would. It would be madness for far too many reasons—his sailing abilities being the very least of them.

But he cannot stop thinking. Thinking about the regret of the last ten years, and the aching bitterness of their parting argument. The constant replaying of conversations, trying to determine if he might have done something, said something, different, to keep Julia from leaving. And there is nothing to lose. Not a thing. He lost Julia years ago.

He is out of the house and marching towards the boat before his good sense can catch him.

CHAPTER THIRTY-FOUR

This wind has whipped four more tiles off the roof, doing nothing to help Finn's terrible mood. By the time he makes it over to the farm next week to ask about the tiles, there'll be little of the damn thing left. This house has begun to feel far too flimsy, far too susceptible to the elements—and to the storm he can see gathering on the horizon. Has begun to feel like far from the beacon of solidity it has been for so much of his life.

He can't quite make sense of what he's feeling when he looks out from atop the ladder and sees Eva draw the skiff up towards the jetty. Violent relief at her safety, yes, but there's far more anger and bitterness than he has ever felt towards her before. An old anger—the kind Henry Ward had spent two years trying to scrub out of him. He hates that it has returned; hates even more than it was Eva who had sparked it.

Finn had spent most of the hour she had been gone debating whether to go after her. Calculating the risks of piling the children into the longboat and following her to Macauley's; of leaving Noah here to guard his siblings with the weather turning and roof tiles shattering. Eva had made her decision, he had decided finally. And now they have to face whatever is to come.

Since she has been gone, Finn has turned into all the parts of his own father he swore he would never be—short-tempered with his children, barking at their waterlogged boots, their stream of questions, their dropped cups of milk. He was almost relieved when Noah had corralled his brother and sister into the bedroom to get away from him. At least this way he couldn't make things worse.

He climbs from the ladder and waits for Eva on the edge of the jetty. The sea is grey and heaving, spitting up over the edges of the island.

"Did you speak to him?" he asks tautly.

"Yes." She winds the mooring ropes. Doesn't look at him.

"And? What did he do? What did he say?"

He offers her his hand to help her out of the boat. She doesn't take it—whether out of spite or anger, or just a deep distractedness, he can't quite tell. She looks flushed and windblown, her blue eyes full of an emotion he can't quite read. Finally, she dares to look up at him. "I don't know what he's going to do," she admits. "I told him the truth and he gave me little in response." He hears the fear in her words.

Finn had truly believed that Macauley would not act on the information Harriet had given him. Why would he want the truth of what his father had done to become public knowledge? But now, with this fear in Eva's voice, he cannot help but wonder if perhaps he was wrong. If perhaps Martin Macauley is far more vindictive than he had imagined. If perhaps he does not care what the village thinks of his father, as long as he has his retribution.

Finn turns away. He can't look at Eva in case he says, does, something he regrets. The thing is done. She has made her choice. And now all they can do is wait to see if Macauley retaliates.

How hard had he and Eva fought to find peace and security? How many times had they nearly lost each other? How hard have they worked to build this uninterrupted life for themselves and their children? Now all that security is at risk again. Now, they are condemned to going back to those nights of watching the horizon, keeping the beacon burning, and waiting to see who might appear on their island. Easy targets. It feels like this is what they have always been.

His anger, Finn realises then, it's not directed at Eva. Not entirely, at least. Yes, they had had their peace. And it had been upturned.

By her own sister.

Finn sucks in a breath, trying to remain calm. He cannot remember the last time he found it such a struggle. They need Harriet out of their lives. Right now, it's the only thing he can see with clarity. Right now, he feels like he would do anything to make that happen.

"You and the children need to get off the island," he tells Eva stiffly. "There's a storm on the way and I don't know how secure the roof is. I don't want any of you here tonight. It's not safe."

When she looks up at him, he sees the unease behind her eyes. But she keeps her voice level. Expressionless. "What about you?"

"I've things I need to do."

"What things?"

He shakes his head stiffly. "It doesn't matter." This is not a conversation he can have with her now. He doesn't trust himself to keep his anger in check.

Eva is silent for a moment, as though debating whether to press the issue. She keeps her distance from him, arms wrapped tightly around her body. "There'll be no chance of keeping the beacon lit when this rain comes," she says finally.

"No."

She unfurls her arms. Takes a tentative step towards him. "Will you come to the house when you're done with… whatever it is you need to do?"

Finn hesitates. He had intended to come back here to Longstone. Lock himself away and try to let his anger dissipate. But he knows that's a foolish thing to do, now that Martin Macauley has become such an unknown threat. He needs to be wherever his family is—and they'll be far safer in the solidity of Highfield House than on this crumbling sea-swept island.

He nods stiffly. "Aye. I'll see you at the house. But you need to go now. Before the weather gets any worse."

He stands on the jetty and watches them leave. Eva doesn't look at him as she pulls the boat away from the island and it leaves a dull ache in his chest. He hates her leaving with things so strained and bitter between them. Still, it's best this way. Safest.

Finn waits until the skiff has disappeared into the wall of cloud.

He climbs into the longboat. Heads for the mainland to find Eva's sister.

Hours have passed and Ward has not returned. The last of the light is draining from the day, and up here on the deck of her father's boat, Harriet can smell the rain in the air. Gulls soar over the water in perfect formation, stark white against the darkening sky.

She grips the gunwale. Squints into the fading light out across the village of Beal. She sees globes of lamplight behind the windows of the lodging house, and in a couple of cottages further up the hill. No other signs of life.

Her father had moored his boat here at the jetty, across the water from Lindisfarne, and stalked off into the village with his pistol in his pocket. If he has found Lawler—or if Lawler has found him—she has seen or heard no sign of it. The fearful anticipation has made every muscle in her body taut. Her stomach is a constant roll, her skin hot and sticky beneath her shift.

She reaches into her pocket. Feels the weight of Peggy's pistol. And beside it, the brass box, smoothed with time.

Harriet has to admit she is grateful for this second chance she has been given, to see Ward again, especially in the new light of her mother's letter. But having him in her life can only be a fleeting thing. Abigail's letter does not change the fact that she destroys every relationship she ever has. It's far easier, far safer, to keep her father on the fringes of her life. Let him remain this half-mythical figure she thinks of sometimes and tries more often to forget.

She wishes she was a stronger person. Once, she had been so proud of the life she had built, out in the world on her own. That unhemmed-in life that had once felt so unobtainable. But now that life doesn't feel like something to be proud of. Now, all she can think about is all the trouble she has caused. All the terrible things she has done. That poisonous streak inside her that wants to hurt and punish others on account of her own failings.

There can be no rebuilding from here—yes, she understands that. She has damaged things with Eva far too completely for them to ever be rebuilt. There can be no rebuilding, but perhaps there can be some attempt at making things right.

To do that, she needs to get back to Lindisfarne. Right now, the tide is high, locking her out. What an irony, she thinks, that she is standing here on the deck of a boat, looking longingly across the water at an island she cannot reach.

She will find someone to take her over. There will be someone at the tavern she can ask. Someone who owns one of these sorry-looking dinghies knocking against their moorings beside her father's vessel.

She gathers her skirts and climbs onto the jetty. And she follows the curve of the road up towards the lodging house.

In the fading light, something glints on the edge of her vision. She sees a gold pocket watch protruding from the wet sand. Thoughtlessly, she pulls it from the water. Shoves it into her pocket.

Her fingers graze the brass box and she stops walking suddenly.

She cannot take this with her as she goes back to Holy Island, trying to undo what she knows can hardly be undone. She cannot take it with her into a life she does not want her father in. She cannot take this box away, without him knowing what is inside.

She climbs back onto the boat. Steps back down the ladder, hearing it creak beneath her weight.

She takes the box from her pocket and sets it in the centre of the table. Her father will return, she tells herself. And he will see Abigail's letter, and he will read it, and he will know the truth of *I love you* and *you are to be a father, Henry*. And he, like his daughter, will think of faded things that once could have been, and now never will.

CHAPTER THIRTY-FIVE

Harriet hears the boards of the deck creak above her head as she is making her way back to the ladder. Her father has returned, she thinks. Her gaze goes to the brass box on the table. She feels a sudden, instinctive need to hide it. She wants him to read Abigail's letter, yes. But she does not want to be here when he does. Cannot face the vulnerability of what it may lead to.

Before she can reach the table, the hatch groans open. A man appears, swallowing the last of the daylight. He's tall, stocky, his face half-hidden behind a thick black beard. His hand curls around the top rung of the ladder, little finger missing at the knuckle. Harriet hears a frightened murmur come from deep in her throat. She stumbles backwards, clattering against the bulkhead. Lawler lowers himself down the ladder in one swift movement.

"Where is my father?" she asks, hearing her voice rattle.

"I was hoping you might tell me that. It would save us both a lot of trouble."

She tries to read beneath his words. See behind his grim grey eyes. Is he playing with her? Has he already found Henry Ward? Has he already delivered his own retribution for his brother's death upon the gallows?

Harriet's heart thunders against her ribs, fear blurring the edges of the room. But this man will not kill her. That is not what this is about. Lawler wants her because she is Ward's daughter—a far more precious commodity alive. But as she tries to cling to this thought, she realises its blatant untruth. Perhaps Lawler wants to kill her to punish Ward. Her life for his dead brother's.

Perhaps Lawler wants to kill her because he knows she was the one who had sent the authorities after Ward's ship. No. Because the only way he would know that would be if Ward had told him. And somehow, whether foolishly or not, she trusts that her father would not do that to her. Trusts, somehow, that he will do all he can to protect her.

But she has no idea if her father is still alive.

Perhaps Lawler has already found him.

He takes a step towards her, rounding the blockade of the table. Instinctively, Harriet tries to back away, stumbles against the storage chest. She grapples at the bulkhead, hand knocking against a solid weight in her pocket.

She remembers. Peggy's pistol. She fumbles for it, feels it cold and heavy in her palm. Brings it out in a shaking fist. Prays Lawler will retreat at the sight of the weapon.

There's a faint quirk beneath his beard—perhaps he is laughing at her. Perhaps he knows she cannot do this. Perhaps he can see the utter incompatibility of this woman and this pistol.

She pulls the trigger. Sends a wild shot flying into the

ladder, the jolt of the pistol coursing through her body. Lawler ducks. Curses. Pitches towards her. Harriet drops the empty weapon. Instinctively, her hand closes around the spying glass sitting atop the storage chest. She swings wildly. The metal shaft cracks against the side of Lawler's head, broken glass spraying out across the cabin. His torso thuds against the table before he crumples to the floor at her feet.

Dizziness swings over her as she bends to collect the pistol. She scrambles up the ladder, stepping, repeatedly, on her skirt hems. Thudding to her knees against the deck. She bolts the hatch closed. Lurches to the gunwale and empties her stomach into the sea.

She hunches for a moment, shaking, sweat prickling her forehead. Is he dead? Surely not. Surely she did not strike him hard enough. She cannot bear the thought of him being dead. For all he has done to her, she does not want the weight of his death. Does not want to carry him wherever she goes.

Silence from down below. A deafening, sickening silence, but it gives Harriet a moment to breathe.

She is thinking of her sister. Thinking of the weight of death Eva has been carrying for ten years. And Harriet thinks of the letter she herself had written, bringing that weighted truth out into the light.

She gets to her feet, skirts tangling around her legs. She needs to leave this place. Needs to leave before Lawler wakes and forces his way out of the hatch.

But before she runs, before she disappears, she needs to go back to Lindisfarne one last time. Needs to try and make things right.

Harriet stumbles off the ship and down the jetty. Dark water laps against the hulls of the boats tied to the moorings, the sea whipped into peaks by the swirling wind. Somewhere distant, thunder rumbles low. The lights of Lindisfarne village glow behind the cloud.

Harriet puts her head down and strides towards the lodging house, trying to will away the weakness in her legs. She will find someone in the tavern, she hopes, willing to take her onto the island. She glances over the shoulder at her father's boat. Thinks of Lawler's motionless body lying at the foot of the ladder. He will wake soon, surely. Will force his way out of the hatch. Will find her like he has managed to find her so many times before.

Panic rising, Harriet breaks into a run. And as she rounds the bend towards the tavern, she collides with her sister's husband. She has never been more grateful to see him. "A boat," she garbles. "You have a boat?"

Finn blinks in surprise. "Of course." His eyes narrow. "Why?"

"I need to get across to the island. Quickly."

"Why?" he asks again.

Harriet tugs at his arm, pulling him back towards the water. "There's someone after me." Breathless. "Can you help me get away?"

For a second, Finn doesn't speak, and Harriet can practically see his thoughts racing. His eyes reflect his contempt for her, his complete distrust. Finally, the faintest of nods. He strides towards the water. Helps her into the longboat and shoves it out onto the sea.

———⟡———

Eva drags the skiff up onto the embankment beyond

Highfield House, Noah tugging on the gunwale beside her and Archie climbing carefully over the beach with his sister in his arms. The last of the light is disappearing behind the horizon, any hint of starlight lost behind thick banks of cloud. Eva smells the rain, feels the air pulsing cold against her cheeks. Wind slaps at the dunes, bending the grass into rigid angles. The gale had blown up on their way over and her arms are tense and aching from the strain of the journey. She casts a quick glance over the water, hoping to see Finn's longboat. He'd not have sent them over here without him if he'd known the wind was going to strike up like this, Eva knows. She has no thought of where he has gone. But she knows he cannot be far away. For all his anger at her, all that tightly coiled rage she had sensed in him when she had returned from Macauley's farm, she knows he would never leave them.

She takes Maggie from her brother and ushers the children towards the house. Noah pounds the door knocker. A flurry of footsteps, then Theodora pulls the door open.

"My goodness, that wind," she says, as another violent burst careens into the entrance hall, making the lamps flicker. "Did you sail over here in this?"

"Wind picked up as we were on our way over," says Eva, handing the baby to Theodora and bending to help Archie unbutton his coat. "We need to stay here tonight. It's not safe out on Longstone."

At the sound of their voices, Thomas thunders down the stairs.

"Where's Da?" Archie asks, for the third time.

Eva hangs the coats. Can't bring herself to look him in the eye as she rattles out the same empty response. *He'll be here soon. He has things he needs to do.*

"Did you fight with Da?" Noah asks.

"A little. But everything is all right." She knows her words sound anything but believable. She is convinced she can see the doubt in Archie's eyes. Is certain she can see it in Noah's. But neither of them protest.

Theodora leads them into the parlour, where a fire is roaring in the grate. Thea sets Maggie down on the rug and goes to the window. Peeks through the curtains. She's on edge too, Eva can tell. Can sense the unease pouring off her. She joins Thea at the window. Slides an arm over her shoulder. "Are you all right?"

Theodora wraps her arms around her slender body. "I don't know where Papa is. When Tom and I got back from Saint Cuthbert's, he wasn't here. It's so unlike him not to leave me a note. And the boat was gone."

Eva feels a swell of unease at the thought of Nathan at the helm of that rickety sloop. She knows he's been turned upside down by Julia's presence—also knows he would never admit to it. Still, her brother is rarely one to act rashly. Eva can tell the platitudes she churns out to Theodora—*the weather is turning, he's likely decided to wait out the storm*; and, most foolishly, *try not to worry*—are doing little to convince her of her father's safety. And she feels the unease inside her simmering, threatening to tear itself free.

"Were you going to the house?" Finn asks Harriet, pulling on the oars and guiding the longboat away from the Beal jetty. The sea is blue-black, churning. Seesawing the boat and spitting salt into his eyes.

Harriet glances over her shoulder. She's trembling hard—Finn can't tell if it's from cold or fear. Her chest is heaving with rapid breath.

"No," she says. "Just to the village."

"Good."

She eyes him. "Why is that good?"

"Because Eva is at the house and you've done enough to her." He pulls through the swell. Tries to rein in his anger. Letting it out here, with the sea and sky rolling and someone on their tail, will do neither of them any good.

"Is that why you came to the tavern?" Harriet asks. She is without a bonnet or cap, and the wind is whipping her pale hair wildly across her face. "To berate me for what I did to Eva? To tell me to stay away from her? To tell me you don't want me in your lives?"

Finn doesn't answer. Suspects he doesn't need to. Harriet seems to be under no illusions as to what he had been doing at the lodging house. "Eva knows you were the one who gave that letter to Macauley," he says finally. "But she doesn't want to admit it. She doesn't want to accept that her sister would do such a godawful thing."

Harriet looks down. "Eva knows who I am." Her voice is thin.

"Is that supposed to be an excuse?"

"No. Just an observation."

Finn doesn't speak at once. She's impossible to read. Has been for as long as he has known her. He has no thought of who Harriet really is. He wonders if anyone does.

He guides the boat past the Pilgrims' Way. From out here, he can see the lamplight of the village. Cannot see Highfield House. Eva and the children will have made it there safely, he tells himself. She's a competent, confident sailor. Noah is becoming one too. They've both managed far worse conditions than this. Nonetheless, he can't shake the regret at not taking his family over to Lindisfarne himself. He'd not expected the gale to blow up this ferociously. He hates that he had let his anger get the better of him.

His frustration at himself sparks his rage at Harriet. "Why in hell would you do something like this to your own sister?" he demands.

She looks at him squarely. She's entirely Henry Ward, Finn thinks. Age has made her look even more like her father. She's got his hardness too; that dark streak that teeters into cruelty.

"I know it was wrong," she says. "I know it was a terrible thing to do. And I know there is no point trying to explain any of it to you." She looks away. "You're far too besotted with my sister to ever see from anything other than her point of view."

Finn snorts. "I'm sorry you resent us for that."

Harriet wraps her arms around herself. "Just take me to the village," she says. "Please." She looks past him, eyes fixed to the faint glow of light coming from the town. Thunder rumbles dully.

Finn rows in silence for several minutes, relieved when the swell tosses the longboat into the mouth of the anchorage. "Was that Ward's boat by the jetty in Beal?" he asks finally.

Harriet nods.

"He found you then?"

No reply.

"Where is he?"

"He went looking for the man who came after me. I don't

know where he is now. I don't know what's happened to him."

In her voice, Finn hears her fears for her father's safety. The glimpse of genuineness surprises him. "You think he's been hurt?"

Harriet looks down. "Or worse. He went after Mr Lawler. But Lawler found me on his ship."

"Lawler was the man from the wreck? The man with the beard who asked after you?"

"Do you really want to know?" she asks tautly. "Don't you want to wash your hands of me?"

Finn ignores the question. "Is Lawler likely to follow you onto the island?"

A short laugh. "Why do you care? You came to the lodging house to get rid of me, didn't you?"

She's right. He had come out here to demand that Harriet keep her distance from Eva and their family. And he will not let himself be drawn in by the constant chaos of her.

He eases the longboat up towards the Lindisfarne jetty. Harriet grabs at the mooring post and stumbles out, skirts held above her knees. She looks back at Finn for the briefest of moments. "Thank you." And she is off towards the beach without looking back.

Finn hesitates for a moment. He needs to get to the house. Needs to get to his family. The need to see Eva is suddenly overwhelming. Ought he take the longboat around the coast to Emmanuel Head? Or try and cross the dunes on foot?

He pulls on the oars. He knows the coast of this island better than the tangle of inland paths. He'll stay close to land, avoid the worst of the wild weather. With luck, he'll be at the house before the clouds break open.

Another vessel out here, he realises, as he traces the coast out of the anchorage. A small cutter perhaps, barely bigger than his longboat. The sail backs, and the cutter's lamp flashes and flares. Finn lurches across the longboat for his own lantern. He holds it up, out towards the cutter.

A figure is waving him down. Calling his name.

He draws the longboat closer, shoulders burning as he drives the oars through a wall of water. Henry Ward looks down over the gunwale at him, panic in his eyes.

"I took Harriet into Lindisfarne," Finn tells him. "Lawler came after her."

Ward nods. "I know. I found him on my boat. She struck him with my spying glass and locked him below. Where was she going?"

"I don't know. She didn't tell me. Into the village somewhere."

Ward nods brusquely. "All right. Thank you." He hesitates for a moment, gesturing out to the dark water around the Farnes. "What are you doing here, lad? Why are you not on Longstone?"

Finn says, "I can't light the beacon in this weather." But as he speaks, he sees the untruth of it. Rough seas tonight, yes. Thunder and thickening darkness. But so far, the rain has stayed away. The firebasket could still be lit.

"Are you certain?" Ward raises his eyebrows—it's a critical look that Finn has seen all too many times. A look that makes him feel like a child again, hunched at the table in Ward's great cabin, weathering the captain's scolding. "You're needed out there," he says—and those simple words strike a physical blow. Finn hates that, after all these years, his former captain can still affect him so deeply. Why—how—

264

does he still hold such power?

You're needed out there.

He closes his eyes, feeling the longboat careen on the water.

Go to the house. Eva is waiting. His children are waiting.

And he had left Henry Ward behind years ago.

But: *you're needed out there.* Yes, he sees the truth of it.

Lighting the beacon, lighting that treacherous patch of sea—this is the responsibility he has agreed to carry on his shoulders. A responsibility that feels like his dues. *You have your absolution*, Eva had said. And perhaps in some ways, he has. The truth of Oliver's death has long been known, at least by Nathan and Harriet, and Finn has come out of it with his marriage—and his life—intact. But the guilt, both over Oliver's death, and the way he had abandoned his father, is still a sharp, pulsing thing inside him. The blazing beacon has always gone some way to easing that. Some way to fading the image of his father's lifeless body on Longstone; dulling the memory of Oliver's blank eyes and the trail of blood snaking out from the back of his head.

The wreck of the *Cygnus* has only served to remind him of just how crucial it is that he is out there. Of how selfish it would be to turn this boat to the left instead of the right and return to Highfield House. He wants Eva; wants to tell her he is sorry for sending her to the house without him tonight. Wants to tell her they will carry the weight of Donald Macauley together. But: *you're needed out there.* If Henry Ward says it, it must be true. As long as this rain keeps from falling, that beacon needs to light the sky.

CHAPTER THIRTY-SIX

Nathan's legs are a little unsteady as he walks into Bamburgh, wind whipping the hem of his coat and pulling his hair loose from its queue. He's still in some kind of disbelief that he has made it here in one piece. At the back of his mind, behind all the madness, he regrets not leaving a note for Thea. She will worry for him, he knows, especially when she sees the boat gone.

But tonight he feels foolishly reckless. Incapable of rational thought. And that recklessness, it keeps pushing him forward, through the streets towards the narrow end of Church Wynd. Up the stairs to Julia's tenement.

He stops outside the door. Raises his fist to knock.

Christ Almighty, what is he doing? Julia is another man's wife. How could he have lost sight of that, even for a moment? More than that, there is every chance her husband is here right now, beneath this roof, ready to answer this knock at the door.

Nathan turns to leave, the floorboards creaking loudly

beneath his weight.

"Who's there?" Julia calls sharply. She bursts through the door with a knife held out in front of her. Her shortjacket is half unlaced, her hair falling loose and wild over her shoulders.

"It's all right. It's just me."

She lets out her breath. Lowers the knife. "I'm sorry. I'm on edge. The safe, and Calum, and I—" She shakes her head. "Why are you here?" Suspicion in her voice? Anger?

Nathan looks down. "I shouldn't be. It was a mistake. But I…" Her husband is not here, he thinks distantly. She would not be standing on the doorstep speaking to him like this if her husband was here. He tries to silence the thought. It can lead him nowhere good. "I came to apologise," he manages, "for those terrible things I said to you. I did not mean a word of it. I just… I did not know how to let you go." His words fall heavily into the silence and he forces himself to hold her gaze. "I should never have said what I did. And I had no right to get angry at your leaving." His voice is husky. "I had no right to feel anything at all. I had my chance to make you my wife long ago and I didn't take it."

Julia reaches for his wrist. Curls her fingers around it, sending a pulse of energy through his body. She looks at him for a long second. "Do you wish you had?" she asks, voice trapped in her throat. "Made me your wife, I mean."

Nathan swallows. "Of course I do."

Julia doesn't speak. Just stares at him with her lips slightly parted. Her fingers move almost imperceptibly against his wrist. The movement feels enormous, consuming. She tugs him gently into the tenement. Closes the door behind them and sets the knife down on the table.

The feel of her has become almost a part of him now, Nathan realises. He cannot quite tell where her fingers end and his wrist begins. And it's not her who's tugging him forward. He's pulling her towards him. Seeking her nearness. Craving it. He is suddenly breathless for her.

He kisses her without thought. He's had ten years of thinking about Julia and it has led him nowhere but in empty, painful circles. And this, he knows, is by far the most thoughtless thing he could be doing. Her lips part beneath his, inviting him deeper.

He finds the curves of her, his hands remembering, relearning, what it is to feel a woman beneath his touch. He feels her chest straining against her stays, her body seeking his. Wind pounds against the cloth window, makes the beams above their head groan.

"Are you all right?" she asks on an exhalation. "Is it too much?"

Yes, it is too much, but it is also nowhere near enough. And now he has Julia close, he needs every inch of her. But: "Is this what you want?" He can hardly bear to think of him, Calum MacNeill, who might walk through this door at any moment. The thought of what that would mean for Julia is enough to make him loosen his grip on her. Enough to make him step away.

She pulls him close again, fist tightening around the hem of his justacorps. "Yes," she says. "This is what I want." She slides his jacket from his shoulders. Pulls at the buttons on his waistcoat. Nathan's fingers slide though her hair, then trail downwards to the lacing on her bodice. He feels breathless, vivid, almost painfully alive.

And he says, "I love you."

Julia pulls away from him slightly, just enough for him to see the faintest of smiles flicker on her face. "I love you too."

And suddenly her lips are crushed against his, last thoughts, last hesitations gone from his mind. She is consuming him, intoxicating him, tugging him down onto the bed with her, as laces come loose and linen falls with a sigh against the floor. Her hands skim over the blazing skin on his back, untouched for so many years by anyone other than himself. It has been so long since he has felt a woman beneath him like this; not since Sarah, whose memory is beginning to fade.

"I'm not..." he says, unsure of what it is he is trying to say. "I don't..."

Julia silences him with a kiss. And she is everywhere, all at once, shifting and writhing beneath him, her breath hot and short and fast against his ear. Tomorrow, she will go back to being someone else's wife. And though he is certain he has no hope of ever making it so, Nathan knows that this, right now, must somehow be enough.

CHAPTER THIRTY-SEVEN

Harriet is relying on hazy memories to find her way to Martin Macauley's farm. She stumbles around the rim of the village, past Saint Cuthbert's and the ghost of the priory, streets dimmed as the lamplight is snatched by the wind. She heads blindly towards the farmland that feeds into the dunes. Tries one property after another until she finds the place she is looking for.

In the pale light glowing behind the cloth window, she can tell Macauley's farmhouse is in tatters: the grass overgrown, the roof tilted, a second window covered with boards. She shivers hard, wind slicing through the layers of her clothing.

And though her hands are still trembling from her attack on Lawler, she fumbles with the pistol and slides in a fresh ball.

She trudges through the mire at the front of the cottage and pounds on the door, unsure if it will be heard over the rattling of the window frame, or the steady thudding of a tree branch against the side of the house.

Lamplight filters under the large gap beneath the door. It opens a crack, letting out the stench of tallow and damp. Martin Macauley's bristly grey head pokes through.

"Who are you?"

She swallows hard. "My name is Harriet Whitley." Using her husband's name feels bitter on her tongue; it has been years since she has done so. But she suspects that, with hearing Edwin's name, Macauley will remember her. And yes, she sees that look of recognition fall across his face. Not just recognition: anger too. Bitterness.

He spears her with hard eyes. "You're Eva Murray's sister."

She nods. "May I come in?"

Macauley chuckles. "I'm honoured the two of you thought to visit me today."

Harriet feels a pull of dread. "Eva was here?"

He doesn't speak.

"What did you… talk about?"

Macauley snorts. "I don't imagine you need me to answer that."

No. Because the question she really wants to ask is, *What did you do to her?* "Did you harm her?" she blurts.

Macauley tilts his head, considering her. "Is that why you're here? Because you think I harmed your sister?"

Harriet feels the weight of the pistol against her thigh. She would do it, she thinks distantly. Every piece of this is her own doing, yes. But if Macauley tells her he has hurt Eva, she would pull that pistol from her pocket and fire. It could not worsen the guilt she already feels.

"I didn't touch her," says Macauley. "I'm not that kind of man."

271

Harriet swallows down her murmur of doubt. "May I come in?" she asks again.

Macauley hesitates, then pulls the door open, gesturing for her to enter.

He does not offer her a chair at the table. Just stands facing her with his arms folded across his chest, waiting expectantly for her to speak. Unbidden, Harriet finds her gaze drifting around the shadowed interior of the cottage. Searching for lies, she realises. Searching for anything that might suggest Macauley has laid a finger on her sister.

The house is a near ruin, with its boarded window and muddy floor and the sideboard door dangling on broken hinges. Roof beams hang low, as though threatening to swallow this miserable excuse for a house. It bodes well for her, Harriet thinks. This place sings of desperation.

She reaches into her coin pouch. Pulls out the gold pocket watch she had found in the water and sets it on the table. "Take this," she says. "Sell it and use the money to start again. Find a landowner who'll rent you someplace decent."

Macauley looks down at the watch glinting in the lamplight. "I don't know what you're trying to get out of me, lass, but it'll take a lot more than some little trinket."

Harriet narrows her eyes. "It's pure gold."

He snorts. "Do you really imagine me so desperate?"

She hesitates a moment. Her hand slides into her pocket, fingers gliding over the pistol. She pulls her bulging coin pouch from her pocket and sets in on the table. Macauley peers inside, his eyes widening slightly at the contents.

I wrote letter after letter of introduction and I tutored half the young women in London and I stayed up painting every night until my damn eyes gave out. I worked so damn hard for all of it.

Harriet pushes aside the ache. She takes her travel documents from the purse and nudges it forward. "Is this a more suitable sum?"

Macauley eyes her. "In exchange for what?"

"In exchange for you leaving Lindisfarne tonight. Leaving my sister and her family be."

For several moments, he doesn't speak. Just glances between Harriet and the pouch she had placed on the table. "Your sister killed my father," he says finally.

Harriet stares him down. "Your father tried to kill my sister. Eva was just defending herself."

Macauley stares back at the pouch, then shakes his head. "This place is my life. I'm not leaving it."

"This place is on the verge of collapse," Harriet hisses, waving a wild hand at the boarded window. "When was the last time you made a damn penny from this farm?"

Macauley doesn't answer.

"There's enough money in there to start again," Harriet tells him. "Somewhere far better than this." He folds his arms across his chest, making her release a breath of frustration. "This cursed island. Why are you all so tied to this damn place? Can you not see that things could be so much better for you elsewhere?" She reaches down to grab the purse.

"Wait."

Harriet straightens.

"How do I know this isn't a trap?"

"What kind of trap?"

"How in hell should I know?"

She sighs. Lowers her eyes. "I was the one who wrote the letter telling you about Eva and your father," she admits.

"Why would you do that?"

"Because I was angry," she says tautly. "Angry and bitter and jealous. And now I'm just trying to undo a mistake." She nudges the pouch towards Macauley. Without it, she has nothing. Without it, she is that penniless charity case she has always feared being. Without it, her only chance of survival is to rely on the family she has shunned. Pray they will let her back beneath their roof. "There is no trap," she says. "Just take the money."

For long seconds, neither of them speak. Macauley stares down at the coin pouch on the table. The cloth window drums loudly. The fire simmers weakly in the grate. Harriet shivers. Edges towards it.

Finally, Macauley takes the pouch. Shoves it into his pocket.

Harriet nods faintly. "You must leave tonight," she says.

"I can't leave tonight. There's a storm about to hit."

"Then you'd best not delay." He could strike her down; Harriet is all too aware of that. Could strike her and take the money and leave her unconscious out on the island somewhere. He could. And yet, he doesn't. Instead, he shuffles around the cottage, shoving shirts and breeches and underclothes into a bag. He takes a tarred greatcoat from the hook beside the door and pulls it on.

"I've animals," he tells her. "A horse. Sheep. I need to take them over to the next farm. Can't just leave them here."

She nods. "Do what you need to do. As long as you leave once you're done."

Macauley eyes her for one last moment, then turns and marches out of his cottage, leaving Harriet standing alone beside the dying fire.

She waits in the cottage for some time, sitting at Martin Macauley's kitchen table, listening to the tree branch thudding against the window frame. Listening to thunder rolling out across the ocean. She feels an unbalancing lightness at both the loss of her money, and the loss of a fraction of her guilt. She has nothing now. No way of getting back to London. No way of continuing her glittering, unhemmed-in life.

She stands from the table and walks from the cottage. The door groans and sticks as she tries to pull it closed behind her. She lifts the lamp, trying to pick shapes from the inky darkness. Where to now? The wind is swirling and she feels flecks of ice in the gale.

She feels painfully adrift. Untethered. The thought of letting herself blow wild at the mercy of the wind is almost appealing. Where else does she have to go? What else can she do?

She stumbles away from the farm, out towards the dark heart of the island. She is walking towards Highfield House, she realises. Because where else is there to go?

CHAPTER THIRTY-EIGHT

Lamps are glowing in the downstairs windows of the house, the upper storey almost lightless. Harriet stands outside it for a long time, her cloak pulled tight around her trembling body. Wind whips her hair around her face, obscuring her view of those bleak stone walls.

Some fragile part of her, the part of self-preservation, urges her to take the final few steps towards the house. Knock at the door. Step inside and escape the coming storm.

But it feels, suddenly, as though something almost physical is preventing her from doing so.

Eva is in this house. Thomas is in this house; this house where his mother had abandoned him.

This house is not yours. The knowing comes from deep inside her. Not your house. Not welcome here.

Harriet understands the alternatives. The cold. The wind. The untethered wild. But none of that has the power to overrule the knowing that she cannot step through that front door.

Finn ought to be here. He promised he would be here.

Eva is at the window of her childhood bedroom, peering out over the dark sea. How many times, before they had married, had thoughts of Finn brought her to this window, as she sought the reassuring glimmer of the Longstone light?

Tonight, there is no glitter in the blackness. Nothing to assure her of Finn's safety. She can see little through the window, but can hear the sea throwing itself against the embankment. Hears wind rattling the time-worn edges of the house. Beams groan loudly above her head.

She tries to push aside the knot of worry in her stomach. Finn had promised he would come to the house. And he will come. Whatever else had passed between them today, he will come.

Soft footsteps in the passage and she turns to see Noah in the doorway.

"Can you see Da?" he asks, coming to stand beside her at the window. Eva slides an arm over his shoulder, pulling him close.

"Not yet, my love. But he'll be here." Lightning jags, illuminating, for seconds, the empty troughs of the sea.

"The weather's bad. There's going to be a storm."

"I know. But it's not here yet. And Da is a good sailor."

"Shall I stay here and watch for him?"

And this is what she and Finn have raised their son to be: a watcher of the sea; a protector, like his father and grandfather before him. But it's not a weight she wants him to shoulder—not yet, at least.

"Let's go back to the parlour," she says. "See what Tom and Thea are doing. Da will come."

Noah hesitates, then nods finally. Lets Eva walk him back downstairs.

He hurries off to the parlour as she peeks in on Archie and Maggie, asleep in one of the old servants' rooms. When she returns to the parlour, she finds Noah, Tom, and Thea on their knees around the tea table, a pack of cards spread out in front of them.

Noah looks up at her. "Will you play, Mama?"

"In a moment." She can't help going to the window. Can't help lifting the curtain; peeking out onto the dunes.

She sees a flash of movement. Pulls the curtain back further. Squints. Just her imagination? No, there it is again: a shadow moving through the darkness. Person, not animal— she can tell no more than this.

Noah scrambles to his feet. "Who's outside?" he pushes. "Is it Da?" Tom trails him to the window, cards abandoned.

"I don't know." Finn would most likely have sailed straight to Emmanuel Head. Unlikely to have come across the dunes. Unless he had thought it safer to moor in the village.

Noah and Tom chase her into the entrance hall. "Stay here," Eva tells them, snatching her cloak from the hook.

Her son looks up at her wide-eyed. "You can't go out there by yourself. It's so dark. And windy."

She feels a swell of love for him. Presses her hands to his cheeks, his shoulders. "Stay here," she says firmly, meeting his eyes. "I'll be back in a moment. I'm only going out to see who's there."

Theodora steps from the parlour, calling the boys back.

"Go on," says Eva. "Finish your game. I'll not be long."

She steps out of the house and pulls the door closed before her son can protest.

Harriet hears her sister's voice bouncing across the dunes. Sees the light from Eva's lamp struggling and flickering against the wind. She hurries away from it. She cannot bear to face her sister after all she has done to her.

The ground rolls and lurches beneath her feet as she stumbles further from the house. Eva is still following her, lamplight moving through the darkness like a will-o'the wisp. Harriet crouches behind the rise of the earth. Wills her sister back towards the house.

The light of Eva's lamp disappears suddenly, snatched by the wind. With the stars and moon lost behind the cloud bank, the only light is the distant glow behind the curtains of Highfield House. Harriet is far from the manor now; a hundred yards at least. She cannot tell how near to her Eva is. Wind swirls, whipping the hood of her cloak off her head. The cold seeps through to her bones.

"Finn?" Eva calls again. "Are you there?" She is closer than Harriet expected. She sees the shape of her emerge from the dark. "Harriet. What are you doing out here?"

Harriet turns away. "Go back inside. Leave me be."

"Don't be foolish. I'm not leaving you out here. What are you doing?"

And what other response is there but the truth? There is no lie she can conjure up that will satisfactorily explain her being here, crouched behind the dunes, hiding from her sister. Although perhaps the truth will not do that either.

"I thought to come to the house," she admits finally. "But I know it's not my place."

"What do you mean? Of course it's your place."

"No. It's not."

Eva steps close. Wind whips dark hair across her cheeks—Harriet sees now that she has come marching out here without her bonnet or gloves. In a sudden spear of lightning, Harriet can see the tangle of emotions on her sister's face. She wonders if Eva is going to tear her apart for telling Macauley about his father, out here in the dunes, with the weather turning wild around them. Instead, she takes Harriet's arm firmly and begins to stride back towards the house.

Harriet feels her muscles tighten as the manor grows closer. Is not sure she can bring herself to go inside. But what choice does she have with Eva latched to her like this, refusing to let go?

The front door comes into view and Harriet finds a fresh surge of determination. She pulls free of her sister's grip and stumbles away.

"Harriet—" Eva whirls around, but her attention is snatched by Theodora bursting from the house.

"Are they with you?" Thea demands.

"Who?"

"Noah and Tom. I can't find them. Their coats are gone."

Harriet hides herself around the corner of the house. Does not want Theodora to see her. Does not want another voice urging her through that front door.

"I'm so sorry." Theodora's tears spill. "Noah wanted to come out and find you. Help you. I told him to stay inside. But then I heard Maggie crying and I went to her, and when

I got back, I couldn't find the boys…"

Eva squeezes Theodora's shoulder. "It's not your fault." She takes the lamp from her, tries to shield it from the wind. Hands her the lantern that had blown out. "Go back inside. Stay with Archie and Maggie. I'll find the boys." Harriet hears the poorly hidden panic in her sister's voice. And she realises that yes, somewhere deep, she is feeling it too. A flicker of maternal instinct she has not managed to bury. This place is far too dark, far too wild, far too sea-hemmed for children to be running around unseen.

For her child to be running around unseen.

The wind catches the front door and slams it shut. Eva strides back down the path, lifting the lamp and spearing light into Harriet's eyes. "Are you coming?" she asks, steel in her voice.

And Harriet finds herself saying, "Yes."

CHAPTER THIRTY-NINE

"They'll be all right," Eva is saying. "They'll be all right." Over and over. "They're sensible boys. They'll not do anything foolish."

Is she trying to placate herself or her sister? Harriet cannot tell. She doesn't tell Eva that if the boys were as sensible as she believes, they would not have come charging out here like this with wind tearing across the dunes and the sky about to open. Knows she has no right to do so.

Eva calls their names, wind carrying her voice away. "They cannot have gone far," she says. "They won't have gone far. They won't." She lifts the lamp, panning it around the dunes. The light flickers. Catches the rugged scarps on the edge of the headland.

"We should check the water," Harriet says stiffly. "The rocks. In case they…" Fear lurches inside her. Stops her from finishing the sentence.

"They wouldn't have…" Eva says, but she is hurrying towards the violent lash of the sea. *Noah*, she calls. *Tom*.

Harriet feels a sudden, violent urge to call for her son. Stops herself. Thomas had ceased to be her child a long time ago.

Eva stops walking suddenly and lifts the lamp out over the water. "No," she says suddenly. "No."

Harriet feels her stomach dive. But Eva is not looking down at the base of the headland anymore. Her eyes are fixed on the horizon, and the faint glow of light coming from the Farne Islands.

"He promised he would come to the house," she says. "Why is he—" She shakes herself suddenly. "Our boat," she says. "Is the boat still there?" She hurries over the embankment, lamp swaying in her fist. Lets out a breath of relief when she sees her skiff still sitting high on the beach. Waves are hurtling over the sides. "I was afraid the boys tried to get out to Longstone," she said. "Finn was supposed to come to the house. But he... we..." She scrubs a hand over her eyes. Crouches suddenly, as though cowed by the weight of her emotion. Her exhaustion. "We fought." She looks up at Harriet for the briefest moment. "We fought over my going to see Martin Macauley."

Harriet looks away. "I'm sorry." She knows there's no need for elaboration. Knows it will achieve nothing.

Eva is silent for a moment, hunching on the ground with her head bowed. She stands suddenly, lifting the lamp and panning it over the dunes again. "We need to find the boys." She pushes past the rattle in her voice. "They must be out on the dunes somewhere." She calls their names again. Follows the curve of the island past unseen rockpools and streams. "Noah is too protective of me when his father's not around," she says, almost to herself. "He's always been like that. The wreck seems to have made it worse. I don't want him to shoulder such responsibility. Not yet, at least. I'm not sure I ever want that for him."

Harriet doesn't respond. She knows this is not a conversation she is meant to be a part of. Knows this is just Eva's way of making sense of the thoughts, fears, inside her head. She and her sister could not have ended up living more different lives. And yet, for all that, here they both are, stumbling through the darkness, carrying their guilt and their fears, searching for their lost sons.

"Mama." Two small shapes burst from the darkness towards the lamp and Noah throws himself at Eva. She wraps her arms around him, sets down the lamp, pulls Thomas close too.

Harriet hangs back. Just watches, listens as Eva is the one to scold the boys for leaving the house, to tell them how relieved she is they are safe. For a moment, Thomas looks past Eva to catch Harriet's eye. She feels a jolt inside her.

"Mama," says Noah, "the firebasket. You said Da was coming to the house."

"Yes," she says. "I did…" Eva has one arm around each of the boys' shoulders, her voice thin, uncertain. "I…" And then she lifts the lamp from the ground again and shines it out over the sea. There's a boat on the water, not far from shore; Harriet sees its lamp diving, disappearing and reappearing beneath the slope of the swell. The boat is small; seems flimsy, misshapen, almost. It pitches across the water, out in the direction of the Farne Islands. And the sight of that flimsy boat with its misshapen sail, it makes a look of dread pass across Eva's face.

"I need you to take the boys back to the house," she tells Harriet.

Noah looks up at her, eyes wide. "Where are you going, Mama?"

"I need to go back to Longstone. I need to find Da."

Harriet keeps her voice low. "Eva. Are you sure that's a good idea?"

"I've no choice," she hisses.

"Why not? What's happening? Whose boat is that?" Harriet knows she does not deserve the answers to these questions, and Eva does not give them to her. When she looks back at Harriet, there's a look of fierce determination in her eyes.

"Please," she says. "Just take the boys back to the house. Make sure they're safe. Tell Thea I'll be back as soon as I can."

Harriet's stomach knots at the thought of being alone with the boys, but she knows she can do nothing but agree.

"Get yourself warm too," Eva tells her. "You're shivering." When Harriet doesn't respond, Eva takes her elbow. "Promise me you'll not stay out here. Go inside and get warm." She looks at her pointedly. "You belong there just as much as the rest of us do."

And Harriet says, "Of course."

She walks with one hand to each of the boys' shoulders in an attempt to keep them from running again; from following Eva; from attempting more heroics. She tries not to focus on the feel of Thomas's lithe body beneath her fingers. Tries to focus on her footsteps, and the intensity of the cold seeping inside her. Because she cannot focus on this.

She stops at the top of the path leading up to the house. Lets her hands fall. They are both staring up at her, she realises. Wide-eyed. Bewildered. Neither of them seem to recognise her from the two days she had spent at Eva's cottage. "Go," she tells them. "Inside."

"Aren't you coming in?" Thomas asks her.

She swallows. "No. I can't."

"Why not?"

She closes the space between them without even being aware of it. Her hands find his shoulders again, tracing the shape of him. Her icy fingers feel the smooth skin of his cheeks, the soft curl of his hair. Thomas stands motionless, lips parted, eyes meeting hers. It's dizzying and dreamlike, and the moment she catches what she is doing, Harriet steps away.

The sky opens, spilling fat drops of rain across the island.

"Inside," she says. "Go and get warm. Quickly."

Thomas hesitates for the briefest of moments, then turns and chases Noah into the house. Does he look back at her? She would like to imagine so, but it's dark, and she is already backing away towards the embankment, and she's starting to feel those same hazy edges to the world as when she had been shipwrecked. But yes, she wants to believe her son looks back at her. Acknowledges her. And perhaps, on some innate level—recognises her.

The door of Highfield House thumps shut, swallowing the blaze of light pouring from the entrance hall. And where does she go from here?

She should not be out here. Should not be doing this. Eva knows that. She knows this weather, this ocean, the maze of rocks and reefs surrounding her home.

But her fear of what Martin Macauley might do to her family pushes aside every other concern. It's a fear she has had for ten years—a fear that has intensified a hundredfold these past few days. At the sight of Macauley sailing out towards Longstone, she knows she has no other option but to be out here, taking on the wind, the sea, the rain.

What reason would Macauley have for being out here in weather like this, other than to seek his retribution? To reach Longstone, when there is no risk of anyone else being out near the Farnes tonight. No herring fishermen in this weather. No passenger ships passing. Just Finn alone in their fragile house, fighting against the rain to keep the firebasket alive.

Eva leans on the tiller, trying to quarter the waves. Her arms are burning, eyes stinging. She doesn't care. All she can think about is getting to Longstone. Getting to Finn. Warning him about Macauley. Because it's not just her fear that has sent her out here; it's her profound love for her husband. A desperate need to tell him how sorry she is for going against his wishes, and for the hurtful words she had spoken. For letting herself imagine, even for a second, that he might have put Oliver's death behind him.

The knot in her stomach tightens as the lights of Highfield House vanish behind sheeting rain. The sea rolls into castles around her, threatening to consume the skiff. And for a moment, she is back in Donald Macauley's dinghy, alone on the ocean, with his body disappearing into the water beneath her.

She shakes herself out of the memory. She is not the same woman she had been that night, more than a decade ago. She is not helpless at the helm of a boat; she is not lost in this new land; she is capable of far more than she had ever imagined herself to be that day. The night she had killed Donald Macauley, she had made it to Longstone. Had made it to Finn. And she will do the same tonight.

The skiff dives forward into a wall of water, sucking the light from the lamp. Water soaks through her cloak, settles in the bottom of the boat.

Eva keeps her eyes on the firebasket. Tries to let the sight of it steady her, pull her thoughts from the terrified spiral they have begun to career down. The flames of the beacon waver wildly, dimming against the rain.

Eva realises she has lost sight of the boat with the misshapen sail. Has Macauley's lamp blown out too? Is he here on this ocean with her? She cannot even bring herself to consider the alternative. Her arms burn as she throws her weight against the tiller. She feels the sea overpowering her, tossing the boat away from her island. She heaves and lurches, driving the skiff away from the Knavestone.

The rain grows heavier, sucking the last threads of light from the beacon. She is close now. She squints through the rain to catch a glimpse of lamplight inside the cottage. Sees just a faint flicker of light—she can tell Finn has closed the shutters to prevent the windows from breaking. To prevent the sea from finding its way inside their home.

Wind tears through her, tosses the skiff forward. And at once, she is too close, the rugged shards of Longstone coming up on her with far too much speed.

Eva reaches desperately for the oars, trying to steer the boat away from the teeth of the rocks. She is too far from the jetty, waves throwing themselves against the edges of the island.

She shouts for Finn. Cannot even hear herself over the roar of the sea. The skiff lurches and dives. And then she is flying, falling, as the sea grabs her boat from beneath and flings her into the waves.

She will die for this, Eva thinks suddenly. Cold water tightens her lungs as she thrashes and kicks and grabs at her cloak, trying to tear herself free from its tangled weight. Flashes of lamplight and air for a second as she breaks through the surface, but they are sucked away before she can grasp them. The skiff growls as it is thrown against the edge of the island, the mast splintering. And as she kicks hard, trying to keep her head above water, she sees Finn running from the dark firebasket over the rocks towards the sound. Sees him pitch towards the water.

She will die, she thinks. And maybe so will he. For her fear and her love and her most foolish of choices, perhaps the both of them will die.

CHAPTER FORTY

Finn has one hand gripping hers, the other reaching for the rocky shards protruding from the sea.

This is their island; surely it won't let them die. He has a hand on her, now she is stolen away, now he reaches her again. The sea tosses them against rock and pain sears the side of his body. Tears at his hands as he tries to pull himself from the water. Another swell of the sea and the edge of the island slips through his fingers. He digs his hand into the laces of Eva's bodice; tethers himself to her. He kicks, resurfaces; sees dark and dark and dark, unbroken only by the faint flicker of light glowing between the shutters.

He kicks towards the island again and this time the wave lifts him; allows him to feel solid rock beneath his feet. He lurches forward, pulling Eva from the water with the next violent surge of sea. The wave crashes over them and Finn braces himself against the rock, covering her body with his.

He scrambles to his knees. Leans over her. Her eyes are closed. Not breathing. The panic is dizzying, blinding. He sucks down a breath before it consumes him.

They are here, he realises, on this cursed plane of rock where he had once found his father's body, colourless, lifeless, succumbing to the sea. He rolls Eva onto her side, his frozen fingers fumbling as he tries to loosen the laces of her stays. "Evie," he says. "Evie." Maybe if he keeps calling to her, he can bring her back. Stop this from being real. He leans over her, thumping his hand hard between her shoulder blades. Again. Again. Calling to her.

And suddenly she is coughing, gasping, emptying the sea from her lungs. The cry of relief comes from deep inside him.

He wraps his arms around her, legs around her. Holds her as another waves crashes over them. Keeps saying her name. *Evie, Evie, Evie.* His voice disappears into the roar of the sea. Rain pelts down on them from low-hanging clouds.

He hears Eva speak close to his ear; words that sound like *Martin Macauley.*

"What?"

She tries to sit up. "Martin Macauley. He's coming here."

Finn brushes her tangled hair from her face. "No. I saw his boat passing by the islands just now. Heading towards the mainland. Don't know what he was doing out in weather like this." He presses a hand to her cheek. "Is that why you came out here? Because you thought Macauley was coming?"

Eva pulls herself into sitting. Wraps her arms around his neck. "I was so afraid of what he might do to you." She pulls back to look him in the eye. "Why are you here? You promised you'd come to the house."

He nods. "I know. I'm sorry." It is not enough. It is not close to being enough. Had he lost Eva to the sea, it would never have been enough.

He closes his eyes for a moment, feeling a too-familiar chill beginning to pull him down. Feels water pelting him from above, rain and sea. And he hears Eva's voice:

"We need to get inside."

Her words spark him into action and he stumbles to his feet, helping her stand. He wraps an arm around her waist. Guides her slowly, carefully, over the rocks. Crouch low, he thinks, to avoid being swept off his feet by the waves tossing themselves at the island. Wind sweeps across the sea, snatching more tiles from the roof. The lightless firebasket sways wildly.

In the light and the warmth of the cottage, the pain hits, blazing down his side where his body had slammed into the rocks. His hands are stinging, palms flecked with blood. Torn patches on the sleeves of his shirt, washed crimson. He stumbles towards the fireplace and throws two more logs into the grate. He lowers Eva onto a chair at the table, reaches for the lacing on her shortjacket. He shivers hard, his fingers seizing.

She lifts his hand away from her laces. "I can manage, Finn," she says gently. "You need to get out of your wet clothes too. Quickly."

When the fire is roaring in the grate, their wet clothes in a pile on the floor, Eva goes into the children's bedroom in her dry nightshift. Returns with her arms full of blankets. She piles them onto their bed and tugs Finn down onto the mattress beside her. *Shipwreck survivors*, he thinks.

He intertwines his legs with hers, holds her close, feeling her heart beat. Water plinks steadily into the pot he has placed on the floor to catch the drips from the hole in the roof. Another stream drizzles down the wall near the children's room, pooling on the top of the sideboard.

Finn doesn't speak. There is so much he needs to say. He hardly knows where to begin. So he just lies in the silence, feeling her body bring warmth back to his own.

Finally, Eva says, "Why did you come out here?"

"I felt like I had to." Right now, it feels like the simplest answer. He does not want to speak of Henry Ward. Ward has come between them on far too many occasions. And there's also a part of him that doesn't want to admit he had let himself be led out here by his former captain. He's far too ashamed of it. He ought to have stopped taking orders from Henry Ward when he was an eleven-year-old child. And here he is, still bending to Ward's will thirty years later. "I had to light the beacon," he says. "If anyone else came out here tonight, they'd be wrecked without it." There's a hollowness to his words. Finn can sense Eva sifting through them, turning them over in her head. She shuffles back on the mattress, running her finger gently over the gashes in his palm. "How much of you being out here is because you want to save lives?" she asks. "And how much of it is because of your guilt over Oliver's death? Your guilt over abandoning your father?"

Finn knows this is not a question in need of an answer. They both know their shared guilt is tying them to this place. Eva flying out here in Martin Macauley's shadow only makes that far more glaring.

That guilt has always been there in the background. But not until tonight has it led them to such foolish, rash decisions. How much longer are they to led the past define their future?

"Maybe we've done enough," he says. The words make

something tighten in his chest. "Maybe we've paid our penance."

Eva sits up in bed, staring down at him. Wet hair falls long and dark over her cheeks. There's a cut on her jawline that he hadn't noticed before. He reaches up and brushes away a bead of blood with his thumb.

He's struck, suddenly, by memories of all they have been through together out here. Nights of watching the sea; of waiting, of fearing. Nights of holding each other in the firelight; of living so much of their lives with a dark sky above their heads. Impulsively, he closes a hand over hers.

"What are you saying?" Eva's voice is soft.

He lets out a breath. "Keeping the light, it ought to be Trinity House's responsibility. Not ours. It never ought to have been ours. Or my father's. Da never ought to have sacrificed as much as he did."

"Trinity House failed to put a light out here."

"The last petition was more than fifty years ago. And they've never needed another because we've always been here. Surely, if we weren't, they'd have to at least consider putting a lightkeeper out here. Especially after what happened to the *Cygnus*."

Eva nods faintly, noncommittal. Finn can barely believe he has spoken the words, but now they are out, he allows himself to imagine a life without this weighty responsibility in it. A life of dry land and unbroken sleep and a future for their children without lightkeeping in it. Is that the life he wants? It feels so hazy, so unformed he can barely tell. "Us being out here isn't going to change what happened to Oliver, or Donald Macauley, or my father." His words come out husky. He is only half aware of having spoken them aloud. "And I don't want Noah to go running off like I did because he can't stand the life he's living."

"What?" Eva leans forward, meeting his eyes. "How long have been worried about this?"

He doesn't know. Supposes some part of him has been afraid of it since that very first night Noah had spent beneath the firelight. Maybe even before that. "A while," he says.

"Noah is not going anywhere," Eva says firmly. A smile flickers at the corner of her lips. "Not until he's thirty-five at least. Besides," her smile fades, "you've seen what he's been like since the wreck. He's thrown himself into keeping the light."

"I'm not sure I want that for him anymore than I want him leaving." Finn lets out a breath. Scrubs a hand across his eyes. "Christ, I sound like a madman."

Eva smiles. "You sound like a father who cares deeply for his son." She lies back down, twining her legs with his again, their clasped hands held against his chest.

For a long time, neither of them speak. Rain throws itself against the windows, shutters thumping wildly. The rhythmic plink of water in the pot becomes a steady stream. Finn hears the sharp crack of roof tiles splintering against rock. Water drizzles down the chimney, dimming the fire. He pulls the blankets up higher.

"Perhaps you're right," Eva says finally, into the thickening darkness. "Perhaps we have done enough." Her voice wavers. "I don't want to carry this guilt anymore, Finn. I don't want to spend the rest of my life trying to make up for my mistakes." She presses her head hard against his shoulder. "And I don't want to die for them either."

Finn pulls her tighter against him. Holds his lips to hers.

Listens to the steady drumming of the rain besieging their cottage. Their last night here, he thinks distantly. This must be their last night here. Let the roof blow to pieces and water flood the chimney and the sea wear away the solid stones of the walls.

Let them break free from the mistakes of the past before the need for redemption consumes them.

CHAPTER FORTY-ONE

Nathan trudges towards the house in the blue haze of dawn. High above his head, the first snow of the season is falling silently, melting into mist before it touches the earth. The air smells fresh and clean; of cold, of sea, of fragrant soil.

He lets himself inside, exhausted, his head aching. After he had prised himself from Julia's bed, he had waited out the storm and the darkness in some regretful corner of the Rose Tavern, bolstering himself with whisky to keep his thoughts from swallowing him whole.

A thick cold has settled into the stone walls of the house; he suspects Mrs Brodie has not yet laid the fires. He makes his way to the parlour. Finds Theodora asleep in an armchair, a cloak pulled to her chin and the laces of her shortjacket hanging open. Thomas and Noah are sprawled out across the settle, legs entangled, their blanket in a pile on the floor.

As though sensing her father's presence, Thea's eyes flutter open. She leaps to her feet and flies at him. Holds him tightly for the briefest of moments, before pulling away.

"Where have you been? I was so worried."

Nathan pulls her back in. Folds his arms around her and kisses the top of her head. "I'm so sorry. I was caught out at Bamburgh. It didn't feel safe to return."

"You took the *boat*, Papa! Without telling me! If *I* ever did that, you would lose your *mind!*"

Nathan nods, chastened. "I know." Can't help a faint smile at her violent punctuations.

"What were you thinking?" she demands.

"I wasn't." It feels like the only appropriate answer.

Theodora eyes him for a moment and Nathan steels himself for her questions. But all she asks is, "Are you all right?"

He is sure the ache of leaving Julia is showing in his eyes. Sure he has not managed to hide his concern for her, about what she will face when her husband returns home. But he does not want Thea to carry any of that. "I'm all right," he says. It's the truth, in some small way. He does not have Julia, but he has never had Julia. And he has his daughter with him, at least for now. And that is enough. Has always been enough.

Nathan glances over at the two boys, chests rising and falling steadily. He picks the blanket up off the floor and tosses it over their sleeping bodies. "Are your aunt and uncle here?" he asks Theodora.

"No. They're out on Longstone." She pulls her cloak from the armchair and wraps it around her shoulders. "We've had quite the night."

Nathan feels a pull of regret. "What happened? Is everything all right?"

"Noah and Tom got out of the house when I wasn't looking. Went running about out there in the middle of the storm. They came back raving about how they saw the Lady in the Dunes."

Nathan smiles faintly, putting a hand to her shoulder. "Perhaps you ought to be more careful about who you tell your stories to," he says gently. He ushers her out of the room so as not to wake the boys. "Why don't you go upstairs and get a little more sleep? Sounds as though you've not had much."

Theodora nods wearily. Trudges up to her bedchamber.

Nathan moves quietly through the house, lighting the fires in the bedrooms, the dining room, the parlour. Trying not to think about Julia. How many hours of his life has he spent trying not to think about Julia? He hears Mrs Brodie stirring, heading for the kitchen. Finds more of Eva's children in one of the downstairs bedrooms.

The knock at the door yanks him from his thoughts. Eva and Finn, no doubt, come to wrangle their family.

Nathan goes to the foyer. Pulls open the door, covering a yawn.

The man on the doorstep is a stranger. He's tall, round-shouldered and bulky, the beginnings of a beard darkening his cheeks and chin.

A stranger, yes, but Nathan has no doubt as to who this man is. Because Julia is standing behind him, eyes full of expectant dread.

A thousand thoughts clatter through Nathan's mind as he stands on the doorstep, eye to eye with Julia's husband. He knows how gravely he has wronged this man. And, yes, how gravely he has wronged Julia.

"Are you Nathan Blake?" says Calum.

"Yes." He looks the man in the eye. Braces himself. For

what? The blow, the brandished pistol, the declaration of a duel—Nathan knows he would deserve all of it. His fingers clench around the edge of the door.

"You laid with my wife. You brought her to stay under your roof."

Nathan swallows heavily. Forces himself to hold Calum's gaze. "Yes."

Calum's dark eyes flash and Nathan grits his teeth, waiting for the fist to the jaw. It doesn't come.

"It was all my doing," Nathan says quickly. "Not Julia's. She's not the one who ought to be punished."

"I know what Julia is like," Calum says thickly. "I know who she is. And I'll not be shamed by her any longer." He reaches into the pocket of his coat for a folded sheet of paper. Shoves it into Nathan's hand.

Nathan opens it with a faint pull of dread. *Bill for the sale of a wife…*

His stomach turns over. He thinks of the wife selling he has seen in the markets and public houses across the country. The halter at the woman's neck, the money changing hands, the gathered crowds. Has Julia not faced enough shame in her life? He dares a glance at her. Her eyes are fixed to the ground. Her chest is rising and falling rapidly, cheeks blazing. "Please don't do this to her."

Calum snorts. "Save me the trouble of taking her to market. She's yours if you wish it."

Nathan feels heat prickle the back of his neck. Feels his heart pound. To do this, to accept Calum's bill and take another man's wife as his own, it undoes every step he has made to regain his family's good standing. He'd make himself the topic of fresh gossip, of whispers, rumours. Shame would hang over his family name again. And this scrawled bill that Calum has clearly cobbled together in his anger, it has not a scrap of legal weight. He could come back at any moment. Reclaim Julia as easily as he is giving her up.

But somehow, Nathan knows that he won't.

In his old life, before Julia, when he was a coffee house frequenter and a Cambridge graduate, and a starched and stilted businessman, he would have been horrified at himself for even considering this. But his old life feels distant. Nathan knows he is not seeing through the eyes of that rigid Cambridge businessman any longer. Now he is stargazer, sailor, lightkeeper's brother—and *before Julia* seems a lifetime ago.

He says, "I do wish it."

Julia says nothing. Just stands with her eyes down, unable to look at either of them.

Calum doesn't speak to her. Doesn't speak to Nathan. Just marches to the wagon waiting outside the house. He pulls out a trunk and dumps it on the wet earth. Scoops Minerva off the bench seat and tosses her out after Julia's luggage. She stalks indignantly across the grass, tail in the air, then disappears inside the house.

Calum leaps into the box seat and grabs the reins. The horse begins to trudge across the wet embankment towards the coast path. Wheels sigh through the grass and Calum is gone.

Julia stands outside the house, breathing hard, watching her husband disappear. For long moments, neither of them speak.

"I'm so sorry," Nathan says finally. "Whatever I did that caused him to find out you and I were together, I…"

Finally, Julia dares to look up at him. Snow settles in her hair and vanishes. "You didn't do anything, Nathan." She keeps her distance from him. Knots her hands together. "I told him."

He swallows. "Why?"

"Because I wanted him to know. I wanted him to rid himself of me." She lowers her eyes. "I'm sorry. He forced me to tell him how to find you. I didn't know he was going to come here. Or ask you to… rid him of me."

Nathan is silent, thoughts rattling. Having Julia here, with him, doesn't feel real. Doesn't feel possible. Feels as though it will all evaporate if he tries to believe it. Finally, he says, "There's no need to stay if you don't wish it. If you wish to go to North Sunderland with Bobby, or look for your brother in London…"

Julia takes a tiny step towards him. "Nathan," she says, voice trapped in her throat, "I told Calum you and I were together because I wanted another chance to have you in my life." She draws in a breath. "However… imperfectly."

Nathan feels a smile on his lips. Imperfectly, yes. But hasn't it always been this? He thinks of all the lies and secrets and moments of distrust that had once passed between them. But there has been none of that, this time around. Now they are free from the shadow of the Rising, there has only been openness and honesty. "I want that too," he says. "So much."

Julia dares to reach for his hand. Keeps her fingers loose around his. "I know I'm asking a lot," she says. "I've abandoned the thieving ring. Calum may tell them where I am. He's angry enough to do so. They may come after me."

Nathan tightens his grip on her hand. Brings their clasped fingers to the place his heart is beating. Warmth spreads through his chest.

He thinks of the letter his mother had written to Henry Ward. Thinks of her confession that she had been coerced by the anti-Jacobite thieves. Thinks of her tearing into the ocean with her children in her arms, leaving this house, this island behind.

The Bamburgh thieving ring has changed the course of his life once before, and he has no intention of letting it happen a second time. No intention of relinquishing this impossible, unlikely life on Lindisfarne with Julia. "Let them come," he says. He's fought for Highfield House in the past. Will do it a second time if it comes to that. He pulls her close, so she might never disappear from his life again. Holds his lips to hers. "I'll not be forced from my home by thieves."

CHAPTER FORTY-TWO

When Finn opens his eyes, he's surprised to find bright white daylight spearing the gaps in the shutters. He can't remember the last time he slept through the night. Can hardly believe he's done so, with the shutters rattling like the gates of Hell. Beside him, Eva is still sleeping deeply. The roof has stopped leaking, but there's a small ocean on top of the sideboard drizzling onto the floor, pools of water in several places around the living area. The rug is soaked through, the ash in the fireplace turned to muck. Finn doesn't quite have the will to inspect the damage to the children's room right now.

A thick chill is seeping into the cottage and he shifts instinctively to light the fire. Stops himself. Are they not to leave this life behind? Leave the fireplace cold and the roof full of leaks, and an ocean rising and falling atop their sideboard?

He sits up, untangling himself from Eva, and wincing at the pain roaring down his side. In the morning light, his torso is dark with bruising, palms flecked with crimson—it feels like an outcome to be grateful for after all they had faced last night. He slides out of bed gingerly. Pulls on a dry shirt and tugs on his wet boots. His coat is still soaked through from the rain last night—he'd flung it aside before he'd dived into the water after Eva—and he makes his way outside in his shirtsleeves. The morning is white and bracing, the sea glassy. The first snow is dusting the sky, disappearing as it reaches the ocean.

He sits on the bottom step for a long time, inhaling the place. Listens to the soft sigh of the sea lapping at the black castles of the archipelago. A faint bloom of sunlight tries to push through the clouds. He can hear the chaotic squall of birdsong coming from the top end of Longstone.

Pieces of the broken skiff are knocking against the edge of the island. One has made it into the rockpool not far from their door and is floating listlessly above the nine-pins ball. Finn sees several more pieces bobbing out on the grey water beyond the firebasket. Mercifully, the longboat is still knocking against the jetty, though he imagines there'll be a lagoon to bail out of her before they leave. Roof tiles lie in pieces across the island.

There's a stillness here that has not existed for years. Those years when he had been alone on the island usually feel impossibly distant. But right now, that alternative life feels so close to hand. Finn is certain that, had Eva not come crashing onto Longstone the night of Donald Macauley's death, he would never have married. Never become a father. And never confronted the memories of Oliver Blake's death. This silent, unpeopled island would have been the rest of his silent, unpeopled life.

He turns at the sound of the door clicking open. Eva is

wrapped in a shawl and thick quilted skirts, dark hair hanging loose down her back. He stands, pulls her close, inhaling the scent of her; sea salt and warmth and familiarity.

She looks down at the shattered tiles, then up at the roof. "Well," she says, "at least the house is still standing." Her eyes drift to the broken pieces of the skiff drifting on the surface of the rockpool. "I'm sorry," she says. "I'm so sorry."

He shakes his head. He doesn't want apologies. He is just grateful they are both still here. Both still standing. Both still breathing.

Neither of them speak as Finn pulls the longboat away from the jetty. Duffel bags crammed with pieces of their lives are sitting at their feet. They've emptied the sideboard of potted meats and jam jars and candles. Flung waterlogged bags of flour and oats into the sea. Cleared the mantel of its candlesticks and quadrant and twine; of all the rocks and shells and driftwood Archie has excavated from the rockpools. Will come back soon to collect the rest of their clothing, and the children's toys, and the furniture that's dry enough to be saved.

There's a heaviness to the thought of leaving that was not here last night. After the storm—and half a century of being pounded by wind and sea—their cottage is still standing. And in the bright light of morning, Finn is not seeing the confined life he had tried to escape as a boy. Is not seeing the frustration and anger of yet another fight with his father. He is seeing the cottage where he had fallen asleep listening to his mother tell stories about selkies and sea spirits. The coal shed where he had first stumbled across Eva. And when he looks at that unassuming plane of rock this morning, he is not seeing the place his father had died, but the place his wife had lived.

He lifts the oars from the water and lets the boat drift. The snowflakes have given way to thick beams of sunlight breaking through the clouds, lifting the water from grey to blue. Finn feels Eva's eyes on him.

"You don't wish to leave, do you."

He tries to read beneath her words. Is she disappointed by the realisation? Relieved? Her voice feels deliberately empty, as though trying not to guide him to a response.

She squints into the sunlight, taking in the silhouette of their cottage on its high stone foundations. The firebasket swaying in the breeze. The creak of the chain reaches them from across the water.

"This is the life I chose, Finn," Eva says, after a long silence. "This is the life I would choose a thousand times over. I've never seen that more clearly." She slides forward on the bench and laces her fingers through his. "But," she says carefully, "if we are to stay, it cannot be out of guilt. Not anymore. It must be because we want it."

He is so desperately ready to release his guilt. Over Oliver. Over his father. So desperately ready for Eva to release her guilt too.

And yes, he realises. He does want it. This life, this island; it has been what he wants for a long time. Who is he without this place? Without the sleepless nights, the sea on the doorstep, the blazing light in the sky. And perhaps the next time he lights the beacon, he might do it out of pride, rather than out of a desperate search for absolution. Because when he takes a step back from his father, and Oliver, and Donald Macauley, Finn can see that yes, he is proud of all he and his family have done out here. He is proud to carry the responsibility of lighting these dark islands. And if this is life his children choose, well, then he will be proud of that too.

"That roof's going to be a real bastard to fix," he says.

A smile flickers on Eva's lips. "I'm sure Nathan will have us at the house for as long as it takes to make the repairs." She shifts on the bench seat, looking over her shoulder at their home. "And Longstone will always be here waiting for us."

Eva cannot remember the house ever being so full, this creaking and shadowed fisherman's cottage grown wild. Full as perhaps it was always supposed to be.

It's a different place to what it had been in those months after her brother had died, when she and Nathan and their mother had been dwarfed and drowned by the enormous silence of the house. A time whose memories have been steadily filtering back to her over the years she has been back in Northumberland.

The parlour is full of voices; the children clinging to her and Finn and talking all at once; Nathan and Julia tucked beside each other on the settle; Theodora, Tom, the golden-eyed cat.

But Eva goes to the bottom of the stairs. Looks up, hesitating. Then she returns to the parlour.

"Where is Harriet?" she asks Thea.

On the journey back to Lindisfarne, Eva had steeled herself against the thought of seeing her sister again. Had convinced herself they could find some path through the bitterness. They had to, didn't they? Especially now, that she has sworn to herself she will let her guilt over Macauley's death fall away. But at the look of confusion in Theodora's eyes, the unease lodged deep in Eva's stomach shifts into something else.

"What do you mean?" Thea asks. "Aunt Harriet never came to the house."

"Yes, she…" Eva feels panic flickering inside her. "She was with me when I went looking for Noah and Tom. I told her to take the boys back inside. I told her to come in and warm herself. She was shivering…"

"The boys came back to the house alone," Theodora says. "They told me you had to go to Longstone. They…" She sucks in a breath. Covers her mouth with her hand. "They were raving about seeing the Lady in the Dunes."

And, *The Lady in the Dunes*, Eva says to Tom and Noah. *Tell me about the Lady in the Dunes. Where did she go?*

The boys go to the window, pointing out onto the embankment, eyes shining with the thrill of the story. "She told us to go inside the house," says Noah.

"She said she couldn't come in."

"We came to the window and watched her from here."

"Watched her do what?" Eva pushes.

"Watched her walk into the water."

Her stomach dives. She thinks of the wrecked ship, of Harriet's story of the bearded man, and the crewmen who had pulled her back from jumping into the sea. She is racing towards the front door as Tom says, "And then the boat came."

Eva whirls around. "Whose boat? Did she get aboard?"

The boys eye each other. "I don't know," Noah says

finally. "It was too dark to see."

Eva rushes from the house. Hurries over the wet rocks of the embankment. Silver pools of the low tide are shining in the pale morning sun. A heron swoops low, wings outstretched.

She is not alone, Eva realises. Finn is just behind her, Nathan and Julia too.

"She's not..." Finn puts a hand to her shoulder. Starts again. "We'd have found her in the low tide if she..."

Eva hears the uncertainty in his voice. Feels a pull of too-familiar fear. The fear of what might lie beneath the surface of her lost and complicated sister. Disappeared into the fabric of this island as she has so many times before.

CHAPTER FORTY-THREE

She wakes to creaks and rattles and that constant unseen hiss of the sea. She is curled up on a sleeping pallet on the floor of the cabin, a scratchy blanket thrown over her shoulders. Eva's storm-cloud grey skirts hang drying over the table. Harriet has dim memories of wrangling herself out of them, trying to shake away the cold, the sluggishness, the haze.

Her gaze is drawn to a shard of glass on the floor, a few inches from her eyes. She thinks of ramming the telescope into the side of Lawler's head. Thinks of the glass exploding across the cabin. Hears the dull thud as he had slumped to the floor. She has not yet found the courage to ask her father what has happened to him. Is afraid of the answer.

The brass box is still on the table. Ward must have seen it, surely. He had helped her down here to the cabin last night after finding her on the edge of the embankment close to Highfield House, dazed by cold, her thoughts tangled. This box that had once been so precious to him—that surely must be still, given what is inside it—there is no way he would have missed it, even in the dark, the chaos, the noise and danger of the storm.

Harriet does not know what had caused her to walk into the water last night. To walk out towards the boat she could see careening over the swell. Confusion, wrought by cold? Perhaps. Somehow, out there in the water had felt like where she belonged. But Harriet can't quite tell if it was a sense of belonging on Henry Ward's boat, or belonging in the dark and silent depths of the sea.

She stands, steadying her legs against the rhythmic tilt of the boat. She climbs into her skirts and laces her bodice, both still far more wet than dry. Takes the box from the table and slips it into her pocket. Then she draws in a breath and climbs the ladder.

Her father is sitting on the bench by the tiller, eyes glassy as he looks out over slate-grey water. He turns as she steps through the hatch. Gives her a faint smile. "How are you?"

It's a complicated question; too complicated for an answer right now. She hands him the box. Ward stares down at it for a long time, running a finger over its tarnished surface.

"Where did you find it?" he asks finally. "When?"

"My brother found it several days ago in Bamburgh. Among thieves." She swallows heavily. Steels herself. "Have you read…"

"Yes," says Ward. "I have." When he finally looks up at her, the expression in his eyes is impossibly weighted. He opens the lid of the box. Peers inside it before closing it again quickly. "I went back for your mother," he says. "A few months after Oliver died, I went back to Lindisfarne for her. I planned to tell her I wanted to make a life with her. I planned to tell her I was leaving the sea."

Harriet sits on the bench beside him. Nods at him to continue.

"The night we arrived on Holy Island, I told my crew I was planning to leave the ship. When they realised that meant cutting their articles of agreement short, they began rioting. I sent one of my crewmen to the house to tell Abigail what was happening. To tell her I'd be there as soon as I could. When Mr Graveney came back, he told me the house was empty."

"Mr Graveney," Harriet repeats. "The man who tried to take the house from Nathan."

Her father nods. He toys with the broken lock on top of the box. "Once it was safe for me to leave the ship, I went to the house for myself, just to make sure. It was dark. Empty. Your mother and siblings were gone."

"They were running from thieves," Harriet says.

Ward nods. "Yes." His voice feels deliberately empty, as though he is doing his best to keep his emotion at bay.

Harriet curls a hand around the gunwale, watching the grey shape of the mainland drift by on their right. Her mind is racing, thinking of that other life that might have been. The life that might have unfolded if Abigail's letter had landed in her father's hands. It's the most pointless of thoughts, she knows. But it is hard to avoid.

She stares at her feet. Can hardly bear the weight of what the revelations in this letter mean for her and her father. But she will not run, she tells herself. Not this time. The life that might have been has fallen away. But she will find the courage to catch hold of this one.

"Mother's letter," she says, "it changes things." Her words come out strained, and suddenly she can't look at her father. "She did not run to keep you from me."

On the edge of her vision, she sees a hint of a smile lighten Ward's face. "No. It would not seem that she did."

Right now, she can go no further than this. Cannot invite him into her life, or discuss what the future might look like. Not yet. The vulnerability already has her heart pounding. Right now, this feels like enough. Feels like everything. "Are you all right?" she asks finally.

Her father passes the box back to her, covering her hand with his for the briefest of moments. "I hardly know." There's a look of bewilderment in his eyes Harriet can tell is reflected in her own.

They sit in silence for a long time. The sea sighs rhythmically against the hull of the cutter, wind piercing Harriet's damp clothes. "Where is Lawler?" she dares to ask. "Did I…"

"No. You didn't. He was like a caged lion when I came back to the ship and found him locked below."

She releases a breath of relief. Swallows heavily. "Do I need to be concerned about him?"

"No."

And she will let this be enough too. She will not pry for answers she does not want. She will give herself permission not to hide a pistol in her pocket. Will let her father carry this for her. She will give herself permission not to go through every inch of life alone.

"Where are we going?" she asks.

"South. Back to London if you wish it. Unless you intend to return to Northumberland?"

She shakes her head. "No. There's nothing for me there." She thinks of her sister, her brother, her son. Thinks of all the memories that hurt to remember. "Rather," she says, pain striking her throat, "there's too much for me there."

Her father gives a her a faint, weighted smile that doesn't quite reach his eyes. "Yes, my girl," he says, glancing over his shoulder to the island disappearing behind a wall of cloud. "I know exactly how you feel."

***

The low tide has given up its secrets: stepping stones and fishing hooks and stolen jewels from a discarded Bamburgh box safe. It has not given up her sister.

Eva has walked the rim of the island; past the rockpools and embankment beyond the windows of Highfield House. Past Saint Cuthbert's Island and the broken shards of the priory, where her eldest brother had dreamed of Viking raids. Past the Pilgrims' Way, where she had fled Lindisfarne in her nightgown, wrapped in her mother's arms.

Searching the island for her sister feels like a piece of both the past and the future—something she is destined to keep repeating. She has been here before. And Eva tells herself she will be here again.

She will choose to believe the best. Will choose to believe Harriet has found her way back to London, to a life that makes her happy. Will choose to believe the boat has finally come for Thea's Lady in the Dunes.

And perhaps in another ten years, Harriet will reappear.

Are you happy? Eva will ask her. *Are your paintings hung in palaces and Parisian salons?*

Yes, she has no choice but to believe in this. To trust there is some part of Harriet that feels, like the rest of them, the tidal pull of these islands; of this silver-black sea that reshapes and scours; that takes and spares lives. To trust that a part of her might be drawn back here by the ghost of that life that might have been. A life that never was, but that somehow, someway, has always been guiding them, starlike, right back to this.

ACKNOWLEDGEMENTS

A very big thank you to everyone who has helped me put together this series: "vibe consultant" extraordinaire Sam Fiorani; beta readers Leanne, Annette and the team at AJC Publishing; and my wonderful cover designer Tim Barber. Thank you to the National Trust team at Lindisfarne Castle and the Northumbrian Jacobite Society for a wealth of incredible information, and to Dave Isom and Denise Yeung for imparting your boat-handling (Dave) and child-handling (Denise) skills.

A big thank you to my wonderful readers' group for coming up with the perfect names for those characters (and cats) I just could not find the right names for; and to Irene Laing—quite possibly the world's biggest fan of these characters—for all your story suggestions (or should that be "demands"?)!

ABOUT THE AUTHOR

A lover of old stuff, folk music, and ghost stories, Johanna Craven bases her books around little-known true events from the past. She divides her time between the UK and Australia, and can be very easily persuaded to tell you about the time she accidently swam with seals on Holy Island.

Find out more at www.johannacraven.com.

Printed in Dunstable, United Kingdom

66377873R00188